GAME
OF
STARS

KIRANMALA AND THE KINGDOM BEYOND

Book One

The Serpent's Secret

Book Two

Game of Stars

Book Three

The Chaos Curse

KIRANMALA AND THE KINGDOM BEYOND

GAME OF STARS

SAYANTANI DASGUPTA

Illustrations by

VIVIENNE TO

SCHOLASTIC INC.

Copyright © 2019 by Sayantani DasGupta

This book was originally published in hardcover by Scholastic Press in 2019.

ISBN 978-1-338-18574-4

10 9 8 7 6 5 4 3 2 1   20 21 22 23 24

Printed in the U.S.A.   40
This edition first printing 2020

Book design by Abby Dening

To the diaspora-born—

you who straddle universes, code switch effortlessly,

zip between dimensions as if on a comet's back.

And to my son and daughter—

born in a new place, a new time, who belong to the world

and who are my world, my galaxy, my multiverse.

You are the heroes we have been waiting for.

Table of Contents

CHAPTER 1

A Demoness in My Room

The first time the Demon Queen appeared in my bedroom, I tried to decapitate her with my solar system night-light.

I was fast asleep, but got woken up by the freaky sound of buzzing. Then I smelled that rancid, belchy, acidy odor I'd come to associate with the rakkhoshi during my adventures in the Kingdom Beyond Seven Oceans and Thirteen Rivers last fall. As soon as I opened my eyes, I saw her outline: pointy crown on her giant head, sharp horns peeking through her dark hair, and evil talons reaching from her long arms. And as if that wasn't bad enough, the demoness had with her some giant, evil-looking bees.

I reached for my magic bow and quiver under my bed, but when my hand came up empty, I remembered I'd left them in my locker at school. So instead, I laced my fingers through the plastic rings of Saturn, yanked my old night-light from the socket, and spun the entire solar system like a flying discus right at the Rakkhoshi Rani's head.

Unfortunately, the sun and orbiting planets never managed to hit her. To my shock, the plastic solar system just sailed through her see-through, sari-clad body, crashing on the front of my Princess Pretty Pants™ dresser, part of the disgustingly princess-themed bedroom set my parents bought me when I was, like, six.

"Honestly, Moon Girl! Is that any way to greet the mother of an old friend?" The rakkhoshi's fangs glinted in the moonlight that streamed through my curtainless windows. As she spoke, bees flew out of her mouth as if carrying her words on their wings. She stretched her clawlike hand toward the fallen night-light, making the plastic explode with a bang.

"Stop that!" I ran out of bed, throwing my bedside glass of water on the place my bubble gum–pink carpet was burning. It did basically nothing to squelch the flames, though. I backed off super quick as the bees swarming around the demoness's head seemed to speed up their swirly flying patterns.

"You're going to burn the whole house down!" The smell of melting plastic gagged me as Mercury and Venus started ooblecking right before my eyes.

"Spoilsport!" the Demon Queen drawled. But she did lean over and breathe an icy gust of wind onto the burning planets—a little mini hailstorm—leaving a charred and smelly solar system on my bedroom floor.

The thing is, being a hero always seems so awesome in the movies. It's all finding your inner bravery and embracing your destiny, fighting monsters and saving the innocent. If you're lucky, you get your own theme song, a wisecracking sidekick animal, or a bunch of heroic friends helping you on your spectacular adventures. But that wasn't the way it worked out for me.

Last Halloween, when I discovered that I wasn't just an ordinary middle schooler from Parsippany, New Jersey, but an interdimensional Indian princess destined to fight demons and monsters (as my parents had hinted at my whole life), I thought I had it made in the shade. I'd always had an allergy to traditional tutu-and-tiara-type princesses, like the nauseatingly sweet Princess Pretty Pants™ franchise, but as it turned out, being a warrior princess was something I could hang with. I figured I'd be going out on weekly demon-butt-kicking adventures with my talking bird sidekick, Tuntuni, and my new posse of friends—the half brothers Prince Lal and Prince Neel and my adopted cousin, Mati. I didn't even mind not having a theme song. Not too much, anyway.

But when I got back to New Jersey from the Kingdom Beyond Seven Oceans and Thirteen Rivers, there were absolutely no heroic perks. I had to keep my identity a secret, make up a bunch of homework I'd missed, and go back to my boring life avoiding the school mean girl, Jovi, and doing stockroom inventory at my parents' convenience store. There was no glory, no fan club, no me-shaped action figure with bendy arms and karate-kick legs. (I was really hoping for a me-shaped action figure with bendy arms and karate-kick legs.) And worst of all, my new friends from the Kingdom Beyond had stone-cold dropped me like I was a demon with bad breath. I knew intergalactic cell service was crapola at best—but my friends hadn't visited or sent a message by flying horse or anything. For *months*.

So when Neel's mom, the Demon Queen, started visiting me in my sleep, I figured my feelings about getting dumped by my friends must have something to do with it. It was a weird, recurring nightmare, that was all. A weird, recurring nightmare in which I was visited in my suburban New Jersey bedroom by a flesh-eating rakkhoshi monster and her personal swarm of venomous insects. No biggie.

"You're not real," I told the flesh-eating rakkhoshi monster. "You're not really here."

"Oh, I'll give you such a tight slap, you dubious dullard!" The Demon Queen rubbed her hand on her chest and shot some bees out of her nose. "I'll tell you what is real—this heartburn! This esophageal reflux! I'd give my left fang for a chewable antacid!"

"This isn't happening." I blinked my eyes, trying to wake myself up. "I'm imagining this."

The demoness belched. Loudly. The bees buzzed even louder. "Loonie-Moonie, you don't have enough imagination to conjure the likes of me!"

Hoping to catch her off guard, just in case I was wrong about the whole being-a-nightmare thing, I launched myself at the rakkhoshi with a ferocious yowl. But she just yawned and let me go flying right through her vaporous form.

I slammed into my dresser, hitting my head hard on a tiara-shaped drawer knob. "I knew you weren't real!"

"Oh, fie on your underdeveloped cranium, you pea-brained tree goat!" The queen picked her teeth with a long nail. "Listen up, I have something important to tell you. It's a matter of life and death. About . . ."

"What?" I prompted from the floor.

"Oof!" The demoness made a choking sound, grabbing at her throat like she wasn't getting enough air. "Oof! Eesh!"

Her image flickered, like she was a broken movie reel. The bees swooped around her. And then they all disappeared.

It went on like this, night after night. The Rakkhoshi Rani showing up in her smelly-but-see-through form along with her insect minions, first insulting me, then trying to tell me something but being stopped by some invisible force. Then she'd disappear.

"Underwater fortress," she said one night.

"Winged key," she managed the next.

"Just one breath," she said another time.

Buzz, buzz, said the bees, zooming in and around the Demon Queen's lips and hair. Yeesh, they gave me the creepy-crawlies. And I'm saying that as someone who's been trapped in an underwater serpent cavern with a bunch of slimy evil snakes.

If the demoness were real, I would have guessed this was all some kind of trick. But since she obviously couldn't be, I could only conclude I should stop sneaking so many chocolate chip cookies before bedtime. Because, wowza, was this a super-weird dream. Every time we got to the part where she wanted to tell me her secret, the rakkhoshi would open her mouth and flap her lips. She would claw at her throat. Her mouth would move, but only bees would come out—no sound. Eventually, her image would flicker and fade altogether.

The closest she got to telling me her secret was one night when she managed to tell me some kind of riddle poem that made absolutely no sense when I first heard it:

Elladin, belladin, Milk-White Sea
Who seeks immortality?
Jewels, stars, eternity
Life and death in balance be
My heart in chains where my soul sings
The prison key a bee's wings
With father's tooth, you crack the case
Humility must wash your face
Fire, water, air, and land
Rakkhosh-kind will lend a hand
Without the dark, the light will fail
Heroes and monsters both will rail
Elladin, belladin, Honey-Gold Sea
Who seeks immortality?

"What is all that supposed to mean? What's that 'elladin, belladin' stuff anyway?"

"Oh, this pancreatic pain! This gaseous gallbladder!" the Queen groaned. "Try to listen between the lines, khichuri-brain!"

"I'm trying!" It was hard to win an argument with a figment of my imagination. "If I figure out your riddle, will you leave me alone?"

"Oh, the intestinal agony of your stupidity!" The rakkhoshi grew so big, her crown grazed my ceiling. She blew green smoke out of her ears and nose, and bee-burped like she was lactose intolerant and had just eaten a cheesy burrito chased by a dozen milkshakes. "This is all the fault of that idiot-boy Lal! And Sesha, that snaky loser! Most of all my ex-husband, that pathetic excuse for a Raja!"

The Demon Queen was so upset it reminded me of something my best friend, Zuzu, and I had read in one of her oldest sister's cheesy self-help books, the one called *Healing Your Broken Heart Chakra: A 17.5-Step Guide.* (Zuzu's sister Athena had *a lot* of books like this because she had *a lot* of experience getting her heart broken. She was practically a professional.)

"So, are you just a manifestation of my angry subconscious telling me I need to bear witness to my . . . er . . . emotional isolation?" I asked, trying to remember the words from the book.

"Bear whoziwhat?" Neel's mom yelled. "Don't give me your touchy-feely psychobabble, you pathetic puppy from Parsippany! Oh, I knew it was a mistake to come to you, you dim-witted moon reptile of a chit! You just can't understand how much depends on you, can you?"

"Of course I can't understand! Because you're. Not. Real!" I shouted so loud I actually woke myself up.

Coming back from the bathroom, though, I couldn't help but stare at the dents in the ceiling, the flakes of plaster on the foot of my bedspread, the half-melted solar system on my dresser, and the charred spot on my carpet. Plus, my bedroom smelled all gassy, like it was at the receiving end of an exhaust vent straight from a garbage dump.

But that was all just my middle-of-the-night imagination. Maybe some cookie-induced sleepwalking. And a night-light so old and decrepit it had just spontaneously combusted. And the smell was probably a combination of melted plastic and some nasty gym clothes that I'd forgotten to wash. Or so I tried to convince myself.

But the thing about subconscious dreams that aren't actually subconscious dreams? Eventually, they come back to bite you in the chocolate chip.

CHAPTER 2

Heroes and Monsters

The Rakkhoshi Queen had been visiting my dreams for weeks, when my mother startled me one Sunday evening, screaming bloody murder. "Kiranmala! Come quick!"

My nerves were a little jangled already, what with all the middle-of-the-night visits from a flesh-eating demoness. So when I heard my mother yell, I couldn't help but imagine the worst. I sprinted from my room and down the shallow steps of the split level, grabbing my father's old cricket bat from the front closet.

"Take that, you fieeeeeeeeeeend!" I shrieked as I dashed into the living room, swinging the flat bat in a huge arc.

If not the Rakkhoshi Queen, I at least expected to find a snot-trailing rakkhosh in the middle of attacking my parents; some kind of bloodthirsty demon snacking on their limbs in the hopes of using their bones as toothpicks. But instead, what I found was a smiling Baba, fiddling with what looked like a small spaceship. Ma, who was closer to the doorway, got the brunt of my attack. Luckily, I didn't actually hit her, but I did knock the aluminum tray she was holding clean out of her hands. The sugary desserts she had obviously just made went flying everywhere, one beaning me wetly on the forehead.

"Darling?" My parents' shock kind of took the wind out of my heroic sails.

"Sorry!" I swiped at my sticky forehead, then scrabbled around, helping Ma pick up the smushed desserts. "I guess I'm a little tense. What with our history of intergalactic demon break-ins and everything."

"Don't worry, sweetheart," said Ma, slapping Baba's hand away as he tried to eat another one of the fluffy white desserts that had fallen on the floor. "There are more chom-choms where that came from! I've been trying out a new recipe!"

I didn't need to look at the February calendar to know that Ma was planning for me to take these treats to school on Valentine's Day. From the drippy rasagollas and sandesh she handed out to unsuspecting trick-or-treaters on Halloween, to the turkey curry and cranberry chutney she made on Thanksgiving, Ma was the queen of fusion holiday celebrations. No matter how many times I explained to her that I was too old to take valentines to school, or that drippy Bengali sweets weren't meant to be put into heart-shaped envelopes, it wouldn't matter. Best ignore the issue for now.

"Why were you screaming anyway?" I asked as Ma finished sponging off the sticky spots from the carpet. "I thought you were in trouble!"

"We wanted to let you know that the Thirteen Rivers satellite company finally sent the new intergalactic remote!" Baba waved the spaceship thing with all its levers, buttons, and weird-looking gears. "We can watch the news from the Kingdom Beyond again!"

My parents may have immigrated to a new dimension, but that was no reason, in their minds, for all of us not to stay up-to-date on the latest news, weather, and sports from the Kingdom Beyond Seven Oceans and Thirteen Rivers. Especially now that I knew the secret of our origins. But that wasn't the reason Baba's announcement made me smile.

As if he was reading my mind, my father said, "Perhaps we will see some of your Kingdom Beyond friends on the television! It has been a while since they have been in touch, hasn't it?"

"It doesn't matter." I tried to sound like I didn't care as I settled on the sofa between my parents. "I'm sure they're just busy."

"But you must be wanting to know how the handsome Prince Neelkamal is doing!" Ma waggled her eyebrows in a totally ridiculous way.

"No," I sputtered, even as I felt my face heat up. "Why do you say that?"

"At your age, you are going to be having many new types of feelings," Ma singsonged. "Maybe we should talk about what happens when you are on the wandering path of your girlhood, and then suddenly blossoming into the garden of your womanhood . . ."

In the movie version of my life, this is the moment that the action would come to a record-scratching halt, and I would look directly at the camera and make a wry confession. Like, *screech*

Okay, fine. Maybe I *had* spent the most time with the half demon Prince Neelkamal when I was in the Kingdom Beyond. And maybe Neel *was* the one who had promised to sneak across a wormhole to go to the movies with me, and maybe I even kind of, not really, well, maybe, just possibly, *like-liked* him. But there was absolutely no reason to admit any of that out loud. I mean, this wasn't one of those celebrity heartthrobs Zuzu and I looked up on websites like Cute Boys Wear Lederhosen Too. (Really, who doesn't like pictures of famous dudes wearing suspender shorts while yodeling?) But what I felt about Neel had no high-pitched goat singing involved. It was real life. And that made it weird, if not downright scary.

Plus, I *so* did not need to hear my mother talk about womanhood and feelings and *blossoming*. I mean, gag. The imaginary movie action resumed with me saying, "I know, Ma! I know what happens. The blossoming. The garden. Everything. I don't need to talk about this."

"Don't need to talk about what?" Baba hadn't been listening, as he'd been polishing off a few more chomchoms. He was also distracted by the complicated remote, which seemed to be making some rattling noises, and also smoking a little.

"Our princess is growing up." Ma wiped a tear from her eye with the corner of her sari.

"No I'm not!" My voice squeaked a little embarrassingly.

"From the moment we found you in that clay pot, floating down the River of Dreams, and adopted you, I knew this day would come." Ma sniffed in a proud way that made me want to absolutely *die*. "If you have any questions, darling, about your feelings, about your body . . ."

"You're having trouble with your bowels?" Baba demanded, entirely misunderstanding Ma's point. "I've told you, sweetheart, fiber intake is very important to maintaining regularity."

"My bowels are fine!"

"Why are you shouting?" Baba looked quizzically at Ma. "Something wrong with her digestion or her hearing?"

Oy. I loved my parents, but sometimes I really couldn't stand them. "Could we just watch the TV show, please?" I pointed to the screen, which had finally come to life.

When we'd started watching the Thirteen Rivers television channel last November, I was surprised at how many bizarre ads they broadcast. Like the one for the energy drink called KiddiePow™: guaranteed to keep kids up all night, and put hair on their chests to boot. And then there was Mr. Madan Mohan's Artisanal Moustache Oil™, a product made by a strange little shopkeeper I'd met on my last visit to the Kingdom Beyond, which claimed to give any user, regardless of age or gender, a moustache that was longer side to side than they were tall. And then there was the company that seemed to be popular across multiple dimensions. The commercial that was on that day.

"Who is the pinkiest girl in the land?" shrieked a little girl in a rosy lehenga choli and sparkling tiara. She was super hyped up, like she'd just downed a six-pack of KiddiePow™ with a side of chomchoms.

"Princess Pretty Pants!" chanted the posse of girls behind her. Each kid had a Princess Pretty Pants™ doll in her hands, but unlike the ones in this dimension, these Kingdom Beyond dolls could walk, talk, poop, and even do gymnastics.

"Sashays, gallivants, and always enchants?" shouted the oversugared lead girl.

"Princess Pretty Pants!"

"Cute and stinky and amazingly pinky! It's who?"

"Princess Pretty Pants!" The girls and dolls cheered and cartwheeled.

The screen froze mid-cartwheel and a male announcer voice said, "Magical batteries not included. Princess Pretty Pants, Inc., and TSK Industries are not responsible for any alterations in self-esteem you might experience with use of this product. If deep-rooted insecurities or increased pressure to conform to patriarchal expectations of femininity arise, please consult someone else, not us. We now return to our regularly scheduled program."

Before the screen switched to the Intergalactic News Network studios, though, I saw something I hadn't noticed before at the end of the Princess Pretty Pants™ commercial. A logo, like a snake eating its own tail, and the words *TSK Industries* in gaudy gold lettering.

I shivered and looked up at the moon, which was streaming brightly through our open living room curtains. For a second, I thought that maybe my birth mother, the moon maiden, was trying to talk to me. But I didn't feel filled up with any of her silvery strength. Instead, I felt trapped, like I was in a cold and clammy cell. I gasped, my teeth almost chattering. And then, just as quickly as it came, the feeling was gone again.

"Are you all right, darling?" Baba put his big palm on my forehead. "Have you been taking your gummy vitamins?"

"Yup! Right as rain!" I said fake cheerily. "Look! The news is on!"

Ms. Twinkle Chakraborty was the glamorous news anchor with ginormous lashes and a dangly nose ring who read the IGNN headlines. Just like in our dimension, there were plenty of terrible things happening in the Kingdom Beyond: ghostly raids on fish markets, rakkhosh attacks during community theater events, a band of khokkosh who crashed a wedding party and ate the caterers. Then there was a news segment on something called the Chintamoni Stone—the so-called Thought Stone—which used to be a part of the Raja's crown jewels, but was stolen by some invaders during a long-ago war. Legend had it, explained the pouty-lipped Ms. Twinkle, that the sparkling white jewel granted wishes, and gave its owner long life. But in combination with its partner, the bright yellow Poroshmoni, or Touch Stone, which the Raja still wore in his royal turban, the stone was even more powerful, and could make it rain precious metals from the sky.

Huh. Twin jewels—the Thought Stone and the Touch Stone—that could make it rain gold and platinum down from the sky. Why did that sound familiar? But I couldn't remember right then.

Ms. Twinkle continued, in her weird, affected accent, "We at Intergalooctic News Network are delooghted to share this IGNN excloosive: there is a chance noo for the Chintamooni Stoon to come hoome at loong last! We join the Raja at the palooce for a highly anticipooted annooncement!"

The image on the television cut to the interior of the palace throne room. Lal and Neel's father was in a shiny brocade jacket and a silk turban. At the turban's crown was an elaborate brooch with what I now recognized as the huge yellow Poroshmoni jewel, and a single peacock feather sticking out from the top. I didn't see any sign of Lal, Neel, or Mati behind the Raja, or even a glimpse of Tuntuni, the talking yellow bird who was also the kingdom's chief minister.

"Mrph pahpa." The Raja was talking, but I could barely understand him. Obviously, no one had told our scatter-brained monarch not to eat while he was making an intergalactic news broadcast. So His Royal Majesty kept reaching into the bags of vinegar-and-chili-flavored chips his ministers held out for him, shoving the nasty chips into his mouth as he spoke.

"My people," he said again with a *crunch, crunch, crackle,* "too long has our most precious Chintamoni Stone been outside our borders. It is time for our national treasure to come home!" Crumbs flew out of the Raja's mouth and onto his thick moustache. "So when our new ally suggested this innovative plan, I embraced it like the visionary genius I am!"

The Raja's white-bearded ministers all jumped up and clapped for at least a full minute, yelling things like, "Hear, hear!" "The jewels in our crown!" "The Raja's a jolly genius monarch!" and "No chips like vinegar-and-chili chips!"

The Raja grinned, waiting for all the applause to die down before he said, "But this is not only a chance to regain our Thought Stone! This is also an answer to our kingdom's demon crisis! Too long have we been terrorized by these ferocious, rhyming monsters, these bloodthirsty rakkhosh, khokkosh, doito, and danav! Our kingdom has fought war after war with Demon Land. We have tried spells and curses, tightening our borders, but to no avail!" The Raja slammed his fist down, crushing some chips. "The time has come for a better solution, never mind what those skateboarding rebels say! On this auspicious day, we hereby announce a revolutionary new opportunity to not only win back the Chintamoni Stone, but rid ourselves of our demon problem once and for all!"

I leaned forward to hear the Raja's announcement. Unfortunately, just at that moment, the TV image cut out, going to a plain green screen with a loud accompanying beep.

"Did the remote break again?" asked Ma as Baba shook the vibrating machine.

Then the TV screen came to life once more, but we were no longer looking at the royal palace, or even the IGNN newsroom. First came some studio logos. A pebble thrown into a still lake caused the words *Undersea Productions* to appear in the ripples. Then a splattering of bright red over a white canvas was the logo for *Lifeblood Pictures, Inc.* Finally, a roaring crocodile indicated funding from *Reptile Studios International.* Then, after a second of pause, a very familiar face came on the screen: my evil birth father, the Serpent King. Baba gave a little shout, but I couldn't say anything. It was like my voice had dried up at the sight of him.

"IGNN viewers, do not be alarmed!" Sesha was in his human form, all oozy handsomeness and flashing green eyes.

Of course, I was alarmed. Seriously alarmed. During our adventure last fall, Neel and I had destroyed Sesha's underworld palace, and then, when we'd had to fight him again, my moon mother had smoked the Serpent King with her magic moonbeams until he was ash. My birth mother had warned me his defeat was temporary, but it was still freaky to see him.

Sesha's shimmery satin smoking jacket glinted with inlaid jewels, which were only outdone by the ruby, emerald, and diamond rings on his fingers. The Serpent King's green-black moustache and beard were trimmed in snake shapes, he had a crown of serpent teeth on his head, and he sat on a throne of gaudy green velvet in a chandelier-filled room. To one side was a rich tapestry depicting that same image of the TSK Industries logo—the head of a snake biting its own tail.

"I interrupt the Raja's announcement of our new interspecies partnership because he has no showmanship! What a bore with all that vinegar-and-chili chip eating, am I right? I mean, I hate vinegar-and-chili chips!"

I saw Ma and Baba exchange a look. Because of course, I hated vinegar-and-chili chips too. It was seriously creepy to realize it was something I could have inherited from Sesha. I put my hand over my snake sign, the scar I had on my upper arm from where my birth father had attacked me when I was a baby. I hated to think he had marked me in so many ways.

"I always say, if you want something done with proper pizzazz, you have to do it yourself!" The Serpent King made fancy jazz hands, then shouted, in a cheesy game-show-announcer voice, "The Serpent King Industries is proud to announce our answer to the Kingdom Beyond's demon problem. Not a war. Not a treaty. Not a foreign infiltration of their internet. But the newest, most exciting reality game show in the multiverse! It's *Who. Wants. To. Be. A. Demon Slayeeer?*"

There were two hooded cobras twisted around Sesha's arms, which now picked up their heads to say, "rahhh!" like a cheering crowd. A bunch of fireworks went off and a logo flashed on-screen of someone valiantly fighting off a drooling rakkhosh with a bow and arrow. The thing that made me pause was the girl doing the fighting, who had green skin, a black braid, and purple combat boots.

Ma gave a choked little gasp, hugging me tight. "Except for the skin, that looks like . . ." She didn't have to say it out loud.

Baba gulped, hugging me from the other side. "I know!"

"Guys!" I protested from the middle of their hug sandwich. "I can't breathe!"

My parents cooled it with the panicky hugging, but still looked visibly shaken. As for myself, I was experiencing a mix of rage, disgust, and confusion. Sesha was back in mortal form, and the first thing he was doing was starting a reality game show in partnership with the Kingdom Beyond? This all had to be some kind of trick. Plus, what was with using someone who looked like *me* as the logo? What a sicko.

"For those of you who survive the three tests of the contest, the rewards are astronomical. Rubies, diamonds, jewels beyond your wildest imaginings." Sesha let a bunch of colored stones fall through his fingers and into a giant chest. "But this is also a friendly contest between our two great nations. If the grand-prize winner is from the Kingdom Beyond, then you get to win your Raja back this." The Serpent King held up a glowing white jewel in his hands, letting it catch and split the light into dancing sparks. "The famed Chintamoni Thought Stone, granter of wishes and long life."

"That must be why the Raja agreed," said Baba. "A chance for the kingdom to get back the jewel. But what is in it for that scummy snake, that . . . that . . . pooper-scooper?"

Needless to say, Baba didn't curse very much, so this was strong talk for him. The thing was, Sesha had made his first seven kids—my brothers—into one awful seven-headed snake, Naga. He'd then tried to do the same to baby me, but my moon mother had stopped him and helped my adopted parents flee across the dimensions to New Jersey with me. Sesha hadn't even known I was still alive until last fall, when the spell protecting Ma, Baba, and me had expired, sucking my adopted parents back to the Kingdom Beyond. When he'd seen me recently, Sesha had again tried to make me into one of his minions. Needless to say, none of this made Sesha very popular in our house.

On the TV, the Serpent King went on, "If the winner is someone from the Kingdom of Serpents, why, then, we win the Poroshmoni Stone." The image on-screen cut to a still of the yellow stone in the Raja's turban. "Either way, the twin jewels will be reunited, in one kingdom or the other."

"It's not going to be a fair contest," I muttered. "Not when Sesha is involved." But even as I said this, I could imagine how good it might feel to win the contest and beat Sesha at his own game. I felt a little dizzy at the thought.

"Thousands of hopeful contestants are filling out their required paperwork at *Who Wants to Be a Demon Slayer?* official registration offices, located conveniently through-out the Kingdom Beyond, the Kingdom of Serpents, and multiple points in between," Sesha said as the screen cut to what looked like miles-long lines of human-appearing and snaky applicants. In one place, there was a stampede as the doors of the registration center were opened. People were pushing and shoving each other in their desperate efforts to get a registration form, ripping papers out of each other's hands.

"Only a lucky few will pass our rigorous applicant selection process. Those who do will face tests both physical and mental. You will fight specially selected demons that challenge your every skill. Already, my minions are rounding up rakkhosh, khokkosh, doito, and danav into a magically reinforced demon detention center specially constructed by The Serpent King Industries!"

The screen switched to some kind of undersea dungeon with row after row of closed steel doors. Even though we couldn't see any of the demons, the sound of moaning and crying coming from behind the locked doors was a little disturbing. And there was the TSK Industries logo again on the steel doors—of course! *TSK* must stand for "The Serpent King!"

"Yes, my modern-day gladiators!" Sesha tossed back his head and cackled evilly, like a movie villain plotting world destruction. "You chosen few will fight these monsters, and those of you who win will become not just heroes, not just reality TV superstars, but demon-slaying *legends*!"

Even though I knew he couldn't see me through the TV, I squirmed under Sesha's gaze. It was like he'd weaseled out my deepest desire—to be a hero, a star, a legend—and made it all dirty. I felt muddled and ashamed. I wondered how anyone related to such a bad guy could ever hope to become something good.

Then, before disappearing into a cloud of green smoke, the Serpent King shouted, "So good luck, you stupid contestants! I'm afraid you'll need it!"

The two cobras on Sesha's arms looked at the camera and said in clipped voices, "Offer valid only for official selected *Who Wants to Be a Demon Slayer?* contestants. Offer for participation in the *Who Wants to Be a Demon Slayer?* contest cannot be combined with other offers to The Snake King amusement parks, vacation cruises, or TSK All-You-Can-Kill chain of restaurants. Use at your own risk. The Snake King, Inc., is not liable for any loss of limb, loss of perspective, or any hospital, tailor, or funeral expenses."

And with a sudden sticking out of the cobra's tongues, they all disappeared. My parents and I stared at each other in weirded-out silence.

The screen shifted back to the IGNN studios, where Ms. Twinkle Chakraborty looked like she was about to burst. "Viewers, remember, yoo heard it here at IGNN first—any oone of yoo coould become the savioor of the Kingdoom Beyoond, and win back the famed Chintamooni Stoone! Just fill oot the handy-dandy application foorm and yoo're on yoo're way to becooming a legend!" The anchor fluttered her fake lashes. "And if that wasn't enoogh yoo will never guess who just paid us a surprise visoot to the IGNN studioos!"

The camera panned out to show Prince Lalkamal, wearing his signature red silk tunic and turban, looking as handsome as ever next to the flushed news anchor.

"Thank you for having me here, Ms. Twinkle." Lal kissed the anchor's hand in a move straight out of a fairy tale. For a second, I worried the woman might faint.

"Oor pleasure, Croown Prince, oor pleasure!" she gushed like a hyperventilating ox. She was rubbing her face against Lal's arm so much her sparkly teep had become un-stuck from the center of her forehead and was kind of hanging out above her left eyebrow.

Then Lal looked directly into the camera, his handsome face all smiles. "I have an important personal message for the Princess Kiranmala."

"What, what, what?" Baba turned up the volume as Ma and I leaned closer to the TV.

"Kiranmala, come stand beside me and be the Kingdom Beyond's champion." Lal grinned and I was filled with a surge of affection for my sweet friend. "I may be the crown prince, but you are already our beloved Princess Demon Slayer."

Princess Demon Slayer, huh? That was the first time I'd heard that name, but I kind of liked it.

"Together, we will win the Serpent King's challenge. We will rid the kingdom of its rakkhosh problem, together. We will win back the precious Thought Stone—together."

Ms. Twinkle Chakraborty now had her coiffed head leaning entirely on Lal's shoulder. I was pretty sure this wasn't professional anchorperson behavior. "Princess Kiroonmala, you looky herooine—if you're watching, your people need yooou!" She winked, then did an eyebrow waggle that put Ma's to shame. "The Crown Prince Lalkamal *needs* yooou!"

Before Baba clicked the newscast off, Lal gave the camera a meaningful stare.

"There are more things to save than you can even know," Lal said in an extra-intense voice. "Remember, Kiranmala, you are the hero your people have been waiting for!"

CHAPTER 3

The Application Ambassadors

can't believe my parents won't let me go to the Kingdom Beyond and join the contest!" I whined for the thousandth time as I got off the school bus the next morning. "It's so unfair!"

"Right, because this *Who Wants to Be a Demon Slayer?* show doesn't sound at all like an elaborate trap set for you by your evil birth dad," Zuzu yelled as we dashed, backpacks held over our heads, toward the front entrance of Alexander Hamilton Middle School. It was horrible weather, even for early February. There were golf-ball-sized chunks of ice falling from the sky, like we were on the losing side of a dodgeball game against the gods. "Didn't the Serpent King say you were, like, some kind of weapon he wanted to use in some upcoming war?"

Sesha had said exactly that. Darn Zuzu and her good memory.

"If this were a trap, why would Lal be asking me to come home?" I asked, my purple combat boots sloshing through the icy puddles. "They need me to get this magic thought stone back! Lal probably knows he can't do it without me! Anyway, all that weapon-in-the-coming-war stuff was just bad-guy talk. Probably."

My best friend's eyes were near invisible behind her rain-smeared glasses. "From what you told me, his brother Neel's no slouch. Let him do it."

I didn't want to admit it, but I was a little confused as to why Neel hadn't been with Lal in the studios, or why Lal hadn't even mentioned him. Or honestly, why it hadn't been Neel asking me to come home and join the contest with him. But still, it didn't change my point. "You know," I shouted over the pounding ice-rain, "super-heroes in stories never have to deal with overprotective parents!"

"Niet, not precisely true. Superman's parents were so protective they put him in a capsule and jetted him off into space, and Wonder Woman snuck off without her mother's permission into the world of men."

That made me pause. "Snuck off, huh?"

"Don't get any dumb ideas, por favor?" Zuzu yelled over her shoulder. She was almost up the entrance steps to the school. "Your parents would kill you if you did something like that. And so would I. That Sesha's a twisted dude. You don't want to mess with him again."

I grumbled a little under my breath. It's not like I didn't appreciate Zuzu's concern. After all, she was the only one at school who knew about my real identity. I'd told my bestie because it was just too big a secret to keep from her. But I hadn't told anyone else. In fact, it had been Zuzu who had warned me to keep all the stuff about the Kingdom Beyond under a tight lid. People probably wouldn't believe me anyway, but worse still, Zuzu was worried about what could happen if people *did* believe me. Would men in black suits take me away to do experiments on my DNA? We'd both seen a lot of TV movies about government agents who went around hunting undercover aliens, and she didn't want something like that to happen to me.

"I can't believe I have to be here doing my homework instead of over there becoming a legend," I finally said.

"Even legends have to pass math." Zuzu laughed as she ran inside the school.

I was just about to follow her, when something made me freeze in place on the entrance steps, my eyes turned upward. Other kids streaming off buses pushed past me, almost toppling me over. Meanwhile, the skies kept pouring down hail onto my head and shoulders, covering the sidewalk beneath my feet in ice. But I couldn't move. Because sitting on top of the slanted roof of Alexander Hamilton Middle School was a sight that almost made me scream: two ginormous, hippopotamus-sized birds, blinking in the rain.

They were both beautiful and terrifying at the same time. Their feathers were ivory at the middle, but darkening at the edges, until each feather ended in a dramatic paisley-shaped swirl. And that wasn't even the weirdest thing about them. Even though they looked like overgrown eagles crossed with pachyderms, the birds' faces were entirely human.

"What is the matter with you? You're going to get pneumonia!" Zuzu ran back out to tug at my sleeve.

"Birds," I managed to blurt out.

"What birds?" Zuzu looked around in confusion.

I gave her a sharp look and realized she really couldn't see them. I knew what must be happening. Last Halloween, when Lal and Neel had parked their flying pakkhiraj horses on my front lawn, the only people besides us who could see them were really little kids. The horses had been under some kind of "the older you are, the less chance there is of seeing me" cloaking spell, and I was sure these birds must work the same way.

"Kiran, are you okay?"

I wasn't. I knew I was getting soaked, but I couldn't feel the rain anymore. I didn't feel the cold either. All I felt was the ancient magic of these creatures from the Kingdom Beyond.

"Who are you?" I whispered. I was talking to the birds, but Zuzu didn't know that.

"Kiran!" she shouted, pulling hard now at my arm. "Basta! You're freaking me out!"

Bangoma and Bangomee, said the birds. They didn't speak out loud but somehow, their words slipped into my brain. *We are here, Princess, for thee.*

I'd seen a lot of brain-boggling things in the last months, but I'd never seen hippopotamus-sized birds with human faces. And I'd certainly never seen magical creatures landing on the roof of my middle school. The birds smiled, each bowing low until its head touched the roof. Then, for what must have been a few seconds, but felt like hours, they just stared at me, their eyes swirling with psychedelic colors—multicolor beacons in the torrential rain. I started to feel myself getting light-headed, and wondered if I was being hypnotized.

"Why are you here?" I whispered, now totally ignoring a frantic Zuzu.

I expected them to say something wise and deep, about the oneness of the multiverse, or the stream of the eternal spirit, but instead, their voices floated into my head in a weird, nasal unison. *Your application is, like, way late. Hold your darn finger out now posthaste!*

"My . . . f-finger?" I stuttered. For who knows what reason, I took off one of my gloves and held out my hand. I only jumped back a little when one of the birds poked my finger with his claw, drawing out a bead of blood.

"Hey . . ." I protested as the bird squeezed my finger, letting the blood drip onto a feather the other bird held out.

We can't tell you how long the processing takes. Sometimes longer, sometimes right away, said Bangoma.

"Processing? Processing for what?" My brain thought the words, but my mouth couldn't seem to make the sounds. It didn't matter, though, because the birds heard me.

Bangomee flapped her wings and answered, *We're application ambassadors, hired by a friend. We can't tell you who, or our jobs will end!*

Don't call us, we'll find you, added Bangoma. *Now scram to class, girl, toodle-oo!*

"Wait, what . . ." I felt dizzy, unable to find words. What had just happened? But the birds didn't seem to have any more time for questions. Flapping their giant wings, the two creatures flew off into the steel-gray sky. As soon as I broke contact with their spinning, multicolor eyes, I felt the whole memory of the giant birds start to fade, like someone had taken a giant eraser to the chalkboard of my mind.

"I don't feel right." I swayed slightly on my feet, and Zuzu grabbed me.

"Does your little friend have a death wish?" I didn't need to turn around to recognize the voice. It was our school-queen-bee-slash-my-evil-next-door-neighbor, Jovi, sparing a second to be snarky as she ran by.

"She's just been standing there, with one glove off and her hand out!" Zuzu yelled. I could finally hear the panic in her voice. "I think she's in shock or something!"

It was true. Something had really done a number on my brain cells. I rubbed my temple. "Why are we standing in the rain?" I mumbled.

"Did she get hit on the head by some hail?" Two people bundled me into the building. "Come on, let's take her to the nurse." I realized with shock that the person speaking was Jovi, and that she also had a hold of one of my arms.

"No, let's take the poor dear inside of here." Someone with a lilting accent was holding open the door of the girls' room, while Jovi and Zuzu helped me inside. "I have something that will mayhap help her regain that girlish glow."

I blinked, recognizing the third girl. Her name was Naya, and she was new to the school, moved here from another country. It was my own fault I'd never asked from where. All I knew was that she spent a lot of time hanging out at Jovi's house. I'd seen her next door a bunch of times after school and on weekends. I didn't know much else about her except that she was pretty, and kind of annoyingly perky.

As Zuzu dried off her glasses with a paper towel, and Jovi stuck the sopping strands of her hair under the hand drier, Naya pulled out a tiny green bottle from her beaded purse. "This will help you."

"I'm not drinking that," I said, backing away. I was still

freaked out by . . . whatever had just happened. Plus, the plain tile floor and terrible fluorescent lights made the bathroom feel like a crime scene.

Naya laughed, showing rows of perfect white teeth. She was short and kind of sickeningly adorable, like one of the girls on the Princess Pretty Pants™ commercial, but grown up. I mean, she wore her hair in, like, a million tiny ponytails with whimsical ties. (Who even owns that many whimsical ties?) Today, she had on a sparkly sweater that said *Bee WHOOO You Are*, with pictures of a bee, an owl, and, inexplicably, a monkey under the letters. I guess it was supposed to be ironic, but I wasn't really sure. Naya seemed like the kind of person who watched a lot of kitten videos on social media. And yet, for inexplicable reasons, super-meanie Jovi actually seemed to like her.

"It's not for drinking! Here, smell it!" Naya uncorked and then waved the little bottle under my nose. It stunk something awful.

"Ew! Get that away from me!" I batted at the new girl's surprisingly strong arm even as the smell of whatever that was totally cleared my head.

"Don't even try with this one, Naya." Jovi narrowed her eyes at me. "The giant chip on her shoulder prevents her from behaving like a normal person."

"Back off, Berger!" I snapped. I was feeling better but was still a little wigged out.

"Most people just say thank you when someone helps them," Jovi shot back.

"Thank you," I said in a gruff voice. "But you didn't have to. I'm fine now."

"No worries, you do you, girl," said Naya in a slow and practiced way, like she'd just heard the phrase from Jovi and was trying out using it. Inexplicably, she then turned around and held up her cell. "Say paneer!" she trilled, before pulling my face down to hers and taking a selfie with me. Then she pressed the Instachat video button on her phone and said, "Another vomitus sickness cured with Stinkopolis brand smelling salts!"

"Don't post that somewhere!" I batted at her arm again, but Naya seemed to think it was a joke, and danced out of my reach. "I probably look awful!"

"What's your problem, Turnpike Princess?" Jovi snapped. "You still living in that dream world of your parents'? The one where they tell you you're Indian royalty in hiding?"

I felt the heat rush to my face. When we were younger, and my mom used to dress me up in silk saris and sparkling jewels every Halloween, it had been Jovi who'd burst my bubble, asking how I could be a princess if my dad owned a Quickie Mart on Route 46. I wished so hard I could rub her face in it now—tell her I really was a princess—but she'd probably just laugh at me. After all, I had no proof. Unless you counted the snake sign on my arm and the crescent-shaped moon mark scar on the back of my neck, which I'm sure Jovi wouldn't.

But Naya didn't seem to share Jovi's skepticism. "Oooh, royalty!" The girl gave a goofy jump up to her perky little toes. "Oh, Your Royal Highnosity, tell me all about it! The gowns! The jewels! And cake! I've heard if you're a princess, there's always a lot of cake!" Naya gave a twirl and a huge sigh that made me seriously concerned for her state of mind. She wasn't just annoying like one of the girls on the Princess Pretty Pants™ commercial, she was like Princess Pretty Pants™ herself.

With a sniff, Jovi pulled Naya out of the bathroom ahead of us. "Come on, we're going to be late for science!"

"Bye, Your Royal Majesty, Your Most Serene Highness, Your Princess-ship!" Naya waved so enthusiastically, I felt like puking again.

Zuzu tugged me along down the hall. "You feeling buena? What was going on with you back there?"

I was about to tell Zuzu about the birds, but she barreled on. "You know, you were being kind of rude, and they did help you. I know you guys didn't get along when you were younger, but Jovi's on the fencing team with me now. She's fantastique at foil, and besides, she's usually pretty nice."

"Okay, thanks for making me feel bad," I mumbled.

"You can't expect to be a superstar all the time." Zuzu threw a wet arm around my shoulder and grinned. "Welcome to your ordinary life, Turnpike Princess. I'm sorry, I mean, Princess Demon Slayer!"

CHAPTER 4

Gold and Platinum Rain

Squishing and squelching all the way, Zuzu and I made it to our science classroom just in time for the first bell. Even though I looked like a rat escaped from a flooded drain, and I was still totally confused by whatever had happened before (I mean, why did my finger hurt so much?), I couldn't help but be excited for class. It was Monday, which meant it was video day.

Outside Dr. Dixon's room was a poster of that great scientist Albert Einstein, someone I'd actually met during my interdimensional travels last fall. I know it doesn't make sense, since Albert Einstein is, of course, dead, but there was something about time and space working differently in different dimensions that allowed him to be alive over there, teaching school to baby stars in an outer space nebula. Yet another awesome experience I couldn't tell anyone about. The quote on the poster was pretty great, and it felt as if Einstein-ji had said it just for me: *If you want your children to be intelligent, read them fairy tales. If you want them to be more intelligent, read them more fairy tales.*

Dr. Dixon was, as usual, at the door to greet us all as we entered his classroom. I shook his hand, grinning up into his warm, moustached face. I didn't know how he did it, but he was so enthusiastic about space, and dinosaurs, and atoms and stuff, he made his students—most of us anyway—love science too. Also, his ugly-funny vests were hilarious. He had one that was all giant microscopes floating through space, another of dogs and cats in astronaut suits, and, my favorite one, the one he was wearing today, of farting T. rexes. (The farts were these green clouds coming out from under their tails, and it made me laugh every time I saw it.)

"Hey, Dr. D.! Did you hear the one about the scientist reading the book about helium?" Dr. Dixon sometimes gave extra credit to people who could stump him with a good science joke, so I'd taken to looking through Zuzu's brother Niko's joke books when I was over at her house.

"No, pray tell, Ms. Ray." My science teacher arched one thick eyebrow. "What about the scientist reading the book about helium?"

"He couldn't put it down! Get it? Because helium rises . . ."

"Yes, thank you so much for that explanation, I am familiar with the properties of helium." Dr. Dixon's eyes twinkled and his moustache even quivered a little, but he kept a straight face.

I launched right into another one as I walked through the door into the room. "I have to tell bad jokes about chemistry because . . ."

Dr. D. joined me for the punch line. "The good ones . . . *Argon*!"

So I tried yet another. "There aren't too many chemistry jokes, so I only tell them *periodically*!"

"That's funny!" It was Naya, sitting near the front of the room with Jovi beside her. "Her Serene Princess-ship's really funny!" she said earnestly to Jovi, who rolled her eyes.

"She's hilarious," Jovi deadpanned, but Naya just kept grinning in that syrupy way. Maybe they weren't very sarcastic wherever Naya came from, but she was in New Jersey now, and sarcasm was the song of our people. Someone was really going to have to explain that to her.

As I sat down in one of the few still-empty seats, Dr. Dixon went to the bookmark for the public television station on his computer, which was already projecting to the screen. He always started every Monday by showing us a few minutes of my favorite science program starring an absolute rock star of a scientist: Shady Sadie the Science Lady. Shady Sadie's public television programs on everything from the super-cool awesomeness of a nebula star nursery to how to explode your toilet with cola and Stop Rocks were pretty much the most mind-blowing-est things I'd ever seen. Last fall, when I'd learned that rakkhosh were actually, in some weird, interdimensional way, the same thing as black holes, it had been the astronomy I'd learned from Shady Sadie that had helped me save my friends and family. Between my demoness nightmares, Sesha's wacky game show contest, and whatever the heck had happened this morning, I felt like I needed some of the Science Lady's insight and wisdom.

"Dr. Dixon?" I shot my hand in the air as an idea came to me. "Could we watch the Shady Sadie show from a couple weeks ago? The one about that new discovery with the colliding waves and . . . falling metal, and . . . uh . . ."

Someone snickered from the back of the room, and I stopped talking, feeling my face heat up.

"You sure you're feeling okay?" Zuzu hissed from behind me. She probably thought I had a concussion, and was regretting not taking me to the nurse before.

But luckily, Dr. Dixon seemed to understand what I was rambling on about. He scrolled through a few of the streaming videos, looking for the one I meant.

"You mean her show about the black hole collision?" my science teacher prompted. I was too embarrassed to say anything but just gave a little nod as I slunk even lower in my seat. To make matters even worse, Dr. Dixon gave me a big thumbs-up. "Sure, Ms. Ray, anything for Shady Sadie's biggest fan!"

"What a dork!" I heard someone mutter, and there were even more snickers from somewhere over my shoulder. I blinked hard, willing the tears away from my eyes. In the Kingdom Beyond, I'd gotten better about showing my emotions in front of people, but middle school was a whole other universe. In some ways, the kids here were just as blood-thirsty as a pack of rakkhosh.

But thank goodness for small miracles, because the classroom lights went low just then. And then there she was on the screen, dancing in to the funny trombone music from her show: My role model! My nerdy girl hero! My scientific rock star! I tried not to look too interested. Nothing put a target on your back in my middle school like looking like you're enjoying a science program.

Shady Sadie was wearing her signature round dark glasses, pantsuit, and bow tie. Today's suit was white with hourglasses all over it. The hourglasses were filled with little multicolor gems that looked like the sands of time. Her bow tie was a giant gem-filled hourglass too. Her short black hair was all spiky in a zillion directions, and she bopped to the beat of her show's theme.

"Heya, young scientists!" Sadie boomed as the music finished. The TV audience yelled back, "Heya, Sadie!"

"The universe is rich with mysteries." Sadie hit a button and the entire room around her became the solar system, so it looked like she was casually walking, in her white pantsuit, through space.

"Just this past year, for the first time in all of history, our instruments began to detect cosmic ripples across the fabric of space-time, the aftershock of two black holes colliding into each other many light-years away."

There was an exaggerated yawn followed by some giggles from somewhere in the room. Dr. Dixon cleared his throat, and the noise quieted down. "You guys are going to like this next part," our teacher said.

The image behind Sadie changed, to two bright white stars circulating around each other.

"Now, just this year, we have detected a remarkable event that happened a hundred and thirty million light-years away. We have seen the beautiful explosion of light—the fireworks—created when two long-ago and faraway neutron stars collided."

"What's a neutron star?" someone in the classroom shouted out.

"Good question." Dr. Dixon paused the video on Sadie's animated face. "Neutron stars are formed when the collapsed core of a very large star explodes out and becomes a supernova, then dies."

Not that I would admit it out loud, but I, of course, knew all about the life cycle of a star—how some suns become red giants, then white dwarves, before becoming black holes. That was because Lal and Mati had actually been transformed into a red giant and a white dwarf last fall during a whole messy disaster where Neel's mom had eaten them, and then vomited them out as golden and silver spheres. Part of the risk, I guess, of having your stepmother be a rakkhoshi-queen-slash-powerful-black-hole.

Dr. Dixon clicked his remote to let the video run again. On the screen, Shady Sadie also clicked on her remote. The two white stars behind Sadie ran into each other, letting off jets of silver and gold sparks. "When these two neutron stars collided," the TV scientist explained, peering at the camera over her dark frames, "they filled the universe with streams of heavy metals, plumes of gold and platinum." To illustrate her point, the sparks danced and glowed on the screen like they were alive.

And just then, my own brain sparked and danced to life too, just like those precious metals. This was what I'd been reminded of when Ms. Twinkle Chakraborty was talking about those magic Thought and Touch Stones—the Chintamoni and Poroshmoni—and how together, they could make it rain gold and platinum from the sky. I felt my breathing speed up. If black holes in this dimension were rakkhosh in the Kingdom Beyond, why couldn't the precious stones the Raja and Sesha both wanted be twin neutron stars?

"So how much gold and platinum did those stars make?" Jordan Ogino asked. Clearly, the talk of precious metals had gotten my classmates interested. They were materialistic, if nothing else.

Dr. Dixon paused the video again. "Oh, just a few nanillion dollars' worth!" He smiled when we all looked baffled. "Well, let me put it this way, it made about twenty Earths worth of gold, and about fifty Earths of solid platinum."

"That's some serious cosmic bling!" shouted out Jordan as everyone laughed.

Dr. Dixon switched off the video and brought up the room lights. "Okay, so who can tell me what alchemy is?" I could tell the teacher was looking straight at me, expecting me to jump in with an answer. But I kept my eyes on my desk. I'd already made a fool of myself enough for one class period. Besides, my brain was occupied thinking about my evil bio father in possession of a neutron star.

"Isn't that, like, when wizards tried to change metals into gold and live forever and stuff?" said Sophie Hiller, popping some gum at the end of her sentence.

"Yes, you're right, young scientist!" Dr. Dixon pointed enthusiastically at Sophie, like she'd just said something brilliant. "Except, maybe, the wizard part. Alchemists were people who spent their whole lives looking for a jewel, sometimes a stone or an elixir, that could transform other metals into gold. They thought this precious stone, if they found it, might also prolong life and cheat death." Dr. Dixon went on, "Now, in light of the fact that these neutron stars actually created gold and platinum and other precious metals, think on this: What if that jewel those long-ago alchemists were looking for was nothing short of the stars themselves?"

My eyes shot up from my desk, catching Dr. Dixon's bemused glance. Then my science teacher held up an image from a textbook, the sight of which almost made me yelp with surprise. There it was, that TSK Industries symbol again, the one that I'd seen in Sesha's broadcast!

"This is an Ouroboros—a snake eating its own tail—from one of the earliest alchemical texts ever known. It symbolizes the eternal unity of all things, the cycle of life and death which the alchemist seeks to break and live forever. The all, as they say, is one."

Isn't that interesting?

I thought for a second maybe my science teacher was reading my mind, or at least in it. But then I realized those last words weren't Dr. Dixon at all.

Hey, Luna Bar! a very familiar voice screeched in my head. *Get out here!*

I stubbornly kept my eyes on Dr. Dixon, who had already started his lesson for the day. But nothing he was saying was registering, because the Rakkhoshi Queen was in my skull again.

So many fresh kiddies in so many rooms! Eeenie, meenie, dummy, dude, in my mouth, you human, you!

She was here, at Alexander Hamilton Middle School! I gasped out loud, hissing, "Don't you dare hurt anyone!"

Zuzu poked me in the back. "Kiran! What's the matter? You okay?"

Loonie Princess, hurry scurry! Or I'll make these kids into a nice curry!

I jumped up from my seat. "No you won't!" I shouted. "Not if I have anything to say about it!"

Dr. Dixon paused, his whiteboard marker poised in midair. "Ms. Ray, are you feeling ill?"

"Yes!" I couldn't stop my voice from shaking. I grabbed my backpack and still-wet coat. "I am! Sick!"

"Do you need to go to the nurse?" Dr. Dixon handed me a hall pass, a worried expression on his face. "Are you going to be all right on your own?"

"Yes, thanks! I've . . . I've got to go . . ." The entire classroom, or so it felt, exploded into giggles. My face was on fire and I couldn't stop the tears from rolling. I heard Zuzu asking me something but I didn't wait to listen.

"I'm fine!" I muttered at her, putting out a hand when she made a motion like she was going to come with me. Then I jetted from the room, away from the laughing voices and toward the demoness waiting outside.

CHAPTER 5

Essence-Tyme

I knew I couldn't go out empty-handed. I needed my bow and quiver, so I dashed as quickly as I could to my locker. I'd left my weapon at school thanks to our gym teacher, Mr. Taylor, still offering archery in spite of the unfortunate incident last year where I'd by mistake hit him in his thigh with an arrow. (His limp was *totally* not noticeable anymore, no matter what Zuzu said.) I whipped through my combination, grabbed my bow and quiver, and ran into the icy rain.

"Where are you, you belching monstrosity of a queen?" I was glad no one was there to witness me with an arrow nocked in my bow, yelling at the air.

Chill out, don't lose your head. I'm over by the gardening shed. The Queen cackled in my mind. I knew it was her because she burped at the end of her sentence.

"Get away from my school, and don't you dare hurt anyone!" I hissed as I ran, slipping and sliding on the icy ground, toward the side of the building with the rickety garden shed. As I passed the cafeteria dumpsters, the smell of rancid sloppy joes and meat loaf almost made me gag. Just beyond, halfway to the soccer fields, was the little gardening shed the groundskeepers used to store stuff. On the far side of the shed was a small overhang. I pressed myself against the somewhat dry wall, away from the rain, and, more importantly, away from the school windows. I really didn't feel like getting caught outside the building without permission. Especially since it might be hard to explain why I had a bow and arrow in my hand. I wondered how long it would take Dr. Dixon to send someone to check up on me and figure out I wasn't in the nurse's office.

"What do you want? Where are you?" I hissed, my eyes wide for any sign of Neel's mom.

The Demon Queen's voice was closer now, and clearer. *Time to go, you pathetic excuse for a hero!*

"Go?" I looked around the deserted, icy soccer fields. "Go where? I'm not going anywhere with you!"

There came an unmistakable smell of some more acidic burps. And the buzzing sound of bees. It was the Rakkhoshi

Rani manifesting herself next to me. She still had the same see-through quality as when she visited my room, like she wasn't really there, even though she was. And she still had her insect buddies along with her.

I was so nervous at seeing her in the middle of the day, and on my middle school grounds, that I let a few arrows fly. Of course, they were useless and just went sailing straight through her to lodge in the icy ground behind her. I blinked hard, second-guessing myself. Maybe I *had* gotten a concussion. Was hallucinating demonesses a symptom of getting bashed in the head by hail?

"Cut the warrior princess act, Moon Shadow." The Queen flipped her long hair over her shoulder as she turned on me. "I don't have time for empty heroics."

"How are you . . ." My words trailed off as I pointed to her transparent form.

"Here but not here?" The demoness cackled, picking her tooth with a long nail. "Essence-Tyme, of course. You 2-Ds don't have it, I suppose? Figures. You really are a limited civilization."

Neel had called me a 2-D once, a word that described how people from this dimension didn't like to think of the universe as a complicated place and wanted a simple and easy explanation for everything. I wanted to tell his mom not to use the insult, to argue with her about all the video-conferencing technology we had in this dimension, but this wasn't the time. "Why are you here?"

"To get you to hurry up and join that dratted contest, *obviously*." The Queen sniffed, loud and wet. "You know, I really don't get what my son sees in you."

My stomach flipped a little at her mention of Neel, but I tried to keep the topic on course. "Join the contest? Are you serious?" I lowered my weapon but still kept an arrow ready and the bow partially pulled back. "Are you seriously here trying to get me to sign up for *Who Wants to Be a Demon Slayer*? What, are you working with Sesha now? I thought you hated serpents!"

"Ack! Ptu! Chi chi!" Acidic smoke, as well as some bees, shot out of the Demon Queen's nose. "Work with Sesha? I have half a mind to rip your tongue out of your head and use it as dental floss! What a disgusting suggestion!"

"Then what? Why are you telling me to sign up for it?"

"Well, they've already approved your bloodwork, so there's that," she snapped, crossing her arms over her transparent chest. At her words, my eyes widened, and I remembered all that had happened that morning.

"*You* sent those giant birds to steal my blood?" I wanted to scream but kept my voice at a level of controlled fury. I may have been arguing with a demoness, but that didn't mean that I wanted to risk getting a detention for being outside of school without a pass.

"Oh, steal, schmeal! They asked and you offered!" The Rakkhoshi Rani snapped her sharp teeth, the bees swirling in and out around her hair. "There was no stealing involved!"

I put away my arrow, shouldered my bow, and then whirled on her with the weapon of my fury. "They *hypnotized* me! And what do you mean 'approved my bloodwork'? Are you telling me you sent my blood sample in to *Who Wants to Be a Demon Slayer?*"

"You should thank me, you ingrate! If I hadn't done that, they would take forever to process your application," said the demoness like it was the most obvious thing in the world. "Their registration offices are a *mess.* Now you'll be through the paperwork lickety-split!"

"I'm not going to the *Who Wants to Be a Demon Slayer?* game show registration office—or anywhere—with you!" I was so frustrated, I could have screamed. "And I'm not competing in it! I mean, the whole show is obviously just a giant ploy by Sesha to trap me!"

Okay, yes, this had been Zuzu's exact point from this morning, and yes, I had been all eager to join the contest back then, but that was before the Demon Queen wanted me to do it. If she wanted me to join, it couldn't be a good idea. The rakkhoshi was the villain in this scenario, and no heroic deed was going to result from following *her* advice.

"Oh, save me from mopey moon chits who live in horrible climates!" The Rakkhoshi Rani shook her fist to the gray sky. Then, with a screech that practically burst my eardrums, she shouted, "Bangoma! Bangomee!" Her voice was so loud I was sure we were going to be caught, and Principal Chen would make it rain detention slips all over me.

"Can you keep it down? I don't know what's going to happen if one of the teachers sees you . . ."

"Shh—ach—uh bup bup! Zip it!" the Queen yelled, making a "shut your face" sort of hand motion in front of my nose. Argh, she was so rude! Even in this half-transparent form.

"Oh, where are those dratted birds? They're always running on avian time. Clearly, they have never heard the expression about the early bird and the worm." She looked up at the skies and shouted, even louder this time, "Bangoma! Bangomee!"

"Shh!" I wanted to clasp my hands over her mouth but (a) her mouth was kind of see-through and (b) see-through or not, she was still a demoness, and I really didn't want to get my hands that close to her fangs. "What is wrong with you?"

The Rani whipped around to give me a red-eyed death stare, but she was interrupted from saying anything by the giant, human-faced birds Bangoma and Bangomee flapping down on the frosty field in front of us. Neel's mother tapped her not-really-there foot and pointed to what looked like a sundial strapped to her wrist. "You birdbrains never have any sense of time, do you? What kind of application ambassador operation are you running, anyway? Your union is going to hear about this, believe you me! Be this late again, and I'm going to give you a one-star review on Cracken's List, and then where will you be?"

Your words are mean, but we will serve you, Queen.

"Show this moon chickie why she needs to join *Who Wants to Be a Demon Slayer?*" The bees around the queen swooped and buzzed.

"I'm not going anywhere with you!" I protested, backing up a little.

"Well then, you're in luck. I've got a workout session scheduled with my new trainer. Got to get in my crunches," the Queen snapped. "Anyway, I can't go. My essence has a block on it from going where they'll be taking you. It's also the reason I haven't been able to tell you the whole story."

"You have a block on your, er, essence?" I wasn't even sure what the words meant.

"Oh, come on!" The Rakkhoshi belched loud and long, sending a bunch of bees streaming out of her nostrils. "You mean to tell me in this dimension, no one monitors your harmonigram conversations and demony-mail? Don't be naive, do you actually believe no one is watching?"

I wasn't sure what to say to that, so I just doubled down on my original point. "I don't care what you have to say. I'm not going to be a contestant on *Who Wants to Be a Demon Slayer?*"

"Oh, you'll change your mind soon enough." The Rakkhoshi pointed a long talon at the birds. "Show her! Now!"

Bangoma and Bangomee shook their rain-darkened feathers and stretched out their wings. I flinched, more than a little cautious since our last dizzying encounter. They opened their eyes wide, and again, I felt like I was falling into their swirling rainbow irises. Those swirly, whirly birdie eyes somehow pulled me out of myself so much that I actually felt separate from my body and my spirit.

Now, Princess, see what you must save.

"No!" I resisted the pull, squeezing my eyes shut at the last minute. "I won't! I don't want to!"

"Oh, yes, by my chin hairs and cracked feet and slowly developing six-pack, you will!" screeched the Queen, shoving my spirit into the birds' irises.

Falling into the giant birds' eyes was the wackiest, weirdest, coolest thing. I felt like I was flying through a movie on super-duper fast-forward. I saw so much—the green fields and rich forests of my parents' homeland, the cawing monkeys and dappled deer. And it wasn't just my sense of sight either. I could smell dizzyingly scented flowers, piled high in the marketplace, hear the mystical possibilities of an early morning raga played on a stringed sitar. I zipped by vivid colors, and people with faces like mine, and the chaotic wonderfulness of a place where history walked hand in hand with modern life. And best of all, I was quickly dry and warm.

Then I felt like I was crashing underwater. Propelled down, down, down in some sort of a bubble to the bottom of the ocean. I wasn't swimming, I wasn't even really there, but I could see it all—the schools of neon fish, the bright coral and the green seaweed dancing about like a mermaid's flowing hair. Then my progress finally slowed down, and I saw him. I couldn't believe it. How could it be? But there he was.

We were standing in a room that didn't look like any-where in the royal palace. It was small, and weirdly familiar, with steel walls and stone floors. And I was right there, in front of him, a boy I had thought was my friend. A boy who had blown me off in the harshest way after promising to be in touch. A boy who made me want to both jump for joy and punch him in the nose.

Neel.

CHAPTER 6

The Underwater Fortress

Well, isn't this a surprise! Where ya been, dude?" Needless to say, when I get mad, I have no sense of chill.

"Kiran!" Neel's dark eyes were wide with shock.

I'd been thinking about this moment for weeks now. What I'd say when I saw Neel again. How I'd be so calm and cool and collected. How I'd pretend it was no big deal that he hadn't been in touch. How I'd pretend like I hadn't missed him at all, and act like I barely remembered him. But all those plans flew right out of my head at the sight of Neel looking so darned surprised.

"Yeah, it's Kiran. Ki-ran." I dragged out the syllables in my name while pointing to myself with a jabby finger.

"Remember me? No, of course you don't. If you did, you would have called or written or ESP'd out some telepathy from your brain like Aquaman, or *something.*"

I thought about Lal, and how he'd gotten himself on intergalactic television to send me a message. A message about how he, and the entire dimension, were waiting for me. A message about how I was the hero everyone needed. Why hadn't Neel made a big old gesture like that? Why had he played it so cool when all I wanted to know was that he remembered I existed?

Neel didn't seem to register how upset I was but kept staring at me in what I can only describe as a doofy way. "I . . . I can't believe you're here."

"Where have you been all these weeks? Why have you been avoiding me?" I bit my lip to stop myself from saying more. Or rather, I tried to bite my lip. Because it was right then that I realized my entire body had the same see-through quality of the Rakkhoshi Rani on all my recent encounters with her.

"Kiran, I . . ." Neel began, but I cut him off, trying to get back in control despite being totally flustered, plus see-through.

"No, never mind. It so doesn't matter. I bet you've been busy, right? So have I. Very busy. So busy! Busy, busy, busy!

Busy with school, busy with your mom, busy with birds. Busy like a little buzzing bee! Bizzy, bizzy!"

"Wait, what?" Neel's mouth twitched a little, and he started chewing on a nail.

"Never mind," I mumbled. I needed to get ahold of myself. This was not the level of cool I'd been going for at all.

We were standing so close, I could practically reach out and touch him. Only, I couldn't figure out how to get my arms and legs to move. It was like my soul was with Neel in the Kingdom Beyond Seven Oceans and Thirteen Rivers, but my body was still back behind Alexander Hamilton Middle School in New Jersey.

"Kiran, listen, you've got to get out of here. It's not safe!" Neel tried to push me, but his hands went right through my shoulders.

"Stop that!"

Then, to my total annoyance, he tried it again. Again, his hands went through me like I was made of mist. I was there, but also not there. It was kind of disturbing.

"Oh, so you can't wait to get rid of me?" My heart was beating fast as the hurt words spilled out of my mouth. "I'm not cool enough to hang with you anymore—is that what all this has been about? You didn't want to be seen with a boring 2-D like me—or is it that I'm the daughter of the Serpent King? You afraid my blood is bad, and I'm going to go all rogue snake on you or something? Then why didn't you just say that to begin with? Why pretend like we were friends at all?"

This whole confrontation thing wasn't going according to plan. When I imagined it, I always sounded much more together, and Neel was usually begging for my forgiveness by now.

"Yeah, that's exactly it—you're a 2-D! Plus half snake! I don't want to hang out anymore! Go home!"

I was about to be offended, but then I saw Neel's eye do a weird twitch thing it always did when he wasn't telling the truth. "You're a terrible liar and a terrible friend!" I shouted. "Plus, what is going on with your hygiene situation here? You *look* terrible too!"

"Gee whiz, *Prin-cess*." He said the word in that drawn-out, irritating way he always used to, that way that made me think I was the furthest thing from a princess in his eyes. "Sorry I didn't spend enough time on my toilette."

I gave a little snort. Immature, I know, but that word always sounded way too much like *toilet* to me.

Neel barreled on. "You know, you always know how to make a guy feel great about himself."

"Stupid head!" I snapped. Honestly, I was feeling bad about my mean words because they were sort of accurate. Neel did look terrible. I mean, he was still handsome, but he also looked skinny and, weirdly for a half rakkhosh who hardly needed sleep, tired. He had big dark circles under his eyes, a fading bruise on his cheek, and one side of his lip looked a little puffy, like he'd been on the wrong end of somebody's fist.

"Look, I'm sorry I haven't been in touch, Kiran," he said, his voice all defeated.

His change in mood gave me the second I needed to take in our environment: the gray walls, the steel door, the sound of moaning and groaning rakkhosh on both sides. Wait a minute.

I took this all in wonderingly even as I asked, "Neel, where are you exactly?"

My friend picked up his hands to show me. Both of his wrists were bound in cruel metal shackles. The chain from his wrists led to shackles that bound his ankles too. They glowed a magical green, which was obviously why Neel, even with his rakkhosh strength, couldn't break out of them.

My feelings were going from angry and outraged to terrified. Neel was a prisoner. More than that, his eyes—there was something wrong with his usually confident brown eyes. They weren't twinkling with laughter, or sarcastic, or teasing. They were scared. Defeated, even. It was an expression I'd never really seen in them before.

"You're in demon detention," I breathed, everything clicking into place in my head. "You got rounded up by Sesha's minions for the game show."

"A-plus, Princess. You move to the head of the class." Neel sat down with a thump on the narrow bed.

In my shock, I'd somehow figured out how to move my transparent body. I paced back and forth across the floor, my legs kind of floating in midair. "You got rounded up to be bait in this terrible reality show! Somebody's going to try to kill you as part of *Who Wants to Be a Demon Slayer?*"

Neel smirked a little.

"Don't smile, this is no time to smile. You're in some serious trouble here," I snapped. But then something else hit me.

"Wait a minute." The terrible truth washed over me like liquid poison, making me dizzy. I had to sit down now too. "You got rounded up for me," I said, hardly believing my own words. "Sesha put you in here because of me."

"I don't know." Neel shrugged, then nodded. "Yeah, maybe. Probably."

I felt like my stomach had bungee-jumped off the top of the Mandhara Mountain. It was my fault Neel was here. My fault entirely. No wonder he seemed so mad at me. He must hate me. How could he not?

Then something else occurred to me. Something else I deserved to feel horrible about. "Wait. Your mom's been visiting me now for weeks through this Essence-Tyme thing, trying to tell me you were in trouble. Only . . . I didn't understand what she was saying. I . . . I didn't believe her."

My voice shook a little as I remembered how many times the Rakkhoshi Queen had tried to get me to understand. Only, I had just thought she was a villain out to trick me. In reality, she was trying to save her son.

"My mother visited you?"

"Of course." I started pacing again. "She wants me to join the *Who Wants to Be a Demon Slayer?* contest and then, I guess, break you out before we're forced to fight each other. Or something. She wasn't super clear on that part."

"No!" Neel leaped up from the bed. "You can't be a contestant. No way."

"What do you mean?" I pointed at my see-through body. "I can't exactly break you out in this form. I'm barely even here."

"No!" Neel repeated. "You've got to stay in New Jersey. Whatever you do, don't come to the Kingdom Beyond."

But I was pacing again, ignoring him. My mind was whirring, making plans. If it was my fault Neel was here, it was my responsibility to get him out again.

"I'll become a contestant, and join Lal like he asked me to. I don't know how much help your mom is going to be. She said something about having a block or something on her. Plus, no offense, she's a little untrustworthy, what with her tendency to eat people and stuff. But together with Lal, and maybe Mati and Tuni, I should be able to hack the contest . . ."

All the details weren't exactly clear to me yet, but the overarching mission was. I was going to get Neel out of here, even if that meant becoming a contestant in Sesha's game show after all.

"Lal and you will break me out?" Neel laughed in a way that made me a little worried about his mental state. "Lal and you?"

"Um, yeah?" I said.

"Kiran." Neel was still laughing, but also, weirdly, kind of crying. "Lal's the one who helped the contest producers put me here."

"Wait. I'm sorry. I must have heard you wrong. Did you just say that your brother Lal helped put you in this . . . this . . ." I gestured around at the cold cell.

"This undersea fortress of a rakkhosh prison? Yeah, that's what I'm saying. Lal's not who you think he is anymore."

Now it was my turn to laugh. "Absolutely, positively no way!" Neel was obviously delusional. The Lalkamal I knew was sometimes a little jealous of his older brother, and definitely in awe of him. But he adored him too. I couldn't imagine gentle and sweet Lalkamal doing anything to hurt Neel. It was totally unthinkable.

"There's got to be some kind of mistake," I said firmly, remembering what Lal had said at the end of the IGNN broadcast. "Lal said something on TV about there being more treasures to save than I knew about. He must have been talking about you. If he wants to save you, he couldn't have put you here. That makes no sense. So, the most important thing right now is for you to tell me how we can find you. Where is this detention center anyway?"

"Under one of the seven oceans, I don't know which. But it doesn't matter—you can't try to find me!" Neel said harshly. "You won't be able to. You'll just make a mess of it anyway! Like you did in New Jersey when you thought you were saving Lal, but then I had to come save you."

"That was only because you were sitting around letting Lal almost get eaten by that rakkhosh!" My heart was beating super fast now. Why was Neel being so mean? "I don't care if you think I can do it or not. I don't need your permission. I'm not going to let you stay a prisoner! And I'm not going to let you keep thinking it was Lal who did this to you!"

What I didn't add was that I couldn't let him blame his brother for something that was obviously my fault. Sesha was my birth father, and his weird issues were all with me.

The Serpent King had been trying to transform me into a magical snake and get me to join his minions since I was born. And the fact that I'd not only gotten away from him last fall but destroyed his underwater kingdom made him furious, I'm sure. He had made Neel bait in a trap for me, and no one else.

The last time we'd fought him, Sesha had trapped Neel in a magical orb of infinite torture. I still remembered the demon prince's horrible, gut-wrenching screams, not to mention Sesha's laugh. My bio father had taken pleasure in causing pain, but I think his real goal was to torture me by hurting Neel. And he didn't hesitate hurting me directly either. I could still feel the burning of my skin where he'd shot me with his green power bolts, trying to burn me alive. We'd barely escaped him then, and only because my moon mother had come to help us. So, I knew perfectly well what Sesha was capable of. And there was no way I was going to let him hurt Neel to get to me again.

"Kiran, don't try to break me out. I forbid you!" Neel was practically growling now.

"Forbid? Forbid! Who do you think you're talking to?" I shouted. "You can't forbid me! I'll rescue you if I want to and you'll be grateful, darn it!"

"No." Neel's face turned stony, making my insides shiver. "You're getting out of here, like ASAP. Who's running your Essence-Tyme anyway? Did my mom hire Bangoma and Bangomee? She shouldn't have gotten you involved in all this."

But I was involved. Why didn't he see that? "Neel . . ." I shouted, angry and sorry all at the same time. "I'm so sorry about everything. So sorry. I didn't know . . ."

But Neel wasn't paying attention to me anymore. All of his attention was now directed toward the cell doorway.

"Neel?" I guess there's really no way to tell someone you're sorry your evil serpent bio dad has captured him and put him in an underwater detention center fortress, all for the purpose of luring you into some yet-unclear doom. There was no greeting card or cute GIF for this, no matter how much I wished for one. But I had to get him to understand how bad I felt, how much I rejected Sesha. "Neel, listen . . ." But he didn't even let me finish my sentence.

"Get out of here, Kiran! Get out of here and don't come back!"

My not-even-present insides felt like ice. It was obvious Neel hated me. And to tell you the truth, I couldn't blame him.

"Move!" he hissed, even as he chewed nervously on the side of his nail.

"Neel . . ." I tried again, not even sure what I could say.

"Get out of here, Kiran! There's someone coming!"

That's when I heard them. The footsteps outside the locked doorway getting louder and louder. Heavy footsteps. Inhuman footsteps. Oh, this wasn't good. This was really, really not good.

"Kiran! If my guard manages to trap your essence, you'll never be able to get home!"

CHAPTER 7

Demon School Dropout

What Neel didn't understand was that I wasn't going anywhere without him. Besides, I couldn't leave even if I wanted to. I had no idea how the Essence-Tyme had gotten me here, and I had no idea how to reverse it.

Neel and I stood side by side, me with my trusty bow in hand, and him with what looked like a big wooden trident that had been propped up in the corner of the room. Wait, not a trident but something with a bit of rice and daal on it.

"A fork?" I hissed. "You're going to fight off whatever that is with a giant *fork*?"

Neel widened his fighting stance, his chained arms and legs clanking. Like me, he didn't take his eyes off the door, but snapped, "You think they let me keep my sword?"

There was no more time for banter then, because the door swung open and someone stepped into the small cell. Someone with multiple horns, skin covered in pus-oozing boils, and a very, very familiar face.

"Hi, Big Bwother!" the young demon bellowed.

"Your prison guard is *Bogli*?" Even though she was bigger now, almost as big as a grown rakkhoshi, I recognized the creature. Bogli had just been born from a well of dark energy back in November, when she'd chased my parents, Neel, and me, almost killing and eating us. Then Neel's mother, the Queen, had shown up and revealed Bogli was her adopted daughter, which meant she was Neel's sister.

"Yeah, Bogli's my personal guard. Someone's idea of a not funny joke, to use rakkhosh to guard rakkhosh." Neel waved his fork at Bogli's belly. We only came up to the young demon's waist now. I realized she'd grown in other ways too, with webs between her toes, gills along her neck, and webbing fanning out beneath her giant arms.

"Hey, you're that girl with the mean pointies!" Bogli bellowed. I rubbed one of my ringing ears. Even though she'd grown up a little, Bogli still didn't have any vocal volume control. And she obviously remembered when I'd hit her with burning, moon-magicked arrows the last time I'd seen her.

"Lay off her, you teenage rebel of a rakkhoshi!" Neel yelled, waving his fork.

I lowered my weapon a little and turned to Neel. "Are we supposed to attack your sister?"

"That monster's no sister of mine!" Neel snorted. "She rebelled against my mom, dropped out of demon school, and then the next thing I know, I see her here." He turned to Bogli. "Hey, rakkhoshi, what happens if Kiran and I try to run away from here?"

Bogli's eyes grew an angry crimson. "You no do that!" she shouted. "You do that, I eat you!"

Bogli lunged at us, her huge claws out, fishy drool streaming out of her mouth. "You stay here, Bwother! Or you die!"

"You see?" Neel called out to me. "Fire!"

I let my arrows fly. Unfortunately, about 50 percent bounced right off Bogli's scales. The other 50 percent that found their mark didn't seem to do much damage, but hung there kind of *boing*ing around.

"Uh, Neel?" But he was already on it, stabbing at Bogli's slimy skin with his fork-slash-trident.

I know it sounds weird, but it felt good, to be fighting alongside Neel again. Like it was where I should be. Well, except for the whole it-being-my-fault-he-was-here-and-him-hating-me part. That part pretty much stank.

"What happened to her anyway?" I yelped as Bogli swiped at me with her algae-streaked nails. I almost lost my balance, slipping on slick stone floor. "What's with all the webs and gills and stuff?"

"Bogli is my name I am," snarled the soggy beast. "A rakkhoshi from the water clan."

"Clan gifts don't appear until rakkhosh are teenagers—which is about two months after they're born," Neel explained as he dived out of the rakkhoshi's snarling but lumbering reach. "When Bogli got her clan gifts, she decided she wanted to be underwater with other rakkhosh like her, not living aboveground with my mother."

I remembered with a flash the listing of rakkhosh clans I'd read about in *The Adventurer's Guide to Rakkhosh, Khokkosh, Bhoot, Petni, Doito, Danav, Daini, and Secret Code* by the famous demonologist Khogen Prasad Das. When I'd left the Kingdom Beyond last fall, Neel had given me a copy of the book by his demonology professor, and I'd gotten into the habit of reading it whenever I'd missed my friends. Which meant all the time. I could see the page about demon clans in my head: .

Elemental Rakkhosh Clans
See Air Rakkhosh
See also Fire Rakkhosh
See also Land Rakkhosh
See also Water Rakkhosh

I'd read the entire section a few weeks ago, during a really boring social studies class. The awful, drooly rakkhosh that had broken into my house last fall to take my parents couldn't fly and liked to eat electric appliances, for instance, because he was a fire demon. On the other hand, the fangirl rakkhoshis who had chased Neel and me during our flight to the Kingdom of Serpents could fly because they were air demons. Of course, Neel's mom was the queen of them all, and therefore, had powers that stemmed from all four elements. So Bogli was a water rakkhosh, huh? Wait, what was that thing about water rakkhosh vulnerabilities?

"You're doing great, Neel!" I sidestepped out of Bogli's reach and fished out my battered copy of *The Adventurer's*

Guide from my backpack. The teenage monster had Neel in a headlock, but he was still managing to stab at her with the fork-slash-trident from under her armpit.

"Stop the stabbing, you! Or I rip your limbs in two!" Bogli's temper hadn't seemed to have improved since the last time we'd seen her. I remembered that back then, it had been the Serpent King who had given Bogli the power to transform herself into a giant whirlpool and almost swallow us. No wonder she'd gone back to him. She'd probably stayed loyal to him this whole time. I flipped quicker through the book, searching for something important.

"This is not a great moment for story time!" gasped Neel, but I ignored him. I knew exactly what I was looking for. My bow still in my hand, I quickly found K. P. Das's scientific diagram of water rakkhosh gills. The page described how rakkhosh gills were as strong as steel and only had a few vulnerable points in between the joints.

"Pwincess like a cozy stowy! When I eat her, she'll be sowwy!" boomed the rakkhoshi as Neel continued kicking and stabbing at her, with no luck.

Before I shut the book, my eyes fell on the next entry.

Elemental Rakkhosh Clans and Alchemy
the creation of precious metals
the quest for everlasting life
the birth of neutron stars
the all is one

I knew there was something important here for me to think about, about the relationship between rakkhosh and the precious Chintamoni and Poroshmoni Stones, but I had to put it out of my mind now and deal with more pressing matters. Like Neel and my imminent death and dismemberment.

Bogli the demon school dropout was drooling long lines of smelly spittle on Neel's head. Neel yelled bloody murder and managed to puncture one of Bogli's scales with the huge fork.

"Nice!" I yelled as I got back into the fight, launching a bunch of arrows to make up for my absence.

The young rakkhoshi ignored my arrows, but the fork must have hurt, because with a roar and a cry, she plucked out Neel's wooden weapon and flung it to the floor. Then she smacked Neel hard across the face. Because of his shackles, Neel didn't have super balance, so he fell hard, unable to use his hands too much to break his fall.

As my friend tumbled down, sure to become demon fodder any second, I shot forward, waving my arms at the beast. "Hey, barnacle head!" I shouted. "Why don't you pick on someone who's not in chains?"

"Girlie mean like electric eel! But pwincess isn't even real!" The rakkhoshi swiped at me, each time, her talons running right through my shadowy essence.

"Neel, are you okay?" I shouted, desperately trying to aim at Bogli's soft spots. I didn't want to kill her, but I certainly needed to slow her down and stop her from hurting either of us.

"Bangoma! Bangomee!" Neel called out to the empty air. "Stop the Essence-Tyme, get her out of here!"

"No! I'm not leaving you here!" I shouted, even as my vision started flickering. Screaming in frustration, I felt myself start to fade from the room, but then the teenage demoness managed to grab my ponytail. Bogli had me now, trapping me in this dimension as she lifted me face high, dangling from her filthy, webbed claws like a girl-shaped piñata.

"Let me go, you stinker!"

Now it was Neel's turn to attack Bogli again, trying to distract her from me. He got in a blow to the monster's thigh with both his shackled hands before Bogli flicked him off like a mosquito, then pinned poor Neel under a giant, warty foot.

"Bangoma! Bangomee! Any time now!" my friend croaked.

In the meantime, Bogli brought me even closer to her head, giving me a full blast of her disgusting bad breath. Her oozy fish drool poured onto me, dripping from my hair, cheeks, and nose. She peered at me with bloodshot eyes. "Who my bwother speak to, dear? Nobody but us fishes here!"

"I am not your dear!" I shot some arrows close range at the monster's head, trying to get her to let a now purple-faced Neel go. Unfortunately, dangling from the air as I was, and only half my actual self, I couldn't seem to steady my hands. The few arrows I was able to shoot went way off their mark, one coming closer to hitting Neel than the rakkhoshi.

"Watch it!" Neel sputtered.

"Sorry!" Concentrating like crazy to control my only halfway-present limbs, I took an arrow out of my quiver but didn't nock it in my bow. Instead, I looked for a soft spot on Bogli's slimy skin. "Hang in there, Neel!"

"Girlie underwater ghost, but I can eat her on some toast," Bogli mused, bringing me ever closer to her rancid breath, her algae- and seaweed-streaked teeth.

"Didn't anyone ever tell you not to snack between meals?"

I stabbed at Bogli's gill-ears with my arrow, aiming for the place that K. P. Das had marked as the most vulnerable. Success! My arrow broke off in the young rakkhoshi's skin, sending something flying. On instinct, I caught a steely piece of broken-off rakkhoshi gill.

Bogli screamed and jumped. Luckily, she moved enough to let Neel roll away from under her foot. Unluckily, she didn't let me go, but tightened her hold on my hair.

"Seafood girl get in me facer! I'll eat you with an oyster chaser!" Giant drops of green-black goo were dripping from Bogli's injured gill even as she drooled more long streams of spittle on my head. I felt like I was trapped at an all-you-can-eat seafood bar. Only, I was on the menu!

"Kiran, your hair!" Neel yelled as he launched himself again at Bogli's giant leg.

He was right. This was no time for vanity. I was no help to anyone as long as the underwater rakkhosh had ahold of my long hair. Or the essence of my long hair. Or however this whole thing worked.

Bogli was so upset now, she was glub-glubbing out giant bubbles as she spoke. "Girlie is a spicy sashimi! I bet she will taste so dreamy!"

Desperately, I brought the broken piece of rakkhoshi gill up to my hair and began to saw.

"I'm no sushi platter, you underwater oaf! More like a big blob of wasabi in your eye!" As I hacked away, I felt the tension from my pony easing.

"Bangoma! Bangomee!" Neel yelled from his position grabbing at Bogli's thick ankle. "Get Kiran out of here!"

"I'm taking you with me!" I yelled, hacking at the last bits of hair that kept me attached to the rebellious teenage rakkhoshi.

"No, Kiran! It doesn't work like that! Get out of here now!"

"Neel, come on!" Did he hate me so much for getting him into this mess that he couldn't let me rescue him?

By the time I sliced through the last bits of my ponytail end, I could feel something otherworldly pulling hard at me, taking me away from Neel. It yanked at my insides with an invisible hand. As I finally cut that very last strand of hair attaching me to the demon's webbed claws, my vision went really wacky—the room started twisting and twirling like I was some kind of Olympic figure skater doing a triple-double-quadruple lutz. I felt my essence being sucked, as if through a giant straw, from this reality back into my own.

"Octopus! Shark! Tuna! Minnow! Where my snakie girlie go?" the water rakkhoshi moaned as my head, face, and body all began to vanish, and all she had left in her hands was a ragged bottom of my ponytail.

"Neel!" I held out my rapidly fading hand. "Come on!"

Neel gave me a look so intense and angry it made me want to cry. "Just get out of here!"

"I don't understand!" I couldn't keep the wail out of my voice.

"Go, Kiran!" Neel spat. "And don't come back!"

"Be careful!" I yelled, even as the nausea swept over me like a tidal wave and everything around me shifted like the inside of a kaleidoscope.

Even in my halfway-present state, I could see what Neel couldn't: that Bogli was advancing on him with venom in her eyes. In a second, the rakkhoshi pinned his arms behind him in a deathly grip.

"Stop!" I yelled, but no one heard my call. The young rakkhoshi had her evil-looking fangs at Neel's throat when my vision clicked off and I was home.

CHAPTER 8

The Secret of the Gardening Shed

N o!" I screamed. "No!"

I wasn't in the underwater detention center anymore, but back behind the gardening shed at school. It had stopped ice-raining, but instead, the tears rained down my cheeks. I wasn't sure if I was crying because Neel was in prison, and maybe in some serious danger right now, or because it was my fault and he so justifiably hated me. Probably all of the above.

His mother, the Demon Queen, had no patience for any of it, though. "Oh, dry your eyes, you simpering snit! Bawling is for babies!" Then she took a closer look at me. "What have you done to your hair? Why is it so uneven, not to mention *green*?"

"What?" I flipped the bottom of my now-uneven, ragged ponytail over my shoulder only to see that the Queen was right. The bottom part, where I'd chopped it with Bogli's scale, had turned a bright, emerald green. What the heck? But I couldn't worry about that now.

"It's a new fashion, okay?" I snapped. "Like you should talk. What are you *wearing*?" Whereas I'd only seen her before in glamorous, embroidered silk saris, now the rakkhoshi queen was in some kind of 1980s workout gear— neon yoga pants, exercise tank, and even a ridiculous headband.

"I told you I was getting in my crunches!" the Demon Queen snapped. I'd never noticed before how much Neel's eyes were like hers.

That helped get my mind back on the important issue. "Neel . . . I saw him. He's in demon detention!"

"Oh, *really*? You don't say, arugula hair?" snapped the demoness with so much sarcasm, I felt my cheeks burn. "Not like it's your fault or anything that he's there. Oh, wait, wait a minute, it *is* your fault!"

I bit at my lip, feeling somewhat grateful I now had a flesh and blood lip to bite. "I'll do whatever it takes to get him out. I promise."

"I don't need stinking promises! Promises aren't going to get my son away from your disgusting reptilian father!" The Rakkhoshi Queen pointed a twisted talon at my chest. "I need *action*!" She flung open the gardening shed door with a dramatic sweep of her hands. "You better get your butt to the registration office, missy misfit, before they're all out of forms! And then you better be the best bloomin' contestant that twisted game show has ever seen! If you don't make it to the final test, when Sesha brings out Neel for you to fight, all of this won't be worth anything! And neither will his life!"

"I'm not going to let anything happen to him, I pro . . ." At a cutting look from the demoness, I let the word *promise* die in my throat. I desperately wanted to ask her if she had a plan of how I was going to get Neel free after I got to the final round, but I didn't dare. I guess I would have to just figure something out with Lal, Mati, and Tuni. Yes, that was it.

"Now get going! Time's a-wasting, Princess Green Eggs and Ham."

As the Rakkhoshi Rani swung the door of the gardening shed even wider, I fully expected to see some sort of psychedelic, swirling portal, or maybe one of those British porta potties that double as time-space traveling machines. After all, she may be half-present but those giant birds were obviously getting in and out of this dimension somehow. But instead, all I saw was an old wheelbarrow, some shovels, and a bunch of empty flowerpots. It was a little anticlimactic.

I ran my hand through my uneven new locks, unable to keep the disappointment out of my voice. "Is this the part when you teach me to ride a flying garden shovel and tell me I'm really a magician?"

"Oh, shove it up your unnecessary literary reference," snapped the demoness. "Your chariot awaits!"

I peered around, but all I could see besides the wheelbarrow, shovels, and a few piled bags of fertilizer and mulch was what looked like a weird yellow-and-black lawnmower. The Queen saw me looking at it and snapped her teeth, making a dramatic hand gesture toward the thing.

"Ta-da!" she said, emphasizing the statement with a bee-filled burp.

I looked a little closer at the machine, which wasn't so much a lawn mower as a little three-wheeled go-kart-slash-golf-cart. It was painted bright yellow and black, and had a roof and windshield but no doors. The top and sides were decorated with shiny plastic streamer things, and there were colorful pom-poms on both sides of the windshield. It didn't have a steering wheel but handlebars like a motorcycle. Unlike a motorcycle, though, there was a broad seat for the driver, and behind that, a bench for passengers. It was an auto rikshaw, kind of an open-air taxi. I'd seen them on my last visit to the Kingdom Beyond but never ridden in one.

The outside of the auto was decorated with tongue-waggling demon faces, as well as spray-painted warning signs for both customers and other drivers:

Keep money safe from thieving hands,
Hide it in your underpants!

Hi, hello, yes you, pip pip!
Do not scrimp on driver's tip!

Slowly, slowly drive with grace,
Fastly, fastly crash in space.

Darling, do not follow close,
Auto rikshaw makes you ghost!

"But . . . there aren't any *walls*," I said doubtfully.

"You aren't going to have a *head* soon if you don't quit your lip flapping and get in!" The Demon Queen pointed a talon to the driver's seat.

"Is there a wormhole nearby? Or a transit point?" Last time I'd traveled to the Kingdom Beyond, I'd had to use a transit station all the way in Arizona, and it had taken all night flying on the back of a pakkhiraj horse to get there.

"Bangoma and Bangomee can make a wormhole. They're magic like that," the demoness explained as she basically pushed me into the front seat of the auto rikshaw with an accompanying burp. "Oof! This ombol!" she muttered, before explaining, "The birds are waiting at the end of this football pitch. It shouldn't be too hard, even for you. Drive toward them at top speed and then head for the vortex they make in between them. Just try not to screw it up."

"But . . . but . . . I don't even have a driver's license!" I protested. I supposed by "football pitch," the rakkhoshi meant the soccer field.

I heard from a distance the faint sound of my name. "Ms. Ray? Kiranmala! Are you out here somewhere?" It was Dr. Dixon's voice, and Principal Chen's too. Oh no, they'd finally figured out I hadn't gone to the nurse's office.

"My teachers are looking for me." I heard my name being called again. Crud. It wouldn't be long before Principal Chen telephoned my parents. And knowing them, they would freak, maybe even call the police. "My parents. They'll be so worried."

"Don't get all acid refluxy about it," the Demon Queen

cackled. "Your adopted parents will figure out exactly where you are when they see you on Thirteen Rivers television, competing in *Who Wants to Be a Demon Slayer?*"

That image was no better than the one where my parents were crying with worry. In my mind's eye, I imagined how angry Ma and Baba would be to see me in the Kingdom Beyond, especially after they had point-blank told me not to go. But that also reminded me of how furious Neel was at me. So furious he wouldn't even leave with me when given the chance. I couldn't leave him in that detention cell, not when it was my fault he was there. Ma and Baba would understand that. I really hoped so anyway.

But I didn't have more time to think about all that now, because Principal Chen's voice was suddenly very close. "Kiranmala? Are you out here?" And then, "Could she be hiding in the gardening shed?"

"Flip on the gas and push the red start button!" the rakkhoshi hissed as she pointed to a little red button on the dashboard. "And don't you dare miss the wormhole! I'm paying those dratted birds by the hour and intergalactic vortexes don't come cheap!"

Without really knowing what I was doing, I pressed the start button and placed my hands on the motorcycle-like handles of the auto. The back bench was covered with a bumpy burlap sack, and I wondered briefly if I should try and get the fertilizer or whatever that was out of the auto before driving off. But then the engine rolled over with a rattling screech, and my heart jumped into my throat. Oh, what was I doing?

"Accelerator on the right-hand side; clutch and gears on the left! Green button to take off!" The Demon Queen indicated the open doorway of the shed, and the long stretch of soccer field beyond. "Time might fold in on itself during the journey, but don't have a meltdown, it won't pass that quickly here."

Time folding in on itself? I had no idea what she was talking about but didn't really want to know either. I reached for the seat belt, only to realize that there wasn't one. Oh, man. If my mom knew about this, she'd totally kill me.

"Kiranmala!" It was Dr. Dixon, sounding so worried it actually made me pause. I wondered if Principal Chen would fire him for losing me. And then, in the distance, I heard it. Police sirens racing toward the school.

"I . . . I don't know . . ." I stammered, but the Rakkhoshi Queen snapped, "Oh, get going already you big nincompoop!" She leaned over me and revved the engine, making the little auto rikshaw shoot out of the shed and start rumbling down the frozen field.

"Kiranmala, is that you?" Dr. Dixon's voice behind me was full of shock and recognition. "What are you doing?

Come back!" I guess the auto rikshaw didn't have the cloaking spell on it after all.

"Go! Straight at the birds!" the demoness screeched. "And don't lift off until the last minute! I'll make a biryani out of your innards if you don't make it—those dratted birds don't give refunds!"

I gunned the engine and drove as fast as I could manage. My hair flew, and my cheeks wibble-wobbled against the frosty, rushing air. At the end of the frozen soccer field, just above the far goal, I could see Bangoma and Bangomee circling around and around each other, and the faint light they were creating between them. At least my teacher and principal couldn't see the magical creatures. Unfortunately, they could see me.

"What is that student doing on that scooter mobile?" shrieked my principal. "This is an unauthorized vehicle driving on school grounds! And a student taking a field trip without a permission slip! And the faking of a nurse's visit! Stop her now!"

I pictured our detention-slip-happy principal running behind me up the icy field, her pregnant belly sticking out in front of her. Oh, this was not good. It was really not good.

"Kiran! What are you doing, young scientist?" Dr. Dixon sounded so hurt and confused I almost turned the auto around. But then I thought of Neel in that cell, and the fact that it was my fault, and kept my eyes on my goal.

I was practically flying over the icy ground now, going too fast to hear my teachers behind me. I hoped I wouldn't crash before I made it to the birds. I really didn't want to deal with the rakkhoshi if I wasted her wormhole deposit. The machine was bumping over the frozen grass, barely in my control. The birds flew faster and faster, the light between them glowing bright now, like some kind of midair sparkly disco ball.

"Faster, moonie!" I heard the demoness yell, and realized she was zipping along right next to me, her see-through body in its workout gear flying on the wind.

The wormhole between the birds swirled at a frenzied pace now, and colors shot off it like sparks of lightning. I saw that there was a blue sphere opening, like an eye, in the center of the space. A portal.

At the sound of another engine, I gave a quick glance over my shoulder. Close behind me, inexplicably, was my pregnant principal, in her giant SUV, off-roading over the frozen soccer field! What was she doing? She bumped and swerved, but was almost on me!

"Drive through the center and into the wormhole as fast as you can!" The Demon Queen gnashed her sharp teeth, rubbing her chest. "Oof! Your incompetence is giving me a peptic ulcer! Go get my son, you little twit!"

That was obviously the closest to a good-bye and good luck I was going to get.

The wormhole was opening, like a giant blue-and-purple mouth. It pulsated with energy and sound, making the very sky seem to vibrate.

"Push the green button!" shrieked the demoness. "Now!"

I pushed the button, feeling myself lift off the ground. Who knew whether Principal Chen or Dr. Dixon could see me. I couldn't worry about them anymore. I gunned the auto rikshaw engine and drove as fast as I could toward the rip in the fabric of space-time.

CHAPTER 9

An Auto Rikshaw in Space

If you have never driven an auto rikshaw through a rip in the fabric of space-time created by two giant, hippopotamus-sized birds, I strongly recommend wearing a bike helmet when you do so. And if your rikshaw doesn't have a seat belt, you should probably consider duct-taping yourself to the seat. Because I have never been on such a bumpy, upside-down, mentally and emotionally disturbing ride in my life. And I've been on some doozies.

First, no matter what that long-haired high school dude who works at the arcade tells you, playing a lot of video games during the summer in no way prepares you for driving a tin can through space. You know those outer space shows where every time they go into warp drive the whole bridge crew goes, "Whoa!" and hangs on to the controls and pretends to shake from side to side? Yeah, it was nothing like that. The motorcycle handlebars were super hard to control, and I felt like the rikshaw was driving me rather than the other way around. I hung on as the machine swung left and right, upside down, and, most of the time, diagonally. Then there was the whole experience of being in outer space. I don't know what kind of magic spell the auto rikshaw had on it, but even though I wasn't wearing a space suit, I could breathe and didn't explode from lack of pressure or gravity or anything, so I guess that part was good. But otherwise the experience was pretty awful. I felt like I was being squished together, until I was practically two-dimensional like a piece of paper. Then my body, spirit, and essence felt like they were being folded up like origami art. Finally, I re-expanded, but still felt my body and spirit in sharp creases and folds. And then the whole thing happened all over again.

It was in the middle of this process of folding and unfolding that I heard it. It was the sound of someone who has to sneeze but is trying to swallow it down and not make any noise.

"Who's there?" I whipped around to look at the passenger's bench behind me.

Remember how I said that the ride was super bumpy and I had no seat belt? Thus, the whole whipping-around-in-my-seat-to-look-behind-me thing? Not smart.

I got knocked clear out of my seat and almost out of the rikshaw, which was unfortunately traveling through the wormhole at a sideways angle at the time. I grabbed on to the only thing I could, holding on for dear life. It was those jingly-jangly decorations on the sides of the machine that saved me from plummeting right into that rip in the fabric of time and space. That and the surprisingly strong hand that Naya extended to me. Wait, what?

"What are you doing here?" I asked after I was done screaming and crying and thanking her for saving my skin.

"Hi, Your Highnosity! Isn't it great? I am—how do you say?—a stower-away!" Naya helped me sit back down in the driver's seat, grinning like the clueless cupcake full of sunshine she was. "I probably should have told you already, but before I lived in New Jersey—"

"You're originally from the Kingdom Beyond?" I sputtered, realizing that no one who wasn't could take in all this without freaking.

"Yes! So I thought I would keep you company! Because you weren't feeling well!"

"You thought you would keep me company?" I repeated.

"Yes! This will be great! It'll be like a sleepover! We can thread each other's eyebrows, paint our nails . . ."

"We're in an outer space *wormhole* and you want to paint our *nails*?" Was this girl for real? But I didn't have time to ask her more—why she'd lied about being from the Kingdom Beyond, how she knew I was traveling by auto rikshaw—because right then a comet whizzed by us and on our far, far left an enormous star looked like it was ballooning out into a super red giant. The light coming off it was tremendous. And yet, Naya was here talking about manis and pedis and eyebrow threading, as if we were doing nothing more than strolling through the Short Hills mall.

But interpreting sarcasm was not on Naya's list of skills. "We could do facials too!" she enthused, slapping a sticky thing on my nose that looked like a piece of masking tape. Then she looked at my pony with a critical eye. "Did you dye your hair like that on purpose? An interesting choice! Very, uh, unique! But let me make it even at least."

Naya pulled out some nail scissors and a bottle of gel from who knows where, evening out my pony and then braiding it. She tilted her head to study the effect. "Quite green, but still nice!"

"I don't care about my hair!" I shouted, desperately trying to hold on to the steering as the auto rikshaw barely avoided a small asteroid field. "I just don't want to die!"

"Oh, pshaw, Your Majestic Serenity, you're such a jokester!" Naya yanked the tape off my nose, making me yelp. Then her face grew serious. "But blackheads are no joking matter. You really should consider taking better care of your pores. They'll thank you for it!"

Naya pulled my face around for a selfie. Under the picture, I saw her type *Just me and my new BFF having a spa day in our outer-space rikshaw!* before sending it off to her Instagreat account. Almost immediately, a bunch of "likes" floated across her screen. Wait, she was getting data bars out here? What kind of phone service did this girl have? I felt madder than ever that my parents *still* wouldn't let me get a cell phone—not even a stupid flip phone—before I remembered I had more important things to worry about.

"How are you not freaking out?" I asked her, indicating the fact that we were, you know, in deep space. "You realize where we are, right?"

Naya blinked in a surprised way, but she didn't manage to answer, because just then, as if just driving an auto rikshaw through space-time wasn't strange enough, things got *really* funkalicious. The rikshaw banked hard left, then right, then shuddered, practically dislodging both of us again. Then we drove into such a bright, blinding light that I could barely see.

"Downshift! Upshift!" yelled Naya. "Pull fuel pin! Crank the space gear!"

I had no idea what any of that meant, but tried to just hang on to the motorcycle handles with both hands.

This wormhole was clearly not just any wormhole, having been formed by two giant, magical birds. Traveling through it was not just the experience of getting from one dimension to another, but more like rewinding the history of the entire multiverse. Of course, I only realized that later. As I tried desperately to control the machine, with Naya shouting useless instructions from the back seat, I felt again like I was being folded up. Only this time, I was being smushed together with Naya, the rikshaw, some moons and planets and stars—basically everything in all of space. Then, boom! Or rather, splaaat! The big bang. But instead of an explosion, as the name implies, it was more like being a really, really tightly folded up little paper that then gets smoothed out over billions and trillions of miles. Except in three dimensions. I guess the best way to describe it is feeling like a chocolate chip all glommed together at the center of a giant dough ball that then spreads out as it heats—distributing chips light-years apart as it stretches itself out, creating a giant cookie universe.

But the big-bang-slash-great-chocolate-chip-cookie theory of the 'verse wasn't the only origin story we experienced. As we passed from our universe through many others, we lived through other beginnings, other ways to understand the birth of the cosmos. We traveled through a solar system that looked like it was revolving around fire, saw the sun rising from an infinite sea, the chaos of the universe morphing into an egg that was then split in balanced two by an ax-wielding god, resulting in earth and sky, murky and clear, yin and yang. Even as we saw all of these possibilities, I knew there were an infinite number of other stories we didn't see, stories that whirred by us too fast for my brain to comprehend; beginnings and beginnings and beginnings without end.

The last thing we saw floating by us in space-time were some gods and demons churning an ocean of milk. They pulled on a familiar-looking snake wrapped around a mountain that operated as a churn. Out of the ocean rose medicine and poison, light and dark, good and evil, and then a sparkling white stone and a glowing yellow one. Holy smokes! We were watching the birth of the Chintamoni and Poroshmoni Stones! Hadn't the

Rakkhoshi Rani said something about this in that poem? Something about seeking immortality from the milk-white sea? I remembered her next words, "Jewels, stars, eternity. Life and death in balance be." Those stones must be more powerful than the Raja knew, and that's why Sesha was after them. That's why he'd set up this whole game show. He wanted the power of the stones to grant him wealth, and maybe even the ability to cheat death! Maybe this whole thing wasn't about me at all, but about Sesha's greed and those two jewels!

But then the black void and distant stars of space became the bright blue sky and the humid air of a hot summer's day. I felt like I was choking in my winter coat, and struggled to get it off. In the meantime, the rikshaw kind of floated and hopped, like a plane making a rough landing. Naya and I couldn't really talk anymore because of all the dry wind whipping by our ears, but soon enough, the rikshaw practically crashed down in a field in front of what looked like a high barbed-wire fence. We were finally in the Kingdom Beyond Seven Oceans and Thirteen Rivers, outside of the same bazaar where I had first entered this dimension.

"Oof!" Naya exclaimed as the auto came bouncing down. "Your Princessness, no offense, but you really must work on smoother landings!"

I didn't bother arguing with the girl, but instead looked around, taking in where we were.

Everything looked really different than when I'd walked through a field of flowers last fall, crossed a bridge over a babbling brook, and strolled into the quirky little market. Sure, the crooked streets and colorful, haphazard houses were still there, but where there had been lush green grass, now the land looked dry and parched. The brook too, just beyond the new twelve-foot-high barbed-wire fence, seemed all dried up and full of trash—empty chip bags, chocolate wrappers, plastic coffee cups, and soda cans. But that wasn't the strangest thing. The strangest thing was the game show recruitment slogans plastered everywhere we looked. Hanging from every lamppost and tree were banners for *Who Wants to Be a Demon Slayer?* with the TSK snake-eating-its-tail logo and contest logo of the bow-wielding girl with her braid, green skin, and purple combat boots. Each banner had a slightly different recruitment slogan for potential contestants, obviously written by the government of the Kingdom Beyond:

Get Off Your Rear End and Become a Real Legend!
Make Demons Groan, Win Back Our
Thinking Stone!

Embrace your Hero's Fate (Plus You'll Get a Lot of Dates!)

"Um . . . Your Majesticness?" Naya ventured, pointing an unsure finger up at the green-skinned girl.

"I know, it looks just like me—except the skin!"

"Well, you do have the green hair," said Naya. Then she pointed at my arm, which was exposed now that I'd taken off my coat and sweatshirt. "And there's the green scar on your arm."

"Green scar?" I looked down with alarm, and sure enough, the snake sign on my upper arm had taken on a faintly green hue. I whipped out a bandanna from my backpack and slapped it over the mark. This must be a side effect of Essence-Tyme, or traveling though the wormhole, or something. "I can't believe that game show logo looks so much like me!" I repeated as I tied off the bandanna.

"Shhh," Naya cautioned. "Maybe it is better that you don't let on to everyone here who you are."

That's when I realized we weren't alone.

CHAPTER 10

Who Wants to Be a Demon Slayer?

The auto had landed us in a giant line with hundreds— maybe thousands—of other people. There were people on foot, in cars, in rikshaws, and in taxis, people on horses, elephants, and even one person on what looked like a giant flying crocodile.

"I'm sorry, Uncle, what is this line for?" I respectfully asked an old man on a unicycle.

"Why, to sign up for *Who Wants to Be a Demon Slayer?* obviously!" The man pointed a gnarled finger in front of us. "Or have you been asleep this past month?"

"The contest's been going on a month?" I asked in alarm, remembering what the Demon Queen had said about time folding in on itself.

The old man wrinkled his hooked nose. "Yes, since the Raja made the announcement on television!"

I took a big gulp. Okaaaay. It had taken us a month to get here. I could only hope the Rakkhoshi Rani was right about time not moving as fast back home. I looked around me. At the front of the line, I could see a bunch of colored lights and streamers decorating a big cement building— like for a Bengali wedding. Only, instead of a sign above the doorway made of flower petals that read something like *Gargi weds Ashish* or *Tumpa marries Bunty*, there was a huge hand-painted sign that read *GAME SHOW RECROOTMENT CENTAR*. My skin prickled with sweat and discomfort, but also foreboding. I was going to have to join Sesha's contest and beat him at his own game. Could I do it? But if all he wanted was the jewels anyway, maybe I could. Maybe I could somehow trade the Poroshmoni for Neel's life? But even as I thought this, I shook my head. What was I thinking? That I'd steal the jewel from the Raja and give it to Sesha? I couldn't do something like that. Could I?

In the line were people of all ages and genders waiting to sign up for the Serpent King's game show. There were entire households—from bent-over grannies to crawling babies. And if that wasn't strange enough, some people were wearing costumes. Well, one costume in particular.

Not everyone, but a bunch of people in the line had on green makeup, braided wigs, and purple combat boots. A lot of the people in costume were girls my age, but there were some adults too! A portion of those who were dressed up were also carrying homemade bows and arrows—some out of tinfoil and sticks, and some looking like they could actually do some damage. The answer to the question "Who wants to be a demon slayer?" was obvious: everyone.

Each group of contestants in the line was in a frenzy of activity. Moms, dads, and even what looked like professional tutors were coaching hopeful kid contestants, quizzing them on riddles, making them warm up their voices with scales: "sa-re-ga-ma-pa-dha-ni-SA! SA-ni-dha-pa-ma-ga-re-sa." A few older kids were practicing stylized-martial-arts-slash-yoga-type moves, one group with swords. Another bunch of contestants in their twenties seemed to be practicing crying spontaneously on camera. "They're going to take the contestants who can give them the most drama," I heard one woman say as she burst into tears and then proceeded to pull at her friend's hair, calling her terrible names. The two hair pullers were pulled apart by a brawny, tattooed dude, and then all three started screaming really foul insults at each other, until the brawny dude called time. "Arré, 'pooper-scooper' is not a real curse word!" he told one of the hair-pulling drama queens.

The good thing about so many people being dressed up in "Princess Demon Slayer" costumes was that no one actually recognized me. It was obvious that they just thought I was a cosplayer like them. A middle-aged, glasses-wearing woman in spray-painted boots and a braided wig (which looked like it was made from an old mop—seriously!) gave me a sneer. "You've got the boots, bow, and arrows right, but your hair is completely wrong! The green highlights in your braid—as if!"

"Um, thanks for the advice?" I managed.

Naya gave me a look, and we both collapsed into giggles. Even though I still had a bunch of questions about her, I was actually really glad Naya had stowed away with me. It was nice to have some company.

But the fun didn't last long. The sun was so hot that soon the parked auto rikshaw started to feel like an oven. We stored our winter coats under the passenger bench, since even looking at them made me sweat. Even though we weren't too far from the Salty Ocean of Forgetfulness, there wasn't even a drop of a breeze. Before long, I felt like we'd be here forever, baking in the sizzling sun.

"How long will it take us to get through this line, you think?" I was just asking Naya, when we both saw the cameras.

Naya gave a little squeak and dived under her burlap sack again. What was she doing? The girl was going to burn up in this heat!

Coming toward us, down the line, was a man with too-pale makeup all over his face. I could tell it was makeup because his throat and hands were much browner than his face. He was wearing reflective shades, a very tight kurta that showed off his chest muscles, and some even tighter jeans. I recognized him, I realized, from the IGNN program. It was Suman Rahaman, Twinkle Chakraborty's co-anchor! He was super famous and very charming, and since he'd been the Kingdom Beyond's cricket team captain at one point, everyone referred to him as "Sooms"—like he was their personal buddy.

Behind Sooms were two umbrella holders, who shaded the star from the sun, and two sweating camera people, whom no one was shading. The anchorman was interviewing the contestants in line, who were going wild—cheering and waving and hamming it up for the cameras.

"What brings you to this *endless* line today?" The anchor flashed his toothy smile as he talked to one of the families with young kids. "Money? Glory? The chance to drop-kick some rakkhosh on live TV while the entire kingdom cheers you on?"

"We want something better for our children," the father answered, gripping his son and daughter by the shoulders. "We want them to be like the crown prince or the Princess Demon Slayer—brave and strong, fierce and true!"

"Arré, lovely! How nice! How quaint! Cho cho chweet!" Suman Rahaman gestured to one of his umbrella holders, who handed the kids some melty-looking chocolate bars.

As the kids licked their chocolate from the wrappers, I followed the father's gaze upward and realized there were a bunch of billboards overhead that I hadn't even noticed yet.

The giant billboards weren't for movies, but rather, starred two very familiar people: Lal and me—Lal and me fighting the rakkhosh on my front lawn, Lal and me flying on the backs of the two pakkhiraj horses. There were even images of Lal and me doing things for which he wasn't actually around—like fighting Bogli in her whirlpool form. In all the posters, we'd been made to look older than we actually were. They'd photoshopped bulging muscles on Lal's arms, given him a six-pack that for some reason showed through his clothes, and pasted a flowing moustache on his face like the Raja's. As for me, I had slightly green-tinged skin, like in the logo, but in addition, my lips were big and red, my eyes huge with curling eyelashes, and my braid was whipping behind me almost like a—dare I say it?—snake. The billboard sayings all had to do with the two of us:

Princess Kiran and Prince Lal
Will slay the rakkhosh one and all!

She's half snake, we'll admit, to be fair
But she's still our Princess Demon Slayer!

In between killing demonic thugs
Kiran and Lal steal kisses and hugs!

Make the kingdom pure, kill the rakkhosh dead
The only good demon is one without a head

Kisses and hugs? What was that about? But I didn't even have time to think it through, because just then Suman Rahaman was jabbing a microphone in my face, and the bright lights from his camera crew were making me see spots.

"Young lady, I see you've tried to dress like Princess Kiranmala, the legendary demon slayer! What brings you here today to join the multiverse's number-one mega-popular super-hit game show?"

I blinked against the light, shading my eyes. "I'm here because, um . . ." What was I supposed to say? I couldn't say I was here to rescue Neel, certainly not on live intergalactic television. So I decided on another part of the truth. "I'm here because I want to be the hero I know I am."

"Oh, my, my! How honorable! How sincere! Well, good luck to ya with that!" Sooms made a tsk-tsk noise with his mouth, like he thought I was so deluded. Then one of the helpers opened a small cooler and handed Suman Rahaman what looked like an ice-cold cola. Ignoring me and looking directly into the camera, Sooms took a long sip, smacking his lips at the end with a satisfied "ah."

I'm not ashamed to say I almost drooled at the sight of the cold drink. It was hot out here.

"This interview was brought to you by ice cold *Thumpuchi*, carbonated beverage to cricketers and stars," said the anchor man into the camera with a sparkling grin.

I was almost going to ask him if I could have a sip, but then he chucked me under the chin and continued on down the line.

"Maybe you shouldn't have done that, Your Highness! Gotten yourself on television!" Naya hissed from the back seat. "Someone is sure to recognize who you are soon!"

"So what?" I countered. "Why do I need to hide my identity anyway? I do enough of that back in New Jersey. Why should I do it here?"

"Until we find your friends!" Naya argued. "Until we have some more support!"

I supposed the girl had a point. I couldn't very well save Neel if Sesha caught me and imprisoned or killed me right now. I was about to tell her that, when she gave a little peep and dived under her sack again. I realized someone else official was coming down the line. This time it was a skinny little man driving a water-buffalo cart. He (the man, not the buffalo) was in a threadbare hotel bellhop jacket worn over a dirty dhoti and kurta. Someone who didn't know how to sew very well had haphazardly stitched a little patch with the *Who Wants to Be a Demon Slayer?* logo on his jacket. On his bald head was a triangular topi, and in the open cart were piled folders, rumpled and stained papers, some type-writers, and even a large, broken filing cabinet.

I saw that as he stopped at each group of contestants, he handed out some numbered tickets, like they do in that really popular bagel shop on Route 46 during the breakfast rush.

"Number five thousand three hundred and twenty-two!" I exclaimed when the little man handed me my number.

"Yes, be ready to have your blood sample drawn in, oh, say, two or three hundred hours," he snapped from his cart. He clicked his tongue at the sleepy water buffalo, who swished its tail to chase away some flies before slowly starting to walk away.

"But I've already had my blood drawn!" I said. Then I remembered what the Rakkhoshi Rani had told me. "And it's been approved!"

"You already have an approved blood sample?" Both the old man and his buffalo gave me hard looks. "Do you have the paperwork—signed in quadruplicate?"

"Um . . ." There was nothing for it but to tell the truth. "No?"

The old man rolled his eyes and sighed. "Here, fill these out," he handed me a giant sheaf of smudged papers from the cart. "Oh, these too."

As I took the bundle from him, he handed me one of the

ancient-looking typewriters too. "Fill them out in quadru-plicate! Four times!" said the old man. "Then go get them countersigned by Laltu-da up in the countersignature office! Oh, but make sure to first get it verified by Rama-di down in verification. That's critical."

"Rama-di, then Laltu-da," I repeated. "Verification office, countersignatures."

"Oh, but Rama-di won't be back until two, and Laltu-da's only here until one," shouted the man, almost as an afterthought.

"Then how am I supposed to get their signatures in that order?" I protested.

"So impatient, you young people! Such linear thinkers!" The man shrugged and seemed about to go on, but I reached out and grabbed the buffalo's harness. The animal blinked at me sleepily, chewing on some cud and drooling a long line of disgusting spittle onto my foot.

"Hey!" I protested as I shook the buffalo spit off my boot. I remembered something else the Rakkhoshi Rani had said. "I thought getting my blood sample in early was supposed to speed up the paperwork process."

"Well, if you're going to be that way about it, fine." The man snapped his reins again. "Follow me, then! You've been parked in the wrong line this whole time!"

The little old man gestured that I should follow him out of the ginormous line. I started up the auto rikshaw and, ignoring the dirty looks I got from the other hopeful contestants, put-putted off behind the man, his cart, and his water buffalo.

The old man led us to a gate on the far side of the registration office. Here, we were totally alone, with no other hopeful contestants in sight. "Wait here!" he ordered, before he and his water buffalo headed off again. I picked up one of the pieces of paper he had handed me at random. It had *Who Wants to Be a Demon Slayer? Hopeful Contestant Form* written on top in giant letters. I threaded the paper into the ancient typewriter and began to type.

"How come this typewriter doesn't have all the letters of the alphabet?" I muttered, hunting around the unfamiliar keyboard. "And why are there so many emojis?"

"Let me see . . ." Naya began, starting to come out from under her hiding place. But she scooched right back under again, because just then, the sunlight that had been streaming into the rikshaw was blocked by someone's thick shadow. Naya gave a little squeak from under the burlap.

"Hark! Who goes there?" bellowed the big shadow-creating someone.

CHAPTER 11

The Password

My hands froze over the typewriter as the person shouted, "Please supply your paperwork, signed in quintuplicate! And it better have Rama-di's and Laltu-da's signatures on it!"

Automatically, I handed over my barely filled-out paperwork. But when I looked up, I almost screamed. The scowling face of the man looming above me was actually familiar. And not in a good way. It was the barrel-chested police constable who had wanted to arrest me last fall for the ridiculous crime of stealing someone's moustache. (Which I totally hadn't done, obviously.) And now he was looking like he was regretting his decision to let me go.

"I'm sorry, I didn't finish," I admitted. "And I haven't gotten anyone's signature yet."

"Unfinished paperwork! No signatures! Why are you in this line? In that case, tell me the password!"

I glanced back at Naya, who was being totally unhelpful by staying hidden. What was with this girl? One second, she's stowing away to keep me company on an intergalactic journey, and the next, she's scared of anything that moves. I sighed with frustration.

"What. Is. The. Password?" the constable repeated, emphasizing every syllable while baring his teeth. His dark brown face was dripping with sweat, and I was starting to feel dizzy from heat exhaustion and fear myself.

"The . . . um . . . password?" I squinted against the scorching sun, my hand over my eyes.

"Yes, the password! Must I get you a de-waxer for your ears as well as a sentence in a jail cell?" Even though it was ridiculously bright outside, the constable shone a big flashlight in my face. I really hoped he didn't recognize me.

"No, no, I was just trying to remember it . . . the password, I mean . . ."

"Just as I suspected!" the constable snapped. Turning over his shoulder, he called out, "Captain Buddhu! Captain Bhootoom! We have a waxy-eared spy! Probably from one of the competing networks, here to gather secrets about

Who Wants to Be a Demon Slayer? We must take her to the cotton swab room for an interrogation!"

"I'm not a spy!" Being interrogated by two captains cleaning my ears did not sound like fun. Plus, being called waxy-eared kind of hurt. "Really! I'm not!"

"It doesn't matter if you deny it!" The police officer's chest was so big, his khaki uniform buttons threatened to pop off with each indignant word. "Truth? That's a relative term these days anyway!"

As he continued to yell about how his serpent affiliates had warned him this might happen, how he didn't tolerate any shenanigans on his watch, and how dare I not know the password, Naya mumbled some nonsensical words to me. When I didn't say anything, she whispered a little louder, "Your Royal Celestialness—it is the password! Please repeat!"

I could see the glow of Naya's phone shining through the rough material she was hiding under. She must be looking up the password on that Kingdom Beyond search engine—what was it called?—Shmoogles? Still, I hesitated. She couldn't be serious. *That* was the password this guy wanted? That couldn't be right!

It wasn't until the constable was reaching for his handcuffs that I started blurting out the words that Naya kept whispering to me. "Exclamation point! Capital letter! Special symbol! Number!"

"That is not the whole—" The constable's uniform buttons quavered in, I suppose, happy anticipation of arresting me.

But I interrupted him, continuing, "Question mark! Name of my first pet! Mother's maiden name! Three asterisks followed by a tilde and a pound sign!"

"Wrong!"

"Hey ho, there, hi there, hee there, constable! She got it bloomin' right," said a funny little creature who had just come up behind the cop and hopped on his shoulder. It was a cheery-faced monkey with a shiny monocle over one eye. He was dressed in a formal military uniform with gold braids and sashes and all sorts of medals all over the chest. He carried a fancy cane, with a handle shaped like a banana, and wore one of those old-timey galleon-sailboat-type hats on his head. The monkey spoke in a seriously fake British accent, and on his shoulder was a tiny little owl wearing a monocle that matched the monkey's, the chain hanging down over his snowy chest. The magnification of the one-sided eyeglass lens made one of the owl's eyeballs look way bigger than the other, which was more than a little disturbing. That, and the stringy tail hanging out of the bird's beak. I tried not to shudder. Gross!

Clearing his throat, the monkey turned the constable's notebook the other way. "You were looking at the password quite flipetty-floppetty, you flibberty-jibbet! We'll have to mention this in your mid-year evaluation! You know the brass ain't going to look favorably on you trying to read upside down *again*."

"It was an honest mistake, sirs!" The burly policeman shifted from foot to foot, looking downright sheepish. "Please, Captains, don't mention it in your report."

The white owl flapped his wings, swallowing whatever rodent was in his mouth with a loud gulp. The monkey whirled his monocle on its gold chain, saying, "Well, you're lickety-lickin' lucky that we haven't yet learned how to write. Otherwise, this would go directmónt into our report, understandamente?"

"Yes, sirs, yes!" The constable wiped his sweaty brow with the back of his thick arm.

"What is with that crazy password, anyway?" I muttered, intending my words for Naya's ears.

"Come now, come now! It's blickety-bloomin' easy to get hacked these days." The monkey put his monocle back on, then picked some small bug off the police constable's eyebrow and seemed to eat it. "Malware, old chap. Er, chapette. It's a thing." As if in agreement, the owl hooted several times in a surprisingly loud voice and then bit his own little foot with his sharp beak.

"You insolent girl! How dare you insult the *Who Wants to Be a Demon Slayer?* registration office security system!" The constable doubled down on his anger, maybe to impress the funny little animals, who seemed to be his bosses. The man flipped the pages of his now-right-side-up notebook so enthusiastically, I was sure he'd tear the paper. "Would you like a citation for insolence as well as the one you almost got only a couple months ago for facial hair thievery?"

Well, there went my hopes that he didn't remember me. "I'm sorry," I began, but the furious man cut me off, speaking out loud as he wrote down my citation. His notebook was so small he could only fit one word per page, so it sounded pretty ridiculous: "Disrespecting"—flip—"malware"—flip—"moustaches"—flip—"and more."

The little owl flew onto the constable's hat and started pecking at it, like he was a woodpecker. In the meantime, the monkey captain hopped onto the roof of the auto rikshaw. Then his little bristly face popped into view, hanging upside down. Which of course resulted in his ridiculous hat and his monocle falling off. When the policeman wasn't looking, the hairy animal gave me a sparkly-eyed, tongue-out-of-the-side-of-his-mouth grin, and then a hairy hang-ten sign like surfers do. "Namaste, Princess!" he hissed. "The sacred in me, like, greets the sacred in you!" Suddenly, the monkey sounded a lot like Amber, Ma's goofy yoga teacher at the Parsippany Community Center, who liked to speak in Sanskrit, and thought she was super deep.

More importantly, I realized with a start, the monkey knew who I was! But when I looked over at him, about to ask him how, the monkey captain put his finger to his lips, whispering, "Shhhh!" I shut my mouth, but my heart was pounding. Just who was the spy here?

In the next moment, the monkey's British accent was back. "Enough with the ding-dong citations, man, ask her the special questions!" The hairy animal snapped from his upside-down position. "Hop to it! Security of the show at risk, yaar!"

"But, sirs!" the constable protested, but then he cowered as the snowy owl clamped his small beak on the man's ear.

"The jiggety-jaggety questions, old boy, ask her the bloomin' questions!" the monkey yelled, jamming the fallen hat and monocle back on.

"Don't think this lets you off the hook, you pre-criminal." The constable rubbed his earlobe with one hand even as he shook his pen at me. It was one of those bouncing novelty-shop things with a long-tongued snake on the top, so when he shook the pen, the snake head bounced around, waving its little rubber tongue. Anyone would have found it creepy, but with my personal history with evil serpents, I was seriously weirded out.

"No, I won't." I gripped the rikshaw handlebars, my palms sweaty.

The policeman flipped some more through his notebook, which was tricky, because the not-all-there-in-the-head owl had apparently thought the snake-headed pen was a real snake and so was attacking it with little aggressive cries. In the meantime, the monkey jumped around, from the rikshaw roof to the constable's shoulder and back again.

"I do like your pen. That snake on it. Very tickety-boo, and all that! First-class creepy! Yes, sir! Yes, sir! Have you ever fought a snake? Well, not anymore because of our partnership with the Kingdom of Serpents, but before that, my second cousin on dear old mummy's side, Honu Bhai, once had a terrible encounter with a boa constrictor. Well, we think he did because he was never seen again. They found just his rainbow-colored suspenders. Must not have tasted very good, those. Not a pleasant scenario, let me tell you, yaar. I mean, boyo. I mean, old chap." Then, as if remembering his dignity, the monkey Buddhu stopped, cleared his throat, and found his English accent again. "Terribly, terribly sorry. Got a tad mentally hornswoggled there. Yes, yes, carry on."

"Sirs?" The poor policeman seemed baffled.

The owl Bhootoom vomited up what looked like a little pre-digested fur pellet on the man's notebook, which he shook off with a grimace. At the same time, the monkey snapped, "The questions, my man! Ask the suspect the special questions!"

"Yes, sirs! Immediately, sirs!" The constable gave a quick salute, which the monkey returned.

"By the order of the magical banana," the policeman solemnly intoned. Naya giggled a little from her hiding place, but it was me who was at the receiving end of the constable's glare.

"As I was saying!" The man cleared his throat. "By the order of the magical banana, I will hereby ask the suspect the extra-special security questions."

Extra-special security questions? I had barely made it past the password. How was I going to answer anything else?

CHAPTER 12

The Order of the Magical Banana

The constable flipped through his notebook, until he found the page he was looking for. Reading one word per page, he asked me, "Why"—flip—"does"—flip—"a"—flip—"banana"—flip—"wear"—flip —"sunscreen?"

It took me a minute to even understand that the security question was in the form of a stupid joke about bananas. It didn't take much imagination to realize why.

If I had any remaining doubts as to the joke's origins, they all disappeared when the monkey captain started jumping around and waving his long arms. "Oo la la! Oo la loo! I know! I know! Hey, over here! Pickety pick pick me!"

"But, sir!" The constable looked embarrassed. "With all due respect, of course you know the answer! You wrote the question!"

In the excitement, the owl started flying around in circles. For whatever reason, he only seemed to be able to fly backward. Meanwhile, the monkey captain jumped from the rikshaw to the chain link of the fence and back again. Then he did an acrobatic swing-around so he was hanging, one-armed, from the side of the vehicle, his body halfway in the cabin with me.

"Why does a banana wear so much blinkin' sunscreen?" Buddhu repeated, his hat and monocle now back on. "Because . . . because . . ." The monkey was laughing so hard he hardly could get the words out. "Because he peels!"

The policeman hid his annoyance by looking at the sky as the monkey dissolved in a fit of laughter, and the owl hooted in short bursts that sounded like giggles.

"Please, sirs! Do stop laughing!"

"We . . . we . . . can't, yaar! That was a good one! Oh, the hardy to the har, har, har!" wheezed the monkey. I was having a hard time keeping a straight face myself, not so much at the joke, but at the animals' reactions to it. Meanwhile, the constable looked downright pained.

"You know about my ailment, sir! The many tonics I am taking for it! The pills! The creams! The suppositories!" begged the policeman, and the monkey stopped, shamefaced.

"So blisteringly sorry, old chap. That was not very kar-
mic of me. You know I always forget. I apologize, old man.
Really." Looking at me, Buddhu explained, "He is not
allowed to laugh. Strict instructions by the doctor. It's
frightfully bad for his tibulooloo. And his right frontal uvu-
lala. His patété too." At a gesture by the owl to the constable's
throat, the monkey added, "Also, his nasoforeignix."

I'm no doctor, but I wasn't sure any of those things were
actual body parts.

"I have a condition!" sniffed the constable. "And, sir,
you have to let the suspect answer the question! We've
talked about this before!"

"Correct! Indeed! You are utterly and most totally
righty-ho-ho!" The monkey cleared his throat and climbed
down off the rikshaw onto the ground. He bobbled his head
a little left to right, losing a bit of his original accent. "Thik
achhe. Thik achhe. Please, deep pranayama breaths, in and
out through your nose. In for four, hold for four, out for
four," he said in a pseudo-deep Amber-the-community-
center-yoga-teacher voice, demonstrating as he did so. "All
right, then, carry on. Proceed."

"How about this one? It's much harder. That was just
a warm-up anyway." The constable gave me a hard stare,

ignoring Buddhu's advice about deep breathing. "Why"—
flip—"are"—flip—"bananas"— flip—"never lonely?"

The answer was on the tip of my tongue, but an over-
excited Captain Buddhu shouted out, "Because they love a
good party!"

"Oh, Captain, my captain!" groaned the constable. The
owl spit out another disgusting furball.

The monkey, who seemed to be chewing on one of the
auto rikshaw pom-poms, snapped, "All righty! All righty!
Don't get your government-issued knickers in a bunch!"
Then, to my annoyance, the military monkey swung himself onto my shoulder and started picking through my hair.
But he had—maybe by mistake—told me the answer to the
question.

"A banana is never lonely because they're always in
a . . ." I started, but Buddhu interrupted me with a loud
laugh.

"I haven't said the punch line yet!" I hissed.

"Arré, hurry up, then!" the monkey retorted. "What's
taking you so flimflamming long?"

Now the owl joined the monkey, and both animals were
perched on my shoulders, picking through my hair.

I took a big breath, trying not to be irritated. "A banana
is never lonely because they're always in a bunch."

"Lucky guess," the policeman groused, even as the monkey collapsed in a fit of laughter, actually falling off my shoulder.

"In a bunch!" he snorted, rolling around and clutching at his stomach. "Oof! Orré baba! That's a good one! In a bunch! Like his knickers!" His tiny claws digging into my shoulder, the owl squawked and flapped his wings as if laughing too.

"Sirs! I am prohibited from vocalizing my mirth! Think of my condition!" The constable's face looked puffed and red, and even his eyes had begun to water, as if he was holding in a laugh with huge effort. "Just consider my cardiothorazine! Think of my duodenumnumnum!"

"Wait, wait! Please, at least one more question for the suspect!" The monkey Buddhu snorted from the dusty ground, where he was still laughing and wiping his eyes. "I'm worried she's a security risk!"

It was obvious he wasn't worried about any such thing and just wanted to hear another banana-related joke, but the constable had other ideas. Or maybe he just wanted to protect his internal organs from his laughing disease.

From the breast pocket of his uniform, the constable pulled out an even tinier notebook than the first. With a dramatic gesture, he turned the notebook toward me and began flipping through it. On each page was a badly drawn stick figure with crooked eyes, an off-center nose, and, from what I could tell, only one ear. But as the man flipped the pages, it looked like the stick figure was not just growing taller but also dancing.

"Very . . . uh . . . artistic!" I said. "I like how it looks like he's moving."

"My style is influenced by an artist from the 2-D dimension," said the policeman as he kept flipping the pages. I could tell he was pleased.

"Oh, I know!" I remembered some pictures I'd seen in art class about a painter who put people's eyes where their noses should be and stuff like that. "Picasso!"

"Ehhh!" The policeman made a sound like a buzzer. "No, it's Van Gogh! Can't you tell? That's why there's only one ear!"

I exchanged confused looks with Buddhu, wondering if this had something to do with the security question. The owl made a series of loud burbling noises. I was pretty sure he'd fallen asleep on my shoulder. I couldn't help worrying if he'd poop while he was perched there.

Naya made a little sound from the back seat. The poor girl was probably melting.

"What did you say?" The constable fingered his handcuffs.

"I was just thinking how much I liked your artistic style!" I volunteered, wiping the beads of sweat trickling from my hair down my neck. "The symbolism! The metaphors! The, uh, earless-ness!"

The constable smoothed down his moustache with a pleased look. "All right, suspect, I will give you one more question to answer before we have to take you in for interrogation." He turned on the monkey, who looked like he was about to say something. "And no, you cannot help her, sir! If you think she is a security risk, then it's my duty to investigate!"

Buddhu gave me a little shrug and then sat right on my dashboard with his legs crossed and hands on his knees, first fingers and thumbs lightly touching. He started breathing deeply, and then making an *Om* noise.

"What are you doing?" I hissed at the meditating monkey.

"Achha, communing with your consciousness, yaar," hissed the monkey back without opening his eyes. "So I can help you with the answer."

I rolled my eyes. Half the time the monkey was all snotty and British, and half the time he was all one with the universe Mr. Yoga Butt. I didn't get him at all, but then again, he was a talking monkey, so we were probably operating on a fairly un-understandable plane to begin with.

The constable cleared his throat and flipped through the notebook, making the stick figure dance again. "Brothers and sisters have I none, but this man's father is my father's son."

"I couldn't just answer another one about bananas?" I asked.

"This is your last chance, suspect," barked the constable.

I snuck a look at the monkey, who still had his legs crossed but had somehow flipped into a headstand. He had one eye open and was hissing answers through the side of his mouth.

"A split! A pair of slippers! Apeeling!"

"It's not about bananas!" I snapped.

"Aw, blast and blimey!"

"Sir, please!" said the indignant constable. "You must let the suspect answer the security question alone!"

I thought carefully about the policeman's question, wondering if I'd heard this one from Niko before, or read it in one of his books. I didn't think so. I'd have to try to logic it out myself. He had no brothers or sisters, so he was an only child. Okay. So, the stick person in the moving pictures' father was the constable's father's son? Was this one of those riddles where the answer was that the surgeon was his mother? No, that didn't really make sense. I bit my lip, thinking through what this family tree might look like. And then it came to me.

"That's your son!"

For a tense moment, the policeman consulted his larger notebook, flipping it this way and that.

"She's right, boyo! She's right, old chap!" Buddhu the monkey jumped up from meditating now to assume his bossy upper-crusty voice. Bhootoom the owl woke up and hooted. "I recognized little junior constable sahib right away!" Buddhu went on. "Blimey, that one ear! The posh clothes! The fly dance moves! Absolute, blinkin' genius!"

The constable looked pained. "My son has two ears, sir. This was artistic license."

"Of course, it blingety-blangety was! Artistic license! Also, artistic credit card! And artistic bill fold! Artistic loose change!"

I gave the monkey a jab with my elbow and he stopped blathering.

The constable gave a *harrumph* and then saluted. "Fine. You pass. I will escort you through the gate and into the registration office."

"No worries, 'enry 'iggins! No need to get chuffed, guv'nor! I got it sorted!" Captain Buddhu jumped onto my motorbike handles, while the owl Bhootoom dug his claws uncomfortably into my left shoulder. "I've still got some more questions for this contestant—er, spy—er, suspect! I think I'll take her to the cotton swab room after all!"

The monkey gave me a little wink, and I wished he'd be less obvious. Luckily, the constable didn't notice, as he was still stuck in a salute, looking pained.

"Don't you have to tell him 'at ease' or something?" I whispered.

"Arré, right on. Thanks, yaar." The monkey returned the constable's salute, and the poor policeman could finally put down his hand. Before I could reach for it, Buddhu pushed the rikshaw's start button with his tail, and the engine turned over.

The police constable began opening the chain link fence's many locks. Some were opened by keys he wore on a giant chain hooked to his pocket. Others were combinations, which he opened after mumbling the numbers to himself, like a little kid who can't read without moving his lips. Finally, the constable seemed to be looking around in the dry meadow grass for something. After a couple failed attempts, he reached out and grabbed something small and striped and buzzing. A bee!

"Got you!" yelled the policeman before ripping off one

of the bee's little wings. I shrieked. But not as loud as the bee, which screamed with a bloodcurdling yell that sounded more like a hairy beast than an insect.

Naya gave a little yelp. The bee, with its full-throated, monstrous voice, cried and wailed.

The policeman inserted the bee's almost-see-through wing to open the last, slot-like lock on the fence. He then swung open the gate with a clang. I shuddered as the poor bee kept screaming. I didn't like bees. In fact, I'd always hated them, and I was even more freaked out by them after the Rakkhoshi Rani started showing up in my bedroom with the buzzing creatures. But no one deserved to suffer like that. Naya seemed to feel the same way, because she kept up a low whining in the back seat.

"By the order of the magical banana, get a blingety-blangety move on!" hissed the monkey. And so, I drove the auto rikshaw slowly through the open gate, only to have it clang shut behind us again. As we drove, I realized there wasn't one fence but a whole bunch of barbed-wire-topped fences around the registration office. There were cameras on top of every one, and at first, I thought I was imagining it, but the camera lenses swiveled, following us as we drove by. It was seriously creepy.

As I puttered along, the monkey whispered in my ear, "Be cool, Princess Kiranmala, we're just taking a little detour before the cameras are on you all the time."

"But how do you know who I . . ." I began, but the monkey put up a hairy hand, directing me away from the registration office rather than toward it.

"My brother Bhootoom and I have been waiting for you for weeks, Princess. We even took these spiritually bankrupt jobs in the registration office so we'd spot you first."

"Wait. What?" I put on the brakes, then shifted in my seat to stare at the monkey on my shoulder, and the owl now on his shoulder. Both animals blinked back at me.

"Keep going! Stop attracting so much attention." The monkey put his hat at a jaunty angle, balanced his goofy monocle against one eye, then leaned out of the auto rikshaw, waving and smiling at the cameras. "Arré, yaar, do you want to save our big brother Neel or not?"

CHAPTER 13

The Owl and Monkey Princes

Y ou can't be Neel's brothers!" I blurted out. Conscious of the cameras, I did my best to keep the auto rikshaw put-putting unsuspiciously along.

"We are all brothers and sisters, are we not?" Buddhu said in his fake yoga-teacher voice, directing me away from the registration building rather than toward it.

"I didn't think that's what you meant," I said as I turned down the main street of the market.

"You're right, it isn't," the monkey agreed, doing some kind of one-leg-in-the-air downward dog on the dashboard. "We're his actual brothers."

"So, explain," I demanded. "How exactly are you both related to Neel and Lal?"

"Squawk!" The tiny owl blinked at me a little creepily right before barfing out a nasty little furry pellet onto my lap. Yuck. I shook it off as quick as I could, sending the rikshaw jerkily back and forth as I did.

"Well, when the Raja wasn't having any heirs, he called upon a rishi, one of those sadhu-sanyasi guys who meditates on the mountaintop and knows all sorts of magic shajik."

As we drove on through the bazaar, Buddhu directing me down a few smaller alleys, I was amazed at how empty it was. The last time I'd been here, the market had been a chaotic but joyful place, overloaded with flower merchants and bangle sellers, jostling pedestrians and on-foot rikshaw wallahs seeking customers. Now it seemed practically deserted. We made a quick stop by a lone roadside green coconut vendor. I slurped the refreshing coconut water greedily through a straw, balancing the awkward nut in my lap as I drove on.

"So, anyhoo, this guy gave the ranis a super-magical fertility root to share so they would all have babies," Buddhu said as he slurped his own coconut.

This story sounded familiar. I felt like Baba had told it to me before, or at least a story very much like it.

"Anyway, the two youngest queens were majorly ripped off. They only gave them the leftovers—the ekdum dregs at the bottom of the bowl after everyone else ate more than their share. This was not very Yogic of them. You know, yaar, we all have to be the love we want to see in the universe."

We were far away from the gate now, so Buddhu took off his monocle and fancy jacket, revealing a tie-dye kurta with a peace sign in the middle. He put his galleon hat away too in favor of an embroidered square cap, which he wore at a jaunty angle across one ear. Across his chest he wore a hand-stitched cloth jhola—a bag in which he now shoved his other costume, as well as his banana-handled cane. Bhootoom, who'd fallen asleep while perched on the auto-rikshaw horn, kept his monocle on.

Buddhu the monkey continued, in much more laid-back tones, "Schmanyhoo, everyone else got healthy human—or half rakkhosh—kiddos except my mom and my brother Bhootoom's mom—the two youngest queens. Typical inter-rani fighting, yaar."

"Yeah, I've met your stepmoms. They're really special."

"Full of charm *and* sharm, amirite?" laughed the monkey. "They banished us from the palace right when we were born.

Didn't want animal-shanimal types around, I guess. Despite the fact we can do the most awesome things like this."

Buddhu flipped up to the ceiling, then hung from his tail. He let out an awful screeching sound, clattering his teeth together while simultaneously scratching his armpits.

"You really are the Princes Buddhu-Bhootoom?"

I'd almost forgotten about Naya. As I apologetically handed her our last green coconut, I saw that she was looking at the animals all worshipful, like one wasn't a slightly smelly and very hairy hippie of a monkey, and the other wasn't a nonverbal owl in a monocle. I also realized the owl and monkey on her *Bee WHOOO You Are* T-shirt looked a lot like the animal princes.

"Arré, you know of the legendary Buddhu-Bhootoom, I see, my secretive and sweaty sister? Yes, indeedie-to-the-celebrimax do!" Buddhu shouted so loud that Bhootoom gave a start, clamping his claws on the horn, which let out a loud beep.

The owl squawked as the monkey went on, "We are the Princes Buddhu and Bhootoom, first of our names, eaters of bananas and also—occasionally, not me, but my brother— of mice. We are the savers of the Kalabati maiden with storm-cloud hair, sailors of peacock barges, and practitioners of sun salutations."

The monkey gave me a sidelong look. "I have heard the people of your dimension will pay plenty for what they think is mystical and spiritual, yes? You think I could make a side business as a yoga-teacher-slash-spiritual-guru there?"

I was about to tell Buddhu about Athena's *Healing Your Broken Heart Chakra* book but didn't get a chance because Naya basically shoved me out of the way to take like a million selfies with both brothers before furiously sending the photos off into the ether.

"I'm a big fan! Huge! I collected every one of your *Teen Taal* covers!" Naya opened an app on her phone and started flipping through pictures of a teenybopper-type magazine with the most ridiculous headlines:

Prince Lalkamal at Tiffin: Secrets from the Hottest Royal's Favorite Meal

If You Were a Rakkhosh, What Kind Would You Be? Take Our Air, Water, Land, and Fire Clan Quiz and Share Your Results Instantly

Ms. Twinkle Chakraborty's Beauty Care Tips for Teens: How You Too Can Be Gorgeous from Your Armpits to Your Carbuncles

On the Mat with Princes Buddhu and Bhootoom: Tapping into Your Inner Animal to Be a Better Yogi

Underneath these headlines were the faces of the Kingdom Beyond celebrities floating around in space. Buddhu and Bhootoom were doing wacky yoga poses in their shots.

"Oh, look at me! Doing a handstand! A warrior two pose! Flying scorpion!" said Buddhu, flipping from one pose to another as Naya flipped through the pictures. "Oh, I am really so, so flexible, and yet, so strong! Arré, it's a gift, what can I say?"

Bhootoom hooted, and Naya responded, "Oh, no, I think your feathers look terrific in that photo." Okay, so I guess everyone but me could understand the little owl.

Naya giggled as she shot me a starry-eyed glance. "Just wait until the others in my Buddhu-Bhootoom fanfic writing group hear about me meeting them!" Naya gushed, before yapping happily with our new monkey and owl friends about the silly filters she was adding to their selfies.

As she chatted, I drove the rikshaw slowly down streets that weren't even paved, but basically muddy, pothole-ridden lanes. Even though it was blazingly hot, the shutters to the colorful houses overlooking the market streets were almost all closed. A lone woman hanging wet saris on her flat-topped roof hid behind the wet fabric when she heard us driving by. At another point, some schoolchildren passed, uniformed and somber, pulled along in a strange caged wagon behind a bicyclist. One little boy in the cage was singing an off-tune little song, "Elladin, belladin, shoi-lo. Ki khobor ai-lo? Raja ekti ballika chai-lo!" I knew it was a kids' nursery rhyme, but it still gave me the creeps. Especially the part that was the same as the rakkhoshi's poem "elladin, belladin" and the part at the end about a king wanting a girl. Why did it remind me of the Serpent King wanting me to join his minions? I scratched at the skin under my bandanna, which was feeling dry and hot. I tried to wave at the singing boy, but he just stared blankly back as the kid-filled cage rattled away down a narrow alley.

When I saw a curious face peeking down at me through a window, I thought I recognized the kati roll dealer who had sold me a delicious lunch when I was last here. "Hello?" I called out, but the man slammed the shutter tight once again. I wasn't sure, but I thought I heard him mutter, "Good-bye."

"What's the matter with this place?" As we drove down street after street, the thing that didn't seem to change was the thick sense of gloom.

"It's been like this since *Who Wants to Be a Demon Slayer?* began," said Buddhu. "People have, like, majorly quit work, school, sold their houses, taken out loans, done everything to scrape together enough money to start training with expert tutors. I mean, capitalism's gnarly, am I right? Since the game show, you can hire tutors in everything from logical word games to rakkhosh fighting. No one wants to miss out on the chance to be a star!"

Buddhu's words made me squirm a little inside. I'd been having trouble paying attention to anything as ordinary as school since I'd first discovered the truth about my origins. And I'd been whining about missing my new friends the whole time to Zuzu, but never really appreciating her either. Was I that different from these game-show-hungry people?

And then something Naya said made me even more squirmy. "They all want to be like you," she said. "You saw all those people dressed up like you in line! You're what they aspire to be! You're their dream!"

"Wait, that's not true." I stopped the auto rikshaw with a screech. We were by a bunch of empty market stalls, and there was absolutely no one around except for one lone paan wallah on his stall platform. The paan vendor, a middle-aged man with a thick helmet of black hair and a potbelly, was sitting cross-legged on the stand, making triangles of silver-paper-wrapped betel nut. His teeth were stained bright red from chewing so much paan himself. He looked up from the food, his jaw working, and let out a thin stream of betel juice from between his crooked teeth onto the dusty road. Gross.

I turned around in the driver's seat to face Naya. "People want to be like me?"

"Oh, yes," Naya said, obviously thinking she was telling me something I wanted to hear. "Why wouldn't they? You are the perfect hero."

"Perfect?" I gave a snort. "Um, I don't think so!"

But before I could say anything else, something very strange happened.

The paan wallah let out a whistle, low and long. And then, before I could start up the auto rikshaw again, we were under attack.

They were coming down the alley from behind us, shooting out of doorways I hadn't noticed, rolling up from a side street. One even popped out from under the paan wallah's stand. After how deserted the bazaar had been, the sudden ambush by so many people was downright startling. Not just people—skateboarders. Everywhere I looked, there was a skateboarder. Skateboarders here, skateboarders there, skateboarders everywhere. It was like we were drowning in a skateboard sea. I remembered with a lurch how the Raja had said something about skateboarding rebels. This must be them. They were zipping toward us super fast now, their wheels shining sparks in the sunlight. What did they want? Well, this princess wasn't just going to sit around passively and find out.

In a move I'd just learned from Buddhu the monkey, I swung myself out of the auto rikshaw, planting myself on the roof. There, I nocked my arrow in my bow, widened my stance, and stood at the ready.

I had an amazing vantage point and could see them all rolling toward us. As far as I could tell, none of them was aiming a weapon. The other thing that threw me off was how the boarders were dressed. They were all girls—from what I could tell—and all dressed in pink saris. Pink saris draped traditionally, pink saris over jeans, even pink saris worn like capes over T-shirts, shorts, and high-tops. It was kind of an amazing sight, actually. Girls of all heights and shapes and sizes shredding on their skateboards, wearing braids and scarves and bangles in the color I'd always associated with dumb passive princess stuff.

One skateboarder did a crazy trick where she popped up three little cement steps, then jumped out in a high arc. Another girl flew over a sideways trash can on the ground

and landed with a dramatic yelp. A third girl, slim and graceful, was skateboarding with a small bird perched on one shoulder—not just any bird but a very familiar-looking yellow one. The girl herself was wearing one thick-soled shoe because one of her legs was a little bit shorter than the other. The end of her sari draped over her hair and face, but even before it floated aside, I knew who she was.

CHAPTER 14

The Pink-Sari Skateboarders

Mati!" I took the arrow from my bow, then jumped down from the auto roof to give my cousin a hug. "And Tuni!" I laughed as my old friend the talking bird did a little silly dance in midair. "What are you guys doing here? Why haven't you been in touch?"

"Tell me, Princess," squawked Tuntuni, "how does a skateboarder talk to her friends?"

I rolled my eyes. Like Dr. Dixon, and now Buddhu too, Tuntuni loved his punny jokes. "I don't know, how?"

"By air mail!" said the yellow bird, cackling hard. From the handlebars of the auto, Bhootoom the owl spit out a fur ball and rotated his head all the way around. Apparently, he was not a fan of Tuni's humor, although he didn't seem to have a problem with his brother's love of banana jokes.

"Kiran, I'm so sorry we haven't spoken. You must have been so worried!" That was an understatement for sure, but before I had a chance to say anything, my cousin waved at the animals in the auto rikshaw. "Wonderful job, boys! I knew you could find her!"

"Of course, my wheelie lady! We are, ekdum, totally and utterly flibberty-flabberting at your service, as most always!" Buddhu gave an elaborate bow, and even Bhootoom woke up enough to turn his head 360 degrees as if in agreement.

"And now"—Mati pointed to the owl and monkey princes—"you'd better get back to your stations at the registration center, before the game show producers start to suspect anything." Mati's words made the monkey's face fall in disappointment and the owl squawk unhappily.

"Oh, no, Miss Mati, we don't want to go back to those terrible jobs!" Buddhu whined. "They are boring and spiritually unfulfilling! Oh, please don't make us go back! They have terrible senses of humor, and no one there even likes yoga! Or bananas! And everyone steals our food in the tiffin room—even when we label it! We want to be here with you, with the resistance!"

But Mati shook her head like a stern general. Behind her, Tuni flapped in circles and crossed his eyes, obviously egging the brothers on. Bhootoom took the bait, flapping his wings at Tuni. The two birds dived and shrieked, each making "come at me, bro"–type gestures. Unfortunately, Bhootoom kept tumbling through the air because of his "I can only fly backward" problem, so Tuni seemed to be getting the better of him.

Mati ignored the birds and went on, "Prince Buddhu, the resistance needs you at the registration office. Priya will take you back." This was another one of the Pink-Sari Skateboarders, a girl with camo pants and a tank top, her pink sari tied around her neck like a superhero cape.

I was sad to see the little monkey go, but not as sad as Naya, who seemed absolutely devastated. "Be safe," she sniffed as she helped Buddhu back into his military coat, galleon hat, and monocle. "Don't forget me. Keep on with your yoga practice, and never forget that your banana jokes are really funny, no matter what those grumpy guards say."

"They are, aren't I?" The money prince dried Naya's tears with a hairy paw, and even the weird little owl stopped fighting with Tuni to peck at her ponytails.

"Hey, why did the banana go out with the prune?" Buddhu said in a mournful voice.

"I don't know," sniffed Naya. "Why?"

"Because . . . because . . ." Buddhu's lip trembled as he delivered the punch line. "Because he couldn't find a daaaaaaate!" The last word was punctuated by a wail.

Finally, Priya had to pick up both animals and put them forcibly on her shoulders. Buddhu sat there, his tail around the girl's broad neck, crying into his fur. "You take care of yourself, Princess."

"I will," I promised. Bhootoom the owl gave me a mournful hoot. Tuntuni flew in gleeful circles, alternately blowing raspberries and wiggling his tail feathers at the brothers with a rude butt-up-in-the-air motion.

"No wonder you got fired from your job, you bird-brained ex-minister! Your jokes are terrible!"

I almost fell out when I realized this was Bhootoom's parting shot to Tuni. The owl could speak in human words after all!

Then the owl and monkey princes were off, wheeling away down the road on Priya's skateboard.

Naya was crying and hiccupping something terrible to see them go, but I only absently patted her arm, because my head was reeling. "Wait, Mati, you sent Buddhu and Bhootoom to get me? And, Tuni, you lost your job? And what's all this about the resistance? Who are you resisting?"

"I'm sorry, Kiran, it all must seem confusing. There's a lot we have to catch you up on." Mati flipped up her skateboard into her hands in a super-smooth maneuver. "Like why you dyed the bottom of your hair green?" My cousin touched my braid. And then, with a little intake of breath, she touched my arm. "And your arm too?"

I looked down, and saw that while my bandanna still covered my serpent scar, the part of skin showing under the bandanna edge had now turned a little greenish too. I put my hand quickly over the spot. "It's nothing. A side effect of Essence-Tyme."

Mati nodded. "I've heard you can get seasick through Essence-Tyme, but I've never heard of skin color or hair changes. But I guess it's possible."

Around us, the other Pink-Sari Skateboarders spun and jumped and did tricks. Naya, for her part, got busy taking photos of the girls doing aerials. For posting on her Instagreat account, I bet. Some of the girls were leaping with their skateboards high enough to reach some more of the *Who Wants to Be a Demon Slayer?* billboards with Lal's and my faces on them. One of the girls pulled out some pink spray paint and spray-painted the words *Who's the monster now?* over Lal's and my giant faces. Finally, she spray-painted her tag—an image of a pink skateboard with the letters *PSS* on it.

"Cousin, we don't have a lot of time." Mati leaned toward me, speaking urgently. "There's already talk. People recognized you from that five-second Suman Rahaman TV interview."

"You saw that? But it just happened!" I wondered with a start if my parents had seen it too.

"It was live. Everything they record these days is. So you've got to be careful, Cousin. Pretty soon, people are going to realize that person on TV didn't just look like you, it was you. And then everyone in the kingdom is going to come looking for you—Princess Kiranmala! Here to win back the famed Thinking Stone for the Raja!"

Mati said this in such a sarcastic way, and I was a little surprised. I'd never seen my gentle cousin be anything more than sincere and earnest. This was new.

"I just want to save Neel," I said bluntly. "It's my fault he's in that terrible demon detention center. Waiting around there like some kind of an animal for a Roman gladiator to fight."

"I know, Kiran, it's awful he's in there," Mati said, but another one of the skateboarders, a girl with thick arms and her sari draped traditionally, interrupted her.

"This is about more than one prince," she snapped. "This is about injustice to an entire peoples. Or have you forgotten about that?"

I wasn't sure what the girl was talking about. I guess she was worried that the Serpent King wasn't really ever going to hand over the stone to the winner. That this whole thing about him partnering with the Raja and the Kingdom Beyond was a big lie.

"Chandra is right," Mati said, gesturing to the girl. "This is about more than just Neel—it's about injustice. But for now, I just wanted to make sure you were prepared for what comes next. As soon as they put you on the show, all eyes will be on you. There won't be a lot more time to talk openly like this. I mean, you've seen the billboards."

I felt my face get hot. The billboard that the skateboarder had just spray-painted over was the one with the slogan about Lal and me stealing kisses and hugs. I wondered if that's why Mati was acting so weird. Was she jealous that people were mistakenly pairing off Lal and me?

As if reading my mind, Tuntuni made obnoxious kissy sounds with his beak. "Kiran and Lal steal kisses and hugs!" he snickered.

"Oh, shut up, Tuni!" I snapped. "Bhootoom's right. No wonder you got fired!"

The bird sniffed, looking offended. "The royal cabinet was downsizing! It had nothing to do with me! My last-quarter performance reports were top-notch! The Raja let me go with an excellent severance package and references!"

"Never mind all that." Mati grabbed my hands again. "Kiran, once you're in the contest, there will be cameras on you all the time. You can't let on you're competing because of Neel. You can't even let on that you know Neel's been captured."

"Okay," I agreed. "That makes sense."

"There'll be three rounds, or tests, each more dangerous than the last. You'll know they're beginning because you'll get a harmonigram message. I'm not sure about the first two, but the third test is the gladiator round, where the contestants face an opponent in a huge *Who Wants to Be a Demon Slayer?* arena. It'll be set up with TV screens all around so the whole multiverse can watch."

"Do you know anything else?"

"Our spies tell us that Sesha doesn't just have demons involved with the contest. He apparently has hired a lot of daini, petni, and shakchunni in his game show too."

"Witches and ghosts!" I exclaimed. "Well, at least I've read K. P. Das's textbook cover to cover. What I want to know is how do I get Neel out of that underwater prison before we're forced to fight each other in the third test?"

Mati nodded. "You've got to make it past the first two tests, of course. Then the night before they bring Neel up to fight with you, they'll transfer him from the underwater fortress to a holding cell on land. That's when we'll get him out. It's just too dangerous to rescue him while he's at the bottom of the sea."

"And how will we do that?" I asked. "Rescue him from land, I mean?"

"We have a plan," Mati said, but before she could go on, the paan wallah, who was obviously a PSS lookout of sorts, let out a high, shrill series of whistles. With one quick gesture, he wrapped up his spices and betel leaves in a dingy cloth and disappeared down the hole under his stand, the same one that one of the skateboarders had come up through.

"Time to split!" said Chandra, the rough-voiced skateboarder with muscly arms.

"Kiran, I promise I'll explain everything, only right now, we'd better get going—we're about to get some not very nice company." Mati thrust a spare skateboard at me that she'd been carrying on her back.

"Stop there! No escape now, you skateboarding resistance scum! We've finally got you!" I heard someone call, followed by the stomping of many booted feet. It sounded like they were close. The sun beating down on us in the alley suddenly made me feel exposed and unprotected. I didn't know a ton about battle strategy, but I knew for sure it was a bad idea to find yourself cornered by enemies in a narrow alleyway.

Naya was already back in the auto rikshaw, her phone put away. All the other pink-sari girls got on their wheeled boards, which were painted in bright colors with garish designs. The rough-voiced girl even had a snarling, red-horned and blue-fanged rakkhosh on hers. But I made a split-second decision. I was a hero. I wasn't going to run. Be this an army of witches or ghosts or rakkhosh or serpents, I wasn't afraid. Ignoring Mati's advice, and the borrowed board, I stood my ground, nocking my arrow into my bow again. I sighted down the shaft, waiting for whatever it was to come into view.

I heard, rather than saw, the auto rikshaw engine start, then Naya calling out to me. I felt other skateboarders whizzing past, making little breezes in their wake.

"Kiran, don't! You don't want to shoot these people!"

Mati urged, practically shoving me onto the borrowed skateboard. "The best thing to do is get out of here, and fast!"

"Aw, come on!" yelled Tuntuni. "Can't she shoot a couple of them?"

I was about to argue with my cousin, but when I saw who was chasing us, I understood her point. Behind us weren't any demons or monsters, but the Raja's own troops in their turbaned, pantalooned, and moustachioed glory (everyone had such thick whiskers they probably bought Mr. Madan Mohan's Artisanal Moustache Oil™ by the caseload). The soldiers should have been on our side, but they were charging us with their swords raised, their sweaty faces furious.

"Stop, you rebels!" shouted the captain of the guard, a muscle-bound bald man with a loop-da-loop curlicue 'stache. "Stop in the name of the crown prince!"

My mind swirled with confusion. Why were Lal's guards chasing us, especially when Lal was basically Mati's best friend in the world? More to the point, if I was about to join Sesha's contest as the Raja's champion, why should I run from his own soldiers?

But I didn't have time to worry about all that now. Those swords looked sharp, and those guys looked ready to use them. "Come on!" urged my cousin, holding my hand and showing me how to pump my leg to get the board rolling.

The soldiers yelled, gaining on us by the second. Behind the dudes charging on foot were a few on horseback. That really got me freaked out. I started pumping my leg harder, trying to get my board going faster. Mati had ahold of my hand and was basically pulling me along, adding to my momentum. But still, I wasn't exactly going sixty miles an hour. Or even half that.

"Um, Cuz, I hate to be a downer, but how are we going to outrun those guys on horses?" I yelled, trying not to sound as worried as I felt.

The soldiers were gaining on us, even though the road was slanted downhill, so my skateboard was really zipping now. I struggled hard to keep my balance, my thighs straining from the effort. I could hear their yells of "Rebel!" and "Traitor!" close behind.

"Power in numbers!" yelled Mati with a wink. And I realized she wasn't holding on to me anymore, but had tied the end of her pink sari around my wrist. She had a chain of skateboarders behind her, some with their saris attached to the next person, some just hanging on to the next girl in some way. She shoved me forward, toward the auto rikshaw.

"Hold tight, Your Royalosity!" called Naya from inside the vehicle.

"Wait, what?" I sputtered, even as I grabbed on to the back railing of the moving rikshaw. I saw that mine wasn't the only chain of skateboarding girls, but there were three others, each three or four girls long. The leader of each line was holding on to some part of the rikshaw, as I was.

"Okay, Naya, we're all on. Now go! Go!" Mati yelled, and Naya pushed the gas, making the rikshaw zoom away, with all of us on skateboards being pulled along behind, like strings behind a zipping kite.

Riding a skateboard while holding on to the back of a moving auto rikshaw was a little scary, I'm not going to lie. But it was also pretty awesome. I don't know why, but all I could think about was what it might be like to ride on a comet. I know it was just a skateboard, but speeding along behind the rikshaw, pulling along all those other girls, felt amazing. I remembered the first time I'd flown on the back of a pakkhiraj horse and felt the stars above me, the horizon stretching out in front of me, the streets and houses of Parsippany turning tiny below. I felt the same sort of wonder and thrill now. The rough-voiced girl at the head of the next line gave me a joyous whoop, then a tongue-sticking-out surfer's hang ten like Buddhu had done. I gave her a whoop back. I couldn't help it. Even though we were being chased by angry dudes with swords, I felt electric, and powerful, and alive. It was like girl power on overdrive, and I was all here for it.

"Hang on tight!" Naya yelled from the driver's seat, before taking a hard right. I did, my knuckles aching and fingers straining from the effort. I couldn't forget that if I let go there was a line of girls behind me who would get left behind too.

"Mutton curry, twelve o'clock!" yelled Tuntuni, as Naya swerved to avoid a family of sleeping goats in the middle of the road. The yellow bird was flying along right at my shoulder. "Oh, my rotten tail feathers, you're all going to die!"

Our whole bizarre caravan careened straight toward the now panicked and bleating goats. The mama goat, heavy with milk, was standing right in front of me, screaming her lungs out as her wobbly legged babies scattered left and right.

"My line—let go!" I yelled, squeezing myself up and praying for flight. Somehow, we all managed it. One girl after the other after the other, each holding the edge of her board as she lifted up in flight. We were on enough of a slope and had enough momentum that we sailed over the animals like we were playing duck-duck-goat. And then, by who knows what miracle, as soon as my wheels touched earth, I managed to grab on again to the back of the rikshaw.

"Whoa!" "Sweet!" "Beam me up!" yelled the pink-sari skateboard girls behind me. Even the tough-looking girl gave me a wide grin. "Nice!"

I gave another loud whoop, feeling dangerous and free. I was starting to understand how Mati could have thought that skateboarding was more fun than mucking out horse stables.

"Almost there!" said Mati from behind me, and I realized the auto rikshaw was actually slowing down.

We'd been traveling so far on the main road out of the bazaar, but now we were at the top of a sloping riverbank. On the sides of the river were shallow steps—the kind that villagers might use to enter the river for bathing, or washing, or prayer. Today the steps were empty, save for a very familiar old sari-clad woman with a walking stick and only one good eye.

"Chhaya Devi," I breathed. It was the goddess of shadows, who had been Lal and Neel's nanny when they were younger, before she'd gone into business catching and selling the shadows of trees.

Naya put-putted the auto rikshaw toward the old woman, who cackled angrily, "What took you scoundrels so long? My shadows do not like to be kept waiting!" Her one rheumy eye swiveled toward me, and her voice dripped with sarcasm. "You finally made it, I see, Princess. So glad you could find time in your schedule to assist your old friends! We wouldn't want something so small as Prince Neel's imprisonment to inconvenience your social schedule! So many soirees! Cockatoo parties! Rickets matches to attend!"

I gave Mati a quizzical look, and she explained under her breath, "Rickets is rakkhosh cricket. Traditionally played with a human head."

All righty. Chhaya Devi hadn't exactly been super balanced the last time I saw her, but from the looks of it, she'd lost a few more marbles since last fall.

"They're almost here," Mati urged. "Chhaya Devi, please."

"All right, all right, give an old woman a parsec," mumbled the merchant of shadows. She fumbled for something from her dangling drawstring bag as the first of the soldiers came around the bend. It was all I could do not to scream. I'd been chased by monsters and fought back. But how was I supposed to deal with these fellow human beings who I really didn't want to hurt, but who I didn't want to get hurt by either? I nocked an arrow in my bow, praying I wouldn't need it. I noticed the skateboarders around me were getting nervous too, some reluctantly pulling out knives, swords, and bows.

"There they are! Get them!" shouted the soldier.

"Not so fast, you naughty rudeniks!" snapped the old woman as she smashed a vial on the ground. "Fly, my enwheeled daughters, fly like the wind!"

I knew from experience the power of Chhaya Devi's vials. They held the shadows of trees inside. Once freed, the shadows reconstituted themselves, like expanding sponges. Super-powerful, tree-shaped magic sponges, that is. This shadow she'd freed for us seemed to be extra magical. It twisted out of its vial in a shimmering silver mist that created a barrier between the soldiers and us skateboarders. Under cover of the mist, we were all able to ride into a hidden tunnel beneath the stairs and then travel quickly under the flowing river. The soldiers were left on the other side of the magical shadow, yelling curses but unable to get beyond.

When we came out of the tunnel on the other side, Mati turned to me with a grin. "That was fun, huh?"

I rolled my eyes but laughed too. "Not bad."

"Listen, we're not far now from the royal palace. The stable's right on the other side of these woods." Mati pointed. "The safest thing for you to do is to go find Lal and stay by his side. I don't think Sesha will try anything while you're with the royal family and competing on live television. He won't dare."

"But why were those royal soldiers chasing you?" I didn't understand everything that was going on here, that was obvious. "I would think we were all on the same side?"

"Things have been pretty confusing since the Raja and Sesha made the deal to work together, and then everybody got caught up in *Who Wants to Be a Demon Slayer?* fever," sighed Mati. "Just make sure you make it through the first two challenges—we can't have you kicked out before you get to the third."

"What about Naya?" I asked, looking at the girl in the auto rikshaw.

I'd been speaking low enough that I thought she wouldn't hear, but somehow, she did. "I will stay here with Mati-didi," said Naya, using the word for *elder sister* after Mati's name. "The people are expecting the Princess Demon Slayer, not the Princess Demon Slayer and her friend from school."

"Are you sure?" I asked, looking doubtfully from Naya to Mati. I don't know why, but I felt responsible for the goofy girl. I wasn't 100 percent sure she'd be able to take care of herself.

"I'll keep an eye on her, don't worry." My cousin looked at me, her face troubled. "When you go to the palace, check on my pakkhiraj, will you? With Neel and now me gone ..." She let her words trail off.

"Don't worry, I will." I gave Mati a quick hug. I noticed that she didn't ask me to keep an eye on Lal. I knew enough, though, not to ask.

And so, it was settled. I was off to the palace, to fulfill my destiny by becoming the Princess Demon Slayer.

CHAPTER 15

Princess Demon Slayer

I wanted to see Lal as soon as possible, but I had to make one quick visit first to see some very precious friends.

The royal stables were empty of people and felt strange without the familiar, calm presence of Mati puttering around. But the white pakkhiraj horse, Snowy, sensed me right away. He put his head out of the stall, his eyes sparkling and wings folding and unfolding like he was waiting for me to fly away on his back.

Princess, I missed you. Where've you been?

"Hi, boy! How's the hay?" I stroked Snowy's nose, and he blew warm breath on my hand. He wiggled his wings a little, like he always did when he was happy. I'd figured out last fall that I could understand pakkhiraj horses, although I still didn't exactly know why.

That's when I noticed that Neel's pakkhiraj horse, Midnight, hadn't even looked out of his stall. "What's the matter with him?" I asked Snowy.

Since Neel has been gone, he has been so sad, said the horse, adding, *Princess, what is wrong with your hair?*

"It's a long story." I looked down at my braid and realized the green was spreading. I didn't want to look at my arm, but I was pretty sure it was spreading there too. I couldn't let myself think about that right now, so I stuffed my worry into that dark room inside me where I stored stuff like that until I was ready to deal with it.

I peered over Midnight's stall, but the big black horse kept his head down and toward the corner. It was disturbing to see the big, powerful horse so quiet and mournful. I could see that he had a lot of worry stuffed inside him too.

I tried to reach out to him with my mind, or however this whole thing worked, but all I could sense in there was Snowy's happiness at seeing me. I eased Midnight's stall door open and stepped in.

"Hey, boy." I approached him slowly. But the black horse's wings stayed folded over his back, and he refused to look over at me. I felt an ache of sadness as well. The last time I'd really seen Midnight, Neel had been riding him.

"Hey, boy," I said again, my hand held out. I waited like that for a minute, sending calm thoughts toward him with my mind. Then, before I knew what was happening, the big animal took two quick steps over to me. He hooked his head over my shoulder and let out snorts so long and deep, it almost seemed like a human being crying. His sadness crashed in waves through my mind, his spirit trembling in the same way his strong muscles shook under his velvety skin. I felt a little bit like crying too.

My boy, I heard the horse say in my mind. *Gone. Where? My fault? Was I bad?*

"No! Of course it's not your fault, Midnight. It could never be your fault he's gone." But Midnight kept sending out waves of sorrow, making low, groaning sounds in the back of his throat. His sadness brought mine up too, like a tuning fork that starts to make the same sound as another. I felt tears well in my eyes at the thought of Neel in prison, and it being all my fault. Would I be brave enough to keep up the farce of this game show until we could rescue him? I hoped so. I placed my wet cheek against the horse's powerful neck as he continued to shudder and cry.

My boy. My boy. Where is my boy?

I threw my arms around the powerful animal's neck. My instinct told me to address him this time with his Bengali name, not the English version of it. "I'll get him back to you soon, Raat."

The horse shook his mane against my face, then neighed, long and deep, as if he believed me. He even gave me a ticklish little nip on the shoulder. I'd always been a little bit intimidated by his sheer size and strength, but now I felt like I had seen into Raat's soul. The powerful pakkhiraj was unwaveringly loyal to Neel and loved him fiercely. And that sort of loyal love seemed like a pretty precious thing.

You promise, Princess. Promise you bring him home. Bring home my boy.

"I'll bring Neel home to you. I promise," I said.

My heart ached as I closed the stable door behind me on the horses and headed toward the palace. I walked out through the empty royal lawns, past sweet-smelling jasmine and oleander plants, nectarine and mango trees. I walked along the edge of the royal woods, past Tuntuni's favorite guava tree, from where he had pelted Neel and me with unripe guavas when we had come to him for help. The vast courtyard that had once been populated by servants scurrying to and fro was deserted, and by the time I reached the filigree-lined hallways that led to the throne room, I was getting really worried. Luckily, the palace proper seemed to be functioning as it always did, with guards at the doors wearing curved swords and stern expressions.

"Halt, who goes there? What is the password?" a guard in a bright orange dhoti asked me.

Praying it was the same combination of nonsense words I'd used before, I said the password that Naya had taught me. As the guard let me through the doorway into the antechamber, I couldn't help but feel nervous. Here I went, and here it started. Once I went in there, I'd be part of the game show. There was no backing out now.

I was in the familiar crowded antechamber, filled with villagers and courtiers, gossipers and complainers, royal wannabes and fancy-pants. I even saw Lord Bulbul, Minister of Sweets, who had been so mean to me the last time I was here. This time, however, the man practically ran over a few dozen people to get to me.

"Princess Kiranmala!" He bowed, jangling all the silly chains and medals he wore on his chest. "The clip of you in registration line is all over the kingdom! You silly billy! How could you not tell us you were coming today to join the contest?"

The minister of sweets pointed up at one of the new TV monitors lining the antechamber walls, and I saw that he was right. It was on mute, but there I was, on an endless loop, squinting into the sun as I spoke to Suman Rahaman. The words scrolling by under the image read: *Princess Demon Slayer arrives incognito in the Kingdom Beyond. But her green-tinted hairdo wasn't enough to fool her real fans!*

Grabbing my arm, he bustled me through into the main part of the throne room. "The Raja and crown prince will be so glad you're here!" he boomed. "Come with me! Come with me!"

He shoved courtiers out of the way, elbowing one old man in the back and practically knocking over a little lady with pearls threaded into her elaborate topknot. As I speed-walked to keep up with him, Lord Bulbul gestured to a silvery tray carried by a servant. "Would you like a sweet? A pithe perhaps? A coconut naru? Or a syrupy chomchom or rasagolla? What about some creamy mishti doi?"

I stared at the tray of desserts. Each sweet seemed to have a bite already taken out of it. From the silver-lined sandesh, to the little crepe of the pithe, to the pretzel-like

drippy orange jilipi. Even the sweet yogurt, in its little earthen bowl, had a dirty spoon resting in it, and it was obvious someone had carved a corner out of the brown-white pudding.

"But someone's already eaten these!" I pointed out. My stomach was growling, but I wasn't hungry enough to eat someone else's half-eaten food.

"Of course! Each tasted by the Raja himself!" Lord Bulbul beamed. "Normally I charge a small fortune to people who want to eat the Raja's leftovers, but for you, I'll give a fantastic discount!"

"No thanks," I said faintly.

"Suit yourself." The minister of sweets shrugged. "But you don't know what you're missing, young lady! Royal spittle adds a fantastic level of flavor!"

We were finally through the crowd of lords and ladies. Lord Bulbul gestured me forward, toward the king, announcing in a loud voice, "Your Majesty—I have found her! Princess Kiranmala, the Princess Demon Slayer!"

Everyone in the throne room stopped talking, and all the courtiers in their silks and jewels and feathers turned around to look at me. I squirmed inside, feeling like a bug under a microscope. Since my adventure last fall, I'd gotten a bit more used to being in the limelight, but I still really didn't love people staring at me. I felt my face and neck heat up as, after a moment of stunned silence, the entire room burst into applause. There were at least a dozen camera people lining the walls of the throne room, and they all whirled on me now, recording my every step, my every word, my every move. I swiped at my nose and really hoped I didn't have anything in my teeth.

I forced myself to ignore the cameras and walked down the long aisle toward where the Raja was sitting. His moustache seemed more prominent and curly—reaching out way beyond the sides of his face. Mr. Madan Mohan's Artisanal Moustache Oil™ strikes again. The Raja was lounging on his throne with the peacock back and the lion heads for arms, but leaped up when he saw me.

"Lord Bulbul—for this we will present you with another Princess Pretty Pants factory! Two, in fact! Oh, huzzah, huzzah, she has come to save us all!" The Raja clapped his hands. "Welcome, Princess! Welcome!"

I was both surprised at the Raja's reaction and super annoyed that the minister of sweets was acting like he'd somehow found me. When I shot him a questioning look, waiting for him to contradict the Raja, Lord Bulbul just grinned and shrugged, as if to say, who would want to contradict a king?

"Greetings, sire." I bowed low, my hands respectfully together.

"None of that! None of that! Most capital! Most capital!" The Raja clapped his hands together again in delight. "Where is Minister Addabutt Gupshup? Where is our new chief minister?"

A greasy-haired man appeared from behind the throne, like he'd been hiding there the whole time. He had a huge, comical hooked nose, and dark round glasses that helped to hide any expression in his eyes. "Here I am, Your Majesty! At your service!" he said in his oily voice. "And the Princess Kiranmala! Such an honor! Such a delight! Such splendiferousness! Such amazement!"

Adda and Gupshup? Didn't those words mean "chitter-chatter" and "gossip" in Bengali and Hindi? This guy was Tuni's replacement?

"It was of course Minister Gupshup's wise counsel that helped us form this alliance with your dear, dear father, Sesha!" said the Raja.

I stared in amazement at the minister. This guy was responsible for Sesha weaseling his way into a partnership with the Kingdom Beyond?

"So you have come, dear Princess, to be the champion of the Kingdom Beyond?" gushed Gupshup. "You have come to win *Who Wants to Be a Demon Slayer?* for our own dear Raja and not your estranged father, the Serpent King? What loyalty to your friends! What family drama!" The minister said this last part directly into a camera, working himself up so that tears shone in his eyes. Huh. Somebody was good at this whole reality TV show thing.

"I'll certainly try," I said tentatively. "To be a good champion for the Kingdom Beyond, I mean."

"Louder! To the cameras!" hissed Gupshup through a fake, clenched smile.

"I'll try to be a good champion," I said in a louder voice, but I could tell I'd still not done it right from Gupshup's slightly frozen expression of disapproval. Now that I was here, I couldn't help but feel nervous. There were more pairs of eyes on me than I could count. And that wasn't even including the cameras. I hadn't really realized that part of the reason they wanted me to be the champion for the Kingdom Beyond so much was because it was kind of an insult to Sesha—to have his birth daughter competing for the other team. I wasn't sure how that all made me feel, but it wasn't good.

Then my dark thoughts were cleared by a familiar face, a face that was a sight for sore eyes.

"Lal!" I smiled and waved, dorky as a kindergartener spotting her parents during a school play. Dorky as over-enthusiastic Naya, I thought with a laugh. "You asked, and I came!"

"Kiran!" Lalkamal beamed at me. But at a stern glance from his father, he cleared his throat, dropping his voice a little lower to say, "Um, I mean, welcome, Your Highness! We are so delighted to have you join the contest to fight alongside me!"

Lal was different since we'd last seen each other, when he was convinced my name was "Just Kiran" and usually called me that. He'd also been so insecure about his abilities to be crown prince, he was always putting on a fake accent and trying a little too hard to be royal. Now he seemed much more comfortable in his skin. When had my friend grown up so much?

As if noticing me studying him, Lal made his fingers into a little gun and shot in my direction, accompanying the gesture with a cheesy little wink. Okay, that was weird. Maybe Lal hadn't grown up as much as I thought. I looked away. I don't know why but I suddenly couldn't help remembering those silly poster slogans, the ones about Lal and me stealing kisses and hugs. I felt my face heat up as I tried to switch the channel in my brain and get the embarrassing idea out of my head.

"Capital! Capital!" The Raja's eyebrows danced with enthusiasm. "It will look wonderful on the publicity releases!" He waved his hand in a horizontal motion, like he was writing across the sky: "Crown Prince Lal joined by the Princess Demon Slayer in historic game show competition! Who wants to be a demon slayer? Why Prince Lal and Princess Kiran, of course! Crown Prince and Princess Demon Slayer bring home Chintamoni Stone for good!"

"Yes! Yes! Splendid thought, Majesty!" said the greasy little minister. "Splendid! Genius! Brilliant thought!"

I desperately wanted to talk to Lal privately, to ask him how Neel had gotten snatched from the palace and what Lal was planning on doing about it, but I knew that all these cameras meant that everyone in the Kingdom Beyond (and beyond) would hear everything I said. And that included Sesha, who was probably watching me right now from some reality show master control booth. The thought made me shiver inside. This was going to be harder than I thought.

Meanwhile, Gupshup was dashing around the throne room practically in a tizzy. He picked up a microphone attached to the wall and shouted into it, "Code blue. Code blue. Public relations, strategic communications, and beauty teams to the throne rooms STAT. PR, strat comm, and beauty to the throne room STAT."

The minister paused, turning his head in my direction. Then he picked up the microphone again. "On second thought, we might need some extra beauty backup. Alpha and beta beauty teams to the throne room STAT. Alpha *and* beta beauty, STAT."

"Wait, what?" I asked as a gaggle of people slammed into the throne room as if I were having a heart attack.

I was even more wigged out when the beauty, PR, and strategic communications teams started grabbing at me. A tiny woman with large teeth shoved a microphone in my face, asking me a series of perky questions: "How does it feel to be competing for the Kingdom Beyond alongside Prince Lal? Do you feel like you're betraying your birth father by not competing for the Kingdom of Serpents? I heard King Sesha tried to turn you into a snake on your last encounter with him, do you have any feelings about that you'd like to share with our viewers?"

"Um, yes, I'm super happy to be the Kingdom Beyond's champion. My *real* parents—the family who raised me—are from here, after all," I sputtered. "On all the other stuff, um, no comment."

At the same time, a fierce-looking older woman with a center nose ring and wildly curly gray-and-pink hair started measuring me, as if for new clothes.

"Excuse me!" I yelped as she stuck her hand into my armpit.

Then I was blinded by a camera flash. A hipster guy with a brocade vest and a weirdly sculpted beard with all sorts of clips and ribbons in it started snapping my picture like a hundred times a minute. His helpers, a tall woman holding a set of lights and a short man with a tray of makeup, worked like busy bees around me.

"Stop that!" I sputtered as the balding makeup guy poofed a bunch of powder all over my face. I noticed that he had colorful pom-poms and feathers glued to his eyebrows.

"Even heroes must look their best for the masses!" sing-songed the makeup dude. "Beauty is hard work!"

"Her angles! Her ANG-LES!" The beardy photographer was now under me, shooting up my nose, now standing on a stool and taking a picture from above my head. "Think heroic, but foxy. Expert, but an ingenue. Ferocious, but coquettish!"

"Oh, this is going to be so much better than those computerized images!" Lord Bulbul said as he chomped on a few coconut naru. "So much more earthy and realistic!"

In the meantime, I was getting mobbed by all these people grabbing and pulling and poking at me. "Lal!" I looked desperately for my friend. "What's going on?"

"You are an official competitor now." Lal's smile was stiff with warning. "Isn't it glorious?"

"Beautify like you've never beautified before! Work like

the wind!" Minister Gupshup yelled. "I want her ready for the cameras! Fix that hair! Cover up those hideous scars! And those green splotches on her arm! She's got to look the part! Remember, people, you're creating the Princess Demon Slayer!"

CHAPTER 16

Ms. Twinkle Chakraborty's Talk Show

We're so deloorious, Princess Kiranmala, that you have given your name and face and honor to the nawble cause of bringing the Chintamoni Stone back to the kingdom again!"

The TV studio audience, led by Minister Gupshup, broke into applause.

It was kind of hard to believe. I was sitting in the palace's IGNN television studios with Ms. Twinkle Chakraborty herself, the Kingdom Beyond's own favorite TV anchor. Ms. Twinkle was dressed in an outrageously fancy sari—the border heavily embroidered with gold thread and the blouse very short and tight. Her tall bun was threaded with jewels in the shape of small animals—so that tigers and hyenas and peacocks all seemed to be peeking out of her hair. She sported huge diamond earrings, a jeweled teep, and a nose ring so heavy it was only by some miracle it stayed on her nose. The woman also chewed a giant wad of pink gum as she interviewed me, which made it even harder to understand what she was saying.

"Um . . . you're welcome?" I volunteered nervously. "The Thought Stone! Yeah, awesome, wow!" I pumped two fists halfway into the air with fake enthusiasm.

I still hadn't had a chance to talk to Lal about his brother, but I'd gotten the clear impression that I shouldn't ask him anything in the awful Minister Gupshup's earshot. Had it been Gupshup himself who'd imprisoned Neel—without Lal or the Raja's knowledge? I wasn't sure but I had to play it cool until I could talk to Lal alone.

There were bright lights on us, and I was in brand-new clothes—a flowing white kurta-pajama topped by soft body armor that had been made particularly for me. My hair—which seemed to be getting more green highlights in it—had been washed and styled in little braids all over my head with metallic thread woven through. The alpha and beta beauty teams clearly knew their stuff. Despite Gupshup's insistence that they cover up my neck and arm scars, the makeup team had listened to me and let them be. I did, however, let them cover up the green splotches that seemed to be spreading down my right arm from the serpent scar. I didn't want to admit it, even to myself, but I was starting to get a little freaked out by them. But the short, little makeup artist with the feathery and pom-pommed eyebrows, Bhashkar-da, turned out to be a total genius and he had made me look like a real hero—pretty, but tough too, with a little green lipstick to top off my look. It was too bad Naya hadn't been here to appreciate his mad beauty skills.

The team hadn't skimped on my accessories either. The costume lady had given me a copy of my signature arm cuffs, the ones embossed with the image of the serpent eating the moon, and even given me a new pair of combat boots—sparkly silver. I'd felt a little sad at giving up my signature purple boots, but the silver was just so darn pretty and sparkly. Plus, my purple boots were getting small and they pinched.

"You're so foonny, sweetheart! Such genooine charm!" Ms. Twinkle twittered through ridiculously pink lips and the wad of ridiculously pink gum. She was reading the questions off a giant notecard on which someone with terrible handwriting had scrawled some really misspelled questions. She squinted at the cue card now, as if she needed glasses but was too vain to wear them.

"Our viewers have a lot of . . . kwes-tee-ones for you, darling dearie! First, tell us about your storming-hoot romance with Prince Lal!"

I assumed she meant to say "steaming-hot" but either way, her question was awful. "I don't have any romance with Prince Lal!"

"Oh, come on, daaahling!" Ms. Twinkle Chakraborty gave a conspiratorial wink into the camera. "It's just between the two of us spicy muffins, us gals about the toon!"

"I'm only twelve!" I sputtered. It was mortifying to think my parents were probably watching this live broadcast. "I'm not a muffin, spicy or otherwise, and I've never been about any toon—I mean, town! And besides, Lal and I were never really special friends like that, it was more like him and . . ."

"Uh-uh-uh!" Ms. Twinkle singsonged. She tilted her head not so subtly at the cue card holder, who held up a big instruction sign that said,

MENSHONE NOT PIPPLE
WHO SHOOD NOT B MENSHONED!!
(SPESHALLY THAT OUTLAW STABEL MADE)

Okay, by that I guess they meant I shouldn't mention Mati. But how had Mati gone from being beloved and competent stable maid to outlaw?

"Let's go on, shaaal we, babe? I know you've killed many, many, many rakkhoosh. Too many to count." She snapped her gum with a wet thwack.

"I've fought, but I've actually never killed—" I started, but the TV interviewer cut me off yet again.

"What's the story of your bloodiest kill, sweeting?" Ms. Twinkle asked this question with so much enthusiasm it was like she was asking me to describe my favorite homecoming cheer. "Was it when you gootted that rakkhosh's intestoones with an ice cream scooper or the one where you bit the khokkosh's joogular vein clean in two with your very own tooths?"

"That's gross! I never did any of those things!" I protested, but Ms. Twinkle leaned over and pinched my cheek extra super hard. "No need to be so hoomble, darling!"

Then she pushed a button, and a giant screen behind us turned on with an image—my house in Parsippany! There was no sound and the video quality was a little grainy, but I could clearly see two pakkhiraj horses on my front lawn, snuffling our nonexistent grass.

"That was last fall," I exclaimed, wondering how in the multiverse they had gotten this footage. "On my birthday."

"Indeed, it woos. And a sad, sad day it was at that, sweet baby girl." The woman sniffed, biting her suddenly trembling lip. I saw her take something out of a little bottle in her hand and touch it to her eye. It made her giant brown eyes water like she was crying.

"You can weep if you moost, it's all root. Let it oot, doll. Let it all oot." She handed me a handkerchief that seemed to be laced with the same liquid. As I held it close, it made my eyes water. I saw several members of the studio audience lean forward, eager to watch me cry.

"Thanks, I'm okay." I returned the heavily scented handkerchief back, rubbing my eyes. After a collective sigh of disappointment from the audience, I felt compelled to add, "I'll let you know when I need it."

The video kept going and the horrible, drooly rakkhosh who had in fact gobbled my parents up, beginning my whole adventure, broke through the front of my house. He held a porch pillar like a club in his hand. The audio finally came on, and we heard the monster roar, "Dirty socks and stinky feet! I smell royal human meat!"

The studio audience gasped, and even I felt goose bumps break out on my skin as I remembered how scared I had been, and how confused at seeing my first rakkhosh—a monster I had only heard about in Baba's folktales.

On the video, the demon's tongue lolled out of its warty head as it approached Prince Lal. "How he'll holler, how he'll groan, when I eat the mortal prince's bones!"

It was strange to see this all on-screen, but cool too, like flipping through an old yearbook. How did IGNN have all this footage? This was, after all, *way* before *Who Wants to Be a Demon Slayer?* began, and therefore, at least theoretically, back in a time when everything in my life wasn't being recorded.

On the screen, Lal did an outrageous back somersault off a nearby tree and landed on the demon's head, riding him like a cowboy on a steer. "Methinks, sirrah, you need to go on a diet!" exclaimed Lal before attempting to stab the thick-skinned monster with his sword.

The audience gasped again, one woman letting out a faint shriek. It was only when I saw myself in the recording, trying desperately to control the horse Midnight, that I realized there was something seriously wrong with what I was seeing. When this had actually happened, I had been sitting on Midnight behind Neel, and it had been Neel who had been controlling the skittish horse. I hadn't ever ridden any sort of horse before, nonetheless a flying one, but in the video, it somehow looked like I was controlling Midnight all by myself. And Neel was nowhere to be seen.

"Wait a minute, something's not right," I began, and Ms. Twinkle Chakraborty batted her heavily mascara'd eyes at me with sympathy. "I knoo it's not. Your adopted parents had just been killed, their boones crushed to the size of ice cream sprinkles. You had noo idea who you really were, and you had just met the gallant Prince Lal—who was in the process of making you fall head over heels in lurve with him."

"No, my parents weren't killed, and their boones—I mean, their bones—are just fine," I protested. "They were swallowed whole and whisked away to this dimension. And Prince Lal never . . . I mean lurve is really not what our relationship is about."

Ms. Twinkle put a long-nailed hand over my mouth. "Shhh, darling, shhh . . . I know this footage must bring up terrible memooroos, but it will all be all right. Lurve will mend your brooken heart."

"But," I began again, as soon as she removed her hand, and she quickly replaced it, patting me all over my face in a bizarre attempt to shut me up while not looking like she was shutting me up.

"Mrph . . . blargh . . . mraph," I protested

"Shhh, there, there, sweet child," she countered, then louder, "There! There!" She was practically slapping my face now with her open palm.

I shut up, but what I saw next on the footage was so outrageously false, I almost started shouting again. The video showed Lal single-handedly fighting the rakkhosh, then rescuing me from its clutches. Of course, what had really happened was that the demon knocked Lal unconscious and I had rescued him. Then Neel had come in and rescued me when I was in trouble. But I saw none of that happen on-screen. Instead, I saw myself swoon in Lal's arms as he carried me off on Snowy's back. I also saw myself double back to stand on top of the now unconscious rakkhosh's head, delivering a bloody death blow with a long-handled sword. This was a total lie, of course, because I'd never actually killed any monsters—rakkhosh or otherwise. I'd fought them, outwitted them, out riddled them, sure, but killed? No. Yet the recording looked so ridiculously real, I almost believed this alternative version of the truth myself.

"Wait a minute, that never happened. I don't even know how to use a sword very well," I sputtered. "And where's Neel? Why isn't he anywhere in the video?"

Ms. Twinkle let out a giant sigh, then looked at the camera and made a throat-slashing motion. "Cut!" called the director. After the video screen flashed with a sign that said *WE R X-SPEERYUNSING TECKNICAL DIFFICOOLTIES*, my interviewer jumped to her feet, her fake smile dropping from her lips.

"I cannoot work like this!" Her voice was super different now, not dripping with honey but sharp and barbed. She ripped off her lapel microphone and threw it down. "Unprofessional! Bloody amatoors! Who prepped this sad excuse for a princess? Who's responsible for her toorrible answers?"

"I was just trying to tell the truth." But Twinkle's voice was so shrill she just talked right over me. "She made me look like a fewell! I refuse to be upstooged on my own shoow!"

The news anchor swept out of the room, her assistant and entourage in tow. Minister Gupshup jumped up from the audience and dashed after the enraged woman, shooting me an evil look as he ran past. I sat there in the studio chair, feeling stunned. What had just happened?

"Don't fret, Kiran, she's like that to all her guests." Lal came into the studio and sat in the bucket chair where Ms. Twinkle Chakraborty had just been sitting.

"Hey!" I leaned in to give him a hug, and the entire studio audience, who was still there, went "Awwww."

"Let's get out of here, huh? I've got to talk to you about something really important."

"Excellent suggestion," said Lal, ushering me offstage. To which the entire studio audience went, "Oooooo," in a really embarrassing singsong way.

I felt myself heating up and saw that Lal's face was beet red too.

As soon as we were fully offstage, though, Lal leaned very close to me. Way too close for comfort. For a second, I actually thought with alarm that he had somehow bought into the lie about our so-called romance. But he just put his mouth near my ear and whispered, "We've got to get Neel out of detention as soon as we can!"

CHAPTER 17

The First Test

I waited a bit before following Lal out into the palace gardens. I was happy enough not to walk out of the studios together. Too much chance for more silly gossip about us. Here too were the giant posters of Lal and me. Where once had been beautiful carved images of peacocks and lions and flowers, the marble walls of the palace were now covered with gaudy movie-poster-style images. The size you see at an amusement park or something. Lal and I fighting side by side, Lal and I flying on Snowy and Raat, Lal and I laughing over a snack of roadside shingaras served by a smiling, mustachioed vendor as a bunch of happy villagers swirl in a happy, festive dance all around us. The posters seemed so realistic they almost fooled even me. But like in all the other images I'd seen, Neel had been entirely cut out of the picture.

Even though there were so many giant images of Lal, I couldn't see the real prince anywhere. But at least there weren't any camera crew people hanging around either. I sat down on a rock by a small fish pond to wait for my friend.

It was almost evening, which meant the heat was actually tolerable, and the moon was just making herself seen in the sky. I breathed the heavy scent of night-blooming jasmine and realized I was sitting next to a bush about to burst with the tiny white flowers.

And then, looking down at my moon mother's reflection in the tiny pond, I had the strangest feeling. Like I was able to connect to something greater than myself. Something shimmered in the pond, almost like a screen coming to life. That's when I heard it, the voice. It was Neel.

"Kiran! I told you not to come to the Kingdom Beyond! What are you doing in the palace gardens?"

"Neel?" I hissed, halfway convinced this was some kind of trick Gupshup and the *Who Wants to Be a Demon Slayer?* producers were playing on me. But then, at another shimmer of my mother's reflection in the pond, I realized what must be going on.

"How can I hear you? Is the moon connecting us somehow?" I remembered the last time I'd been sitting in the moonlight—in my living room in Parsippany—and that feeling that had come over me then. Like I was in a prison cell. I had the same cold and clammy feeling now, even though the evening air was actually pretty warm.

"Must be. She's pretty powerful," said Neel. "When I look up at the moon through the cell window, I can see you reflected there." He cleared his throat before adding, "Why do you look so different? What in the khokkosh spit are you wearing? Is that green lipstick?"

I bit down my irritation. "I got made up by the TV game show team, okay? I guess they didn't think my regular look was good enough."

"I didn't mean it like that. No need to get all touchy," said Neel's disembodied voice. "You look . . . nice."

"I'm not touchy!" I snapped. "And I don't need your pity compliments!" I squinted up from the reflection in the pool to the actual shining moon in the sky. I couldn't see Neel even though he seemed to be able to see me. It made me feel kind of weird and exposed. Not unlike, I suppose, being on this ridiculous game show.

"Don't be all defensive—" started Neel.

"Listen," I cut him off. "Are you okay? Last time I saw you, Bogli looked like she was going to take a bite out of your head!"

"Well, she didn't. I'm all right, I guess. Fine, I mean," said Neel, not very convincingly. Then he went on, "Kiran, you've got to listen to me. I meant what I said, you can't help me. You're just going to make it worse. Go home! Like, right now!"

I felt the guilt rising in my chest again. The guilt from it being my fault that Neel was in demon detention. He obviously thought it was my fault too, which is why he was so mad at me. "Whatever, dude. I mean, give it a rest with the bitter, all right? I've already joined the contest." I rubbed my arms to get warm. "We have a plan to get you out. Just hang tight!"

"Kiran, I told you, don't!" Neel sputtered in my head. "Go home to New Jersey!"

I was just about to lose my temper with Neel-in-my-head, but I couldn't. Because just then, from around the corner of the studios, came two cameras, their lights focused on me. And with them came the cheesy anchor Suman Rahaman, his hair all pompadoured up with gel, his T-shirt straining over his chest muscles.

"Princess Demon Slayer! All alone I see! Could it be that you're waiting for the Crown Prince Lalkamal?"

"What?" shouted Neel. "I told you not to trust my brother!"

"Um, yes, actually." I tried to ignore Neel's voice and smiled stiffly into the cameras. It was so weird. Now that I knew I was on TV, I couldn't figure out how to smile normally, couldn't figure out what to do with my hands.

"Well, surprise! He's not coming!" shouted the anchorman. "This is actually the beginning of your first round of competition in the multiverse's favorite game show—*Who. Wants. To. Be. A. Demon Slayer?*"

Then, just as Mati had said, there appeared, out of nowhere, a harmonium floating in midair. I couldn't see the hands that played the small set of keyboards or pumped the accordion bellows. The magic harmonium not only played itself, but sang too. The Bengali song sounded vaguely familiar. "Aguner poroshmoni . . ." it warbled in a slightly off-key but very melodramatic baritone. The part that struck me about the song, though, was something about stars illuminating the darkness. Poroshmoni was the name of the Raja's yellow jewel, and this line about stars in the song made me all the more convinced—was I right about these twin jewels really being neutron stars?

My thoughts were interrupted by the anchor dude shouting at me again. As he began to speak, the harmonium disappeared. "Before you begin on your first challenge, I have just one question for you, Princess Demon Slayer. Are you ready to fulfill your heroic destiny?"

"No! Say no!" shouted not-there-Neel in my head. "Don't play their games! Don't follow their rules! They've made the contest for you to lose!"

"Um, yes?" I said, shielding my eyes from the moonlight. "Cut it out!" I hissed to Neel through gritted teeth.

"I'm sorry, Princess, did you say something?" Sooms stuck his microphone in my face again.

"Just that I can't wait!" I fudged, super conscious of how close the cameras were to my face.

"Fan-tas-tic!" shouted the anchorman. "Just remember, act naturally, like you're not on camera! And whatever you do—don't break the fourth wall!"

"The what?"

Suman Rahaman smoothed back his gelled hair with ringed fingers. "Just ignore the fact that the cameras, or the audience, are there. Don't ruin the game show experience for our viewers, just keep acting like there's nobody else there!"

And then the anchor was gone. Thank goodness I had the sense to look at the cameramen, because I realized they had both pulled out poofy silk sleep masks and put them on, like it was naptime. Only, they still had their cameras on their shoulders and were still standing up. Wait, of course! Mati had warned me that Sesha employed a lot of witches and ghosts in his game show. And I knew perfectly well from my extensive reading of *The Adventurer's Guide* that the way that ghosts trapped your soul was when you looked at them after they called your name. Quickly, I pulled out my copy of K. P. Das's book from my pocket and flipped to the right page:

Petni, Shakchunni, and Other Ghosts of the Female Persuasion

<u>Residence:</u> **Tamarind or similar trees. Unless died by drowning, in which case, live in bodies of water like lakes or ponds.**

<u>Desire:</u> **To capture a woman or girl's soul and trap it in a tree trunk. Then to live in her body and take over her life. Souls are forfeit for the taking when a victim turns at the sound of their name. Also, to eat a lot of fish, but avoid paying for said**

fish. Plus, bizarre interest in riddles and logical puzzles. Riddles are the only thing ghosts treat with honor. Also, they cannot resist a challenge.

<u>Anatomy:</u> Feet often face backward. Additionally, have extendible and/or flammable arms and legs. Often caught out when they use said extendible arms to pluck a lemon from a tree instead of walking out to the tree. Alternately, when they light their feet on fire to cook the morning rice, having been too lazy to obtain proper firewood in a timely and humanlike manner.

<u>Vulnerabilities:</u> Can only call a human being up to two times. Also, iron and steel are terrifying to them. They're not terribly bright, and so have been tricked into being trapped into small containers and the like.

As I closed the book, I heard a chilling, nasal voice. I was right—it was a lady ghost. "Should we drink your blood or catch your soul, child? Maybe both! Let's live! Be wild!"

I froze in place, my eyes squeezed shut. Because I knew perfectly well that looking at a ghost face-to-face while it was calling me would make my soul forfeit for the taking. I turned around, my back toward the direction of the ghostly voices.

"Kiranmala! Come! Why do you loiter here in a land not your own?" a ghost cackled, making annoying kissy noises in the air.

A different voice screeched, "Seeing Lal is her only wish! But listen, yo, we need some fish!"

Ugh, this nonsense about Lal again. I wanted to scream at them to shut up, but I knew not to fall for the bait. The voices were coming from all around, it seemed. Each ghost only had two tries to get me to turn around, but how could I know which one of them had called how many times?

But wait a minute, I had some backstage help. "Neel?" I hissed under my breath. "Are you still there? Can you see the ghost ladies? Can you tell me which one's called me how many times?"

When Neel didn't answer, I hissed out his name again. One of the petni must have heard me, because she shrieked, "Who do you whisper to, oh princess dear? Just turn and tell me! Have no fear!"

I felt the panic rising in me. I couldn't hear Neel's voice anymore, so he wasn't going to be any help. I peered into the pond to see if I could see his reflection. But in the dim evening light, all I could vaguely see was my own pinched face. But also . . . wait . . . I could see the wispy shadows of six, no, seven ghosts behind me—their scrawny, sari-clad bodies, their balding heads, their hunched backs, their backward feet, the radish-like front teeth dangling from their mouths.

The sight of the scary ghost ladies freaked me out so much, I didn't even think twice. I, like every other kid in the multiverse, had read the story about the kid who killed Medusa by looking in a reflective surface. Looking ahead of me, I aimed my bow up and back. Using only the reflection in the pond as a guide, I took aim at the shadowy figures, firing my arrows over and over. Unfortunately, I was no Perseus. Not only did I not seem to be able to kill the ghosts, my arrows seemed to be tickling them!

"That's so nice, where your arrow hit! Aim another at my armpit!"

"Princess! Princess! Hit me here! I'm super ticklish by my ear!" they taunted, giggling and laughing.

I fired over my shoulder like that again and again, my

moon-magicked quiver refilling with arrows so I could never run out. But what good was it if all I was doing was tickling some obnoxious ghost ladies? Oh, how was I going to get through this test already?

"A riddle!" I blurted out, remembering what K. P. Das wrote about ghosts loving riddles. "If I can solve a riddle, will you go away?"

I heard the ghostly ladies whispering among themselves, debating this option.

"If you solve three riddles, then you can roll. But if you can't, we trap your soul!"

I shivered. What choice had I but to agree? I remembered what Mati had said about making sure I got through the first two tests. And besides, having my soul trapped in a tree trunk and a ghost take over my body seemed like a real bummer of an option.

"Fine," I said, keeping my back turned to the ghosts. "Three riddles and then you go!"

"Tell me, Princess, if you're so dashed slick," asked one of the nasal, ghostly voices. "What's so delicate, even speaking its name will break it?"

This one was easy. I'd heard this riddle from Zuzu's brother Niko a million times.

"What's so delicate even saying its name destroys it?" I repeated. "Silence, of course. If you say its name, you break it."

I heard the ladies grumbling, and consulting each other. "That was a practice one!" snarled someone.

"No," I said reasonably, as if it was totally normal to be standing outside a palace arguing with a bunch of riddling ghosts all the while being filmed for intergalactic TV. "That was the first riddle, you have two more you can ask me."

There was some more grumbling, and then some whispered discussion. I heard a ghost say, "That one! She'll never get it since it's in Bangla!" before her sisters shushed her again. And then another one of the ladies cackled in a louder voice, "Tell me, Kiranmala, and don't you quibble, which kind of land has no people?"

I bit my lip. I didn't know this one, but still it did sound strangely familiar. Along with stories about rakkhosh and serpents, Baba was always telling me riddles. Most of them were Bengali wordplays. For instance, he usually broke out one of his favorite riddles around Halloween, when he and Ma used to make me wear a sari and be an "Indian princess."

"Tell me, Daughter, which shari isn't worn?" he'd boom out, pronouncing he word *sari* the Bangla way.

The answer to that riddle was *mawshari*—or mosquito net. So, what land had no people? It must be a wordplay on the Bengali word for land—*desh*.

"I've got it!" An image came to mind of the sticky sweet homemade desserts Ma always made for trick-or-treaters. "Which desh has no people? Sandesh!"

"That was too easy!" shrieked one of the ghosts.

"No, it wasn't!" I protested. "You have one more chance, and then I pass this test!"

There was more shuffling and whispering behind me, and for a moment, I couldn't really see their reflections anymore and got seriously nervous.

I guess they'd decided to play fair, because another one of the ghosts cleared her voice and said, "I have arms but no legs or head to behold. My chest is open wide, and I swallow people whole."

Oh, dratty drat pants, I hadn't heard this one before either, and it seemed more complicated than either of the previous riddles. I took a big breath. Okay, calm down, Kiranmala. Think. Think.

"Your soul I will steal and in a tree conceal!" screamed one of the ghosts.

"Hold on to your petticoat! Give me a minute!" I yelled back. All I could think of was some kind of open-chested, headless rakkhosh, but that didn't make sense. And it couldn't be a snake because they had no arms or legs. Despite the cooling evening, I was starting to sweat. And I thought, randomly, how in New Jersey I would have been freezing cold, bundled in a giant winter jacket.

That's when it struck me. "Wait, I know! What has arms but no legs or head, and it swallows people whole? It's a coat!"

"No, the answer's a shirt! You are wrong!" cackled a ghostly voice. "Your soul is ours, now come along!"

"Wait, it could be a shirt or a coat!" I shouted.

But they weren't having it. "Come, Kiranmala, come to my tree!" "No, Princess, come with me!"

Of all the sneaky supernatural tricks, what was I going to do? I was all alone with these ghosts—who weren't playing fair! Then I remembered that I wasn't actually alone.

"Suman-da! Minister Gupshup!" I yelled to the air. I knew the anchor had told me not to break the fourth wall, but as Neel had said, I didn't need to play by their rules. When no one answered, that's when I remembered that Suman Rahaman and Gupshup weren't the only ones who were watching.

"Hey, Sesha! Your ghosts don't play fair! I got their riddle right and they want my soul!" I shouted in the direction of the closest cameraman.

The cameraman took in a big breath of shock. I could hear the ghosts behind me getting restless, cackling in anticipation of being able to spirit away my soul.

"What kind of a game are you running here anyway, Serpent King?" I persisted, dragging out the last two words. "Is it any wonder I'm competing for the Kingdom Beyond and not for the Kingdom of Serpents? Do you want everyone competing on *Who Wants to Be a Demon Slayer?* to know they're not getting a fair deal?"

There was a moment's silence, then a speaker hidden in the jasmine bush came to crackling life, and out came that terrifying voice I knew so well. The voice of Sesha, The Serpent King, my birth father.

"Oh, fine, fine! You win this round, *Princess Demon Slayer!*" drawled Sesha through the speakers. "Oh, get back to your dimension, you annoying ghostie minions! She's right, the answer to your riddle could be a coat *or* a shirt!"

I heard the shakchunni and petni cursing, long and low, but then with a *pop-pop-pop*, they disappeared from the garden. I turned around slowly and let out my breath. As I did, one of the cameramen pushed up his sleep mask to actually give me a grinning thumbs-up.

I'd passed the first test. Only one more to go before I could rescue Neel.

CHAPTER 18

The Instructional Video

I was given an entire suite in the palace overlooking the gardens. After the first test was over, when Lal was allowed to speak to me again, he showed me to the rooms himself. The entire way over, he kept apologizing.

"They wouldn't let me interrupt the filming!" he explained, his handsome face screwed up in concern. "I am so sorry, Kiran, to abandon you like that! I didn't want to!"

"It's okay. It's not like you could help it. At least those ghost ladies didn't snatch my soul and stick it in a tree trunk, so I consider that a win." We were climbing the steep steps up to my tower suite. I couldn't get Sesha's voice out of my head, or the fact that I'd had to rely on him to get rid of those ghosts. "So, what was your first test like?"

"Ghosts too. Only I never thought of asking them for

riddles. That was brilliant!" said Lal. "I managed to fire iron pellets at them, and they left."

"Right, because of their whole afraid-of-iron-and-steel thing. Good thinking!" I pushed the heavy doors to my rooms open. "How many contestants are competing right now anyway?"

"Dozens! All over the kingdom and beyond!" Lal gestured at a giant screen embedded in my sitting room wall, flipping the channel to a sort of scoreboard with a whole line of names on it. Lal's and my names were at the top of the board. His was higher than mine, I saw, and when Lal caught my eye, he kind of blushed.

"It didn't take me quite as long to get rid of the petni and shakchunni," he said kind of apologetically.

I laughed. "Don't worry about it, I'm just glad I got away from them in the end. But how come every other contestant after us is from the Kingdom of Serpents?" I pointed at the screen, noticing the number of green snake insignias after the other contestants' names. "All the contestants from the Kingdom Beyond seem to have been crossed off!"

"No other human contestants have made it past the ghosts, to be honest," said Lal. "No, that's right, one guy went all the way to the second test, but then he had to confront a fire rakkhosh, and well, he got so incinerated, there was not much of him left to find."

"Dang!" I knew that *Who Wants to Be a Demon Slayer?* was a potentially deadly game, but hearing about someone getting flame broiled like a fast food burger didn't make me feel particularly good. "Do you think Sesha has it rigged in favor of the serpents?"

"Well, you and I are at the top of the leader board," Lal pointed out.

"True." I bit my lip, thinking about those ginormous lines at the registration office, the parents enrolling their kids. How many of those people would enter the contest only to get hurt, or maybe killed? This was even more motivation to win the game, and quick. "I can't believe people from the Kingdom Beyond are still signing up after seeing what happens to everyone else who isn't us."

"Indeed, more sign up every day!" said Lal.

"And we have no way of knowing when the next test will be?"

"No, the harmonigram message just arrives without warning." Lal fluffed his already-perfect hair, taking a quick peek at himself in a gilded mirror. I had to hide a smile. "I have been waiting for the second test harmonigram message to come for a while now. But the competition goes through all the different contestants, so you can never be totally sure when it will get to you. A part of keeping us on our toes, I suppose." Abruptly, like he was avoiding talking to me about something, Lal turned to go, stepping back toward the door.

I hesitated, not sure why I felt so weird bringing it up. "Wait. Lal, about Neel . . ."

"It's all my fault." Lal turned back to me, his eyes a little shiny. "Oh, Kiran!"

Oh my gosh, he was crying! I patted his arm as he took out a beautiful white handkerchief and wiped at his eyes and nose. I wondered how that knucklehead Neel could have ever suspected his younger brother of being at fault for putting him in prison. Lal mumbled through his sobs, "I thought—oh, I don't know what I thought, Kiran, but I never believed they were going to take him away to demon detention. When my father told me . . ."

"Your father knows?" I was shocked. The Raja had never been the most affectionate father, particularly after he found out about Neel's mom being a demon. He'd even made Lal crown prince instead of Neel, but I never thought he would stoop so low. "He just let Neel get taken like that? What the heck?"

"I know, I know." Lal gave a dramatic sigh through a couple sniffles. "But I won't rest until we rescue my big brother, Kiran."

"Do you have a plan?" I asked. "You know, I was thinking, maybe we could ask your old demonology teacher for help?"

"K. P. Das? That oddball? He is not even teaching anymore, but off in the woods above the palace calculating formulas and writing equations that make no sense to anyone but himself." Lal was suddenly dry-eyed and full of irritation. "I hated that class. Never even handed in my final."

That startled me. Unless I was wrong, I thought Neel had once told me that demonology was Lal's favorite subject. But I must have been misremembering.

Just then, there was a noise at the suite door. Lal strode up to it and yanked it open. As if they'd been listening the whole time with their ears pressed to the door, in stumbled three maids with trays of food, new clothes, soap, and hair things for me. They didn't even have the decency to look embarrassed at being caught. The three eavesdroppers didn't understand why I didn't want them to stay and help me eat. I noticed that all three of them were wearing combat boots under their kurta-pajamas and one even had her hair styled like mine—including the bottom of her braid being dyed green!

"That's a super-nice offer, but I can manage to feed myself," I said, trying to shoo them out. But it was Lal who got embarrassed and decided to go instead.

"I should probably let you get settled," he said, blushing.

"No, we haven't finished talking about . . ." I sputtered. One of the women jammed a crunchy piece of fish chop in my mouth, so I couldn't talk until I finished chewing.

"Tomorrow," said Lal, raising his eyebrows significantly as he turned back from halfway down the stairs. "We'll talk tomorrow."

I was still fighting off my enthusiastic helpers, so all I could do was nod in agreement.

It took me another ten minutes to get rid of the curious maids, convincing them that, no, Princess Demon Slayer, the savior of the Kingdom Beyond, really could feed herself. Also bathe herself and brush her own teeth. All three of them asked if they could take selfies with me, though, before they left. It was with a sigh of relief that I shut the heavy doors behind them. I guess I'd thought being a famous hero and reality TV star would feel, somehow, more awesome, but the kind of attention I'd gotten since coming to the palace just felt suffocating.

I nibbled on some more spicy fish chop as I looked around my suite. My rooms were beautiful, with a huge mosquito-net-covered carved bed, silver pots of flowers everywhere, carved leaf motifs on the marble walls, and one wall that wasn't even really there but opened out to the balcony. I walked out there now, looking from the balcony over the darkened garden.

I could smell the night-blooming jasmine, heady on the warm evening air. Far in the distance came the sparkle of moonlight reflecting off the distant ocean. Then I was getting goose bumps on my arms, but it wasn't from the warm night breeze. It was the faint rustle to my right that told me I wasn't alone.

"Who's there?" I demanded, my bow in my hand and an arrow nocked and ready.

"Hi, Your Highness-ship!" Naya heaved herself over the dark balcony railing and ran straight at me, barely giving me a chance to put my weapon away before she wrapped me in a bear hug.

"What did that two-faced crown prince want?" snapped Tuntuni, flapping over to my shoulder. "I thought he'd never get out of here."

"He's not two-faced! Lal wants to get his brother out of detention as much as we do." I looked meaningfully at Mati, who had pulled herself onto the balcony just behind Naya.

"Well, congratulations on making it through the first test!" said Mati, ignoring my comment about Lal. I wondered what had happened between the two friends to make her so upset with him. They used to be super close, and now she'd not just left the palace to join an anti-government skateboarding resistance group, but was refusing to even mention his name.

"How did you two climb up here?" I looked over the railing for a ladder but saw nothing.

"We flew," said Naya promptly, but then Tuntuni gave her a peck on the arm and the girl quickly corrected, "Erm, I mean, Tuni flew over here real quick. We were behind him with the auto rikshaw."

That still didn't explain how they'd gotten up so many stories to my balcony.

"We saw the broadcast of your first test," said Naya, hopping up on her toes with enthusiasm. "Congratulations, Princess, you were wonderful!"

"Um, thanks!" I was relieved to see Naya looking like her normal, perky self. Even though I hadn't exactly asked her to stow away with me, I felt responsible for her and was glad to see Mati was taking good care of the girl just like she'd said.

"I for one was sure you were going to get stuck in a tree trunk by those petni and shakchunni," squawked Tuni.

"Thanks for the vote of confidence, buddy!"

"Keep your voices down! We're not exactly here with a royal invitation," Mati shushed. Then she grabbed my arm and pulled me close toward her. "Listen, Cuz, this isn't a social call. We're here because our spies intercepted a message that we wanted to get to you right away."

"Intercepted?" Why was my cousin talking like a movie secret agent? "What do you mean?"

Mati lowered her voice even more. "They're not going to transfer Neel to the on-land holding cell before your third test. So we're going to have to get him out the hard way."

"The hard way?" I repeated, feeling my stomach flip. "What's the hard way?"

"We're going to have to rescue him from the hotel— under the water," explained Mati.

"But he's in a detention cell, not in a hotel," I corrected.

"Oh, you haven't heard?" chirped Tuni, pecking at the plate of food I'd brought out to the balcony with me. A piece of beguni, or battered and fried eggplant, hung from his beak as he went on, "After you and me and Neel destroyed his fortress last fall, Sesha, your lovely birth father, built a huge underwater fortress and casino. The detention center is in the subbasement level, but above is all high rollers, slot machines, and snake-friendly cigar shops."

"There was a huge segment about the casino on TV a few weeks ago." Naya pulled out her phone and typed in something. "Here it is, look!"

The first thing I saw on the screen were the scrolling words *Lifestyles of the Rich and Monstrous.* It was obviously some sort of celebrity lifestyle show, hosted by none other than ex–Kingdom Beyond cricket captain and overall king of pomposity, Suman Rahaman. Reporting from inside a deep-sea diver's outfit, Sooms toured his viewers around the gold-plated outside of the gaudy TSK underwater casino. A few minutes later, he was inside, having changed out of his diving costume into a way-too-tight sherwani suit, marveling at the dripping chandeliers and snake motifs emblazoned in gold everywhere. The place was totally disgusting and so typical Sesha.

"A hotel-slash-casino-slash-fortress so exclusive, no one even knows which of the seven oceans it's under!" exclaimed the fancy host. "Tune in next time on *Lifestyles of the Rich and Monstrous*! Until then, champagne wishes and cadaver dreams!"

"Wow, that underwater casino's really, um . . . something." I fake suppressed a gag, which made Naya at least laugh. "So how did you find all this out, I mean, about them not taking Neel to the on-land place and us having to rescue Neel from under the water?"

Mati pointed to Naya's phone. "They're not transferring anyone anymore to the on-land facility. We saw a video message from Sesha."

"Wait a minute," I sputtered. Zuzu and I didn't watch as many spy shows as we did science fiction ones, but I'd seen enough to learn a couple basic spy things. "If Sesha sent you a video, it's got to be a trap, right?"

"We don't think so." Tuni paced back and forth on the balcony railing with his wings behind his back, like some kind of detective or lawyer. A piece of cauliflower he'd obviously stolen from my dinner plate bobbed up and down from his beak like some kind of flowering cigar. "The Serpent King has been broadcasting this video all over Demon Land—to torture those rakkhosh whose relatives have been taken. But it wasn't in range of anything we would pick up in the Kingdom Beyond."

"If the Pink-Sari Skateboarders didn't have eyes and ears everywhere, we'd never have seen it," explained Mati. "That's why we think it's authentic."

"Our guess is he's trying to make money by running a competing reality game show—*Who Wants to Be a Rakkhosh Savior?* or something equally horrible." Tuni pecked again at my plate, nibbling at some spinach leaves until I shooed him away. "Filming rakkhosh as they unsuccessfully try to save their relatives from the underwater detention center."

Mati shook her head grimly. "It's totally sick."

"Look, Your Serene Princess-ship, here's the video!" Naya hit a button on her phone. I leaned over the small screen, almost giving a shout as Sesha's slimy face filled it.

"Welcome, hopeful rakkhosh, to this instructional

video to entering The Snake King Towers underwater detention center!" said Sesha with a sly smile. "Your sister's disappeared? Your father has a heart condition and doesn't have his medicine? Your little kiddies are crying for you from their detention cells? Why not try to save them? Why not try to, dare I say it, be a hero?" He cackled evilly, petting his hooded cobras that wound around his wrists. Naya visibly shuddered. As for myself, I was experiencing a mix of rage and disgust and confusion. There he was, my biological father. Why was he so evil? And how much of him had rubbed off on me? Could someone who was the daughter of an evil serpent king ever really hope to be good?

"For those of you foolish enough to attempt it, I have created this helpful video to share the many terrible ways you can die in your attempt to enter my detention center without invitation." Sesha casually wound the twisting cobras around his ringed hands. "First of all, only one chosen one per captive may be appointed to rescue said captive. If a captive does not appoint a chosen one themselves, then their nearest relative may appoint a chosen one for them."

"Neel doesn't want me to save him, though," I pointed out.

"But his mother wants you to save him," Tuntuni squawked. "You're the Demon Queen's chosen one!"

Mati raised her eyebrows at me. I sighed. "Okay, okay. I suppose she did choose me."

"You're the chosen one, Princess! Like Captain Lola Morgana on *Star Travels*!" burbled Naya. "Oh, I love that show, don't you? Look!" She pulled something out of her book bag. "I even wrote away through the intergalactic catalog for a Lola Morgana thermos!"

That distracted me for a second. "There's an intergalactic *Star Travels* catalog?"

"Yes! I've been saving up for the Lola Morgana set of solar-powered curling irons!" Naya forced the thermos into my hands. "Here, Majesticness, you take it! To inspire you to be as successful in your mission as Captain Lola!"

"Oh!" I took the thermos from the girl. "Are you sure? I mean, um, thanks!"

"You're welcome!" enthused Naya, clearly super happy I liked her spontaneous gift.

Tuni cleared his throat in a rude way. "Could we go back to the video, please?"

On the small screen, Sesha went on. "Of course, you must figure out where my hotel fortress is, and locate the appropriate ocean."

Mati reached into her pocket and handed me a moving map of the Kingdom Beyond. I looked at all seven oceans—the Milky

Ocean of Time, the Salty Ocean of Forgetfulness, the Honey-Gold Ocean of Souls, the Serpentine Ocean, the Ocean of Star Light, the Ocean of Infinite Knowledge, and the Ocean of Wine and Sorrow. They were spread all around the seven floating landmasses of the Kingdom Beyond (and beyond). Only which one was the Serpent King's hotel-slash-dungeon-detention-center under?

"You must wait for the night of the full moon. Then, once at the shoreline, you must dive under the water with only one breath. Which is when, well . . ." Sesha cackled evilly, like some bad cliché of a movie villain plotting world destruction. His pet cobras seemed to smile as well. ". . . most of you will die."

"Comforting," I mumbled. I was getting a headache. Only a real villain would go to so much trouble to actually make a video like this. It made me barfy to even admit to myself I was related to this guy.

The Serpent King went on: "If you are one of the lucky few who don't drown, you must enter the hotel fortress, and go down to the dungeon level. Then you must get through the guards—answer their questions in order to find the right doorway, in which will be the crystal box holding a rakkhosh soul bee."

Wait, what? Rakkhosh soul bees? Was that related somehow to the Demon Queen's buzzing minions?

"You must crack open the crystal case, rip off the bee's wing, and open the fortress door using that wing as a key. Of course, when you do that, you'll kill the rakkhosh that bee belonged to—but who cares, right? As long as your loved one is all right," Sesha snarled evilly.

"Sick," repeated Mati, shaking her head.

"Oh, and unfortunately, the only thing that will crack open the cases is a very particular kind of tooth from a very particular source." Here, Sesha cackled again, showing off his two frightening front fangs. His pet cobras hissed at the cameras too.

"So, good luck, you stupid rakkhosh! I'm afraid you'll need it!" Sesha waved as the video clicked off, but not before the giant TSK logo flashed on the screen again. That darned Ouroboros. It was showing up so often now it was giving me the creeps. And that was even before I realized there were letters etched into its snaky skin.

The all is one

Where had I seen that before?

I gave a shudder. "So, in summary, this mission to rescue Neel from the undersea detention center is basically impossible." I ran my hand over the cool marble of the balcony. "I mean, if I survive all that diving-to-the-bottom-of-the-ocean-and-getting-past-the-guards stuff, I still won't have Sesha's tooth to crack the case."

"Ah! That's where you're wrong! Look what we have!"

"What's this?" I took a heavy green leather book from Mati. It looked like the old-fashioned day planner Baba kept in the convenience store office to keep track of stock delivery dates and bank payment schedules.

"It's Sesha's appointment calendar, usually kept under incredible security," my cousin explained, her face all hopeful. I kept flipping through the pages, not understanding what I was looking at.

Tuntuni flew over, using his beak to flip me to the right page. "We lost a lot of good people to get you this appointment book, Princess."

"No, we didn't," Mati said, rolling her eyes.

"Well, we might have. It was very risky anyway." The talking bird sniffed. He had a smattering of rice stuck to his beak, but I didn't bother telling him.

I peered at the page Tuni had flipped to. First, I noticed that two nights from now was the night of the full moon—which had both an upside and a downside. The upside was that this was the one day that I could potentially storm the underwater prison. The downside was that since it was the full moon, my moon mother would be high in the sky and couldn't possibly help me.

"What am I supposed to be looking at?" Tuni put his beak down on the page with a swift peck, practically nicking my finger. "Hey!" I protested. But I did notice what he was pointing out. It was one of those sticky round appointment reminders that Dr. Berger, Jovi's mom, gave us every time we had an upcoming appointment for a tooth cleaning. "My bio dad has a dentist appointment tomorrow? The day before the full moon?"

"The Serpent King has terrible dental hygiene," Mati explained, pointing to an X-ray on a light box that Naya had pulled out of her endlessly roomy backpack. Mati pointed to all the black spots on the X-rayed fang. "He can regrow his teeth, but he has to get his fangs pulled all the time, they're so decayed and cavity-filled! I mean, look at that plaque and gingivitis!"

"Say, why do kings go to the dentist?" squawked Tuntuni.

"I don't know, why?" Despite the dire situation, Naya was all chipper enthusiasm and wonder, as usual.

"To get their teeth crowned!" crowed the bird, flying in circles as he laughed.

"Oh, that's a good one!" Naya's eyes were all round with innocence. "But I thought the plan was Princess Lady Kiranmala was going to go steal the Serpent King's tooth while he was at the dentist so that she can use it to crack the bee case and free His Royal Highness Neelkamal, sir."

"It was a joke, Naya," explained Mati. "But yes, that's what Kiran is going to do. We're going to sneak her into the dental office, and she's going to grab that fang as soon as it's pulled."

And then we three put our hands and Tuni put his wing together. With a rallying sort of a cry, Mati raised her fist in the air and shout-whispered, "To the dentist!"

Naya and Tuni joined in, gleefully pumping their fist or wing in the air and saying in less-than-shouty voices, "To the dentist!"

I inwardly groaned. Oh man, what had I gotten myself into now? I wasn't strong enough to confront Sesha again. What if this whole thing failed because of me? Being the chosen one sucked big time.

CHAPTER 19

Mission Ridiculous

The plan was for me to meet my friends in the woods surrounding the palace at dawn. I snuck out of my rooms before the sun rose and made my way down to the grounds, grateful the camera crews didn't seem to be awake yet.

The thought of going to confront my evil snake father was scary enough. The added creepy factor of having to do this in a dentist's office didn't make me feel any better. I hated dentists! Maybe it was the fact that Dr. Berger, my dentist, was also my neighbor and Jovi's mom, but going to the dentist had always made me anxious.

Mati, Naya, and Tuni were waiting for me in the woods with two new additions, those giant birds, Bangoma and Bangomee. Since all dental offices in the Kingdom Beyond (and beyond) were located in Demon Land (fitting!), and since landmasses tended to move a lot around here, the safest way for us to travel was by magical giant bird, as they apparently had magical GPS systems built into their brains. Only problem was, Bangoma and Bangomee were *huge*. My stomach was already doing flips before we climbed onto the giant birds—Tuni and I on Bangoma, Naya and Mati on Bangomee.

"How are the other PSS going to get there?" I'd asked my cousin, who had told me that we'd have skateboarder backup outside the dental office, just in case my bio father brought some henchmen with him.

She'd looked mysterious and just mumbled something about "another way."

I ended up wishing I'd gone with them that "other way," because Bangoma and Bangomee flew so fast that the air battered our faces and made my hair feel like it was going to get whipped off my head. There was nowhere to really hold on, so I gripped Bangoma's slightly oily feathers with all my might, yanking off a few by mistake in the process. I wondered how the others on Bangomee were faring, because on Bangoma's back, my insides felt like they were getting mixed up in a power smoothie blender. Midway to the dentist's office, poor Tuntuni got caught by a gust of wind and almost taken off our ride.

"Save me, Princess! I'm too pretty to die!" yelled the bird.

I lunged for him and grabbed him by a yellow wing. I saw that on Bangomee, Naya and Mati also seemed to be hanging on to each other for dear life.

After what felt like an extra-long dryer cycle of turbulence, the two giant birds began slowing down over Demon Land, that waste-strewn landscape of single-use plastic cartons and discarded yo-yos. The smell of rotten carcasses filled the air, and yet, the part of Demon Land where we landed was nothing like the jungle I'd run through with Neel last fall, or the dry desert where we'd visited his grandmother Ai-Ma. This was a more industrialized part of the country, with strip malls, fast-food joints, and a multilane blacktop highway. In fact, this part of Demon Land looked very eerily like New Jersey.

"The dental region," said Tuni in my ear. "Only dental offices in this entire area. Oh, and the occasional podiatrist too."

A whole area for tooth and feet doctors? Why not.

As we flew even lower, I saw in the distance the familiar shoreline of the Ruby Red Sea. From each direction, there were lines of demons trudging toward the watery border of their country.

"What's going on there?" I pointed.

"Ever since the show producers started raiding demon villages, taking away rakkhosh, khokkosh, doito, and danav to detention centers, the refugee situation has been terrible," said Tuni, his voice unusually serious. "Everyone in Demon Land is leaving their homes, and running away. No one wants to be the monster on a game show, the bait so that someone else can be a hero."

I shivered, not sure what to feel. I mean, these were demons we were talking about. They were evil. They ate people, for goodness' sake. But it was still kind of sad to think about an entire country living in fear of being raided and put in detention.

"What's going to happen to them?" I looked at the endless streams of rakkhosh, khokkosh, doito, and danav, happy that we were well out of the reach of their notice, not to mention their claws and fangs. They were mostly traveling in what looked like family groups, adults carrying children and elders on their shoulders and backs. Plus, a lot of demons seemed to be carrying all their worldly possessions—inflatable life rafts, half-eaten kitchen appliances, broken-down toilet seat covers.

"Some will make it to safety across the Ruby Red Sea, and some won't," said Tuni, as Bangoma landed in a rubbish-filled but otherwise empty parking lot. "There was an entire boat of doito schoolchildren drowned last month. Doito are

scared of water as a rule, and not as strong as rakkhosh.
Those kids didn't stand a chance."

Wow, that was heavy. It was terrible thinking of those
doito kids drowning, but less sad when I remembered that
feeling sorry for demons was something you could only do
from really far away. That's when another thought occurred
to me. What if those refugees started streaming into the
Kingdom Beyond? Or even, gulp, through a wormhole and
into Parsippany? I mean, Naya and her family had somehow immigrated, just like Ma, Baba, and I had. What was to
stop refugee rakkhosh from doing the same thing?

Mati and Naya approached us from where the other
bird had landed, a few feet away. "Ready, Cousin?"

"Hey, how did the dentist become a brain surgeon?"
quipped Tuntuni.

"Tuni, this is really not the time, I really want to know
how . . ." I began, but the dumb bird just kept going.

"His drill slipped!"

Despite myself, I laughed along with everyone else.
Okay, whatever was going on with this rakkhosh refugee
stuff, saving demons was not my problem right now. I just
had to worry about saving the half-demon prince Neel. I
took a big breath and tried to put the image of those drowning refugee kids out of my mind.

Mati went over the plan again with us with the seriousness of a director giving her spies a briefing. "Remember, the dental receptionist is on our side. So, she's arranged for the regular dental hygienist not to be there today. You'll be taking that hygienist's place, Kiran, and helping the dentist with the extraction."

"But there's no way Sesha's not going to recognize me!" I protested.

"Don't worry, you'll be in this fantastic disguise!" Naya chirped, handing me a full hygienist's robe along with a ridiculously bright red wig.

"Um . . . really?" I looked skeptically at the wig, which would do nothing for my skin tone.

She helped me slip into the robe and jammed the wig on my head before saying, "You'll also have this!" Naya handed me an eye patch that looked like she'd stolen it from a Halloween pirate.

I put on the disguise, feeling ridiculous. "But what happens if something goes wrong? Who's my backup?"

"We'll be right there with you—in the air shafts." Mati had pulled out, again from who knows where, a scale model of the dentist's office. "We'll enter here"—she pointed—"and crawl through to here"—she pointed again. "From there, we'll connect the sleeping gas canister pipes to the pipes for the ventilation. So that when the dentist turns on the gas to knock the Serpent King out, he'll knock himself out."

"Won't I get knocked out too?"

"That's where this special face mask comes in, Your Royalness!" Naya chirped, handing me a weird-looking beak face mask that looked like something out of a medieval painting.

"Uh, okay." I eyed the beak mask. "But what about your secret agent? The receptionist, I mean? She's on our side too, right? How will she not get knocked out?"

Naya and Mati exchanged a look. "Oh, she'll be able to handle herself."

"We merry band, we band of sisters," Mati said in an inspiring voice. When Tuni cleared his throat, she added, "And bird, of course. We go now to take the first step in rescuing Prince Neelkamal. They will tell of this day for generations to come in story and song, the day Princess Kiranmala stole the Serpent King's tooth!" Mati was all flushed from her speech, but I didn't blame her. I was feeling pretty pumped up too.

"To the dentist's office!" we all said again, and this time, I actually joined in.

The dental office was easy to spot—a decrepit, factory-like building of filthy, falling-apart brick. On top of the building was a giant neon billboard that first glowed bright with a grinning dentist in one of those mirrored head lamps, a pair of pliers in his hand. Then the sign changed to the patient's mouth, a tooth flying out along with giant neon red splotches of blood. Now the dentist, now the bloody mouth, now the dentist, now the bloody mouth. I understood why all dentists, regardless of species, had their offices in Demon Land.

I put on the beak-like face mask, taking a few tentative breaths. "Here goes nothing!"

Mati pointed me toward the employee entrance as she boosted Naya and then directed Tuntuni into the opening for the building's air shaft. I made my way all by myself through the ramshackle front hallway of the office building, past the broken elevator, and then up some rickety stairs to the dentist's office. There were entire steps missing so that I kind of had to jump and rock-climb in places. The place was so eerie and empty I felt like I was in a zombie apocalypse movie. A zombie apocalypse movie where people still cared about getting their cavities filled, that is.

The front door to the demonic dentist's office was hanging off its hinges, and someone had taken a giant bite out of the wood, but no one had bothered to repair the breach. On the outside of the broken door was a stenciled name plate—*Dr. I. M. Pagol, dental unprofessional,* it read. Well, *that* wasn't reassuring. The door frame and ceiling were huge—at least twenty feet tall—made for rakkhosh patients I supposed. All right, time to go in. I took a big breath. Under my hygienist robes, I still wore my backpack and weapon. I fingered the bow, hoping I'd be able to easily throw off my robes and nock an arrow if this receptionist turned out to be less friendly than Mati said. I charged into the office, ready for anything.

But to my surprise, the receptionist was someone I knew. Someone huge, and strong, and cannibalistic, but someone who still loved me—in her own wacky way. Her gangly pole-like legs were barely tucked under the broken desk and the huge hands on the ends of her fire-hose arms

poked listlessly at an ancient typewriter with no paper in it. She was wearing a stained cardigan with buttons that looked scarily like real bones over her ratty sari. Her bug-encrusted gray wig was fashioned into a bun, and a pair of thick-framed black reading glasses were perched on her nose, attached around her neck with a rusty chain. The lenses were so cracked and smudged, she couldn't see out of them, but the receptionist didn't seem to notice.

"Ai-Ma?" I said, not able to believe my eyes.

Neel's rakkhoshi grandmother took one look at me and leaped up into a fighting stance, knocking over her desk in the process. "Scram! Get away from here, you ginger-haired, pirate bird-beast! We don't want your cargo-stealing, bird-seed-eating, and rum-drinking kind here! Any closer and I'll yo-ho-ho your liver for dinner!"

I laughed, pulling aside the eye patch and beak mask to reveal my own face. "It's me, Ai-Ma—Kiranmala!"

Neel's grandmother's nose twitched as if she didn't trust her failing eyesight.

"Ai-Ma, it is me!" I stepped closer to her, hoping she'd recognize me. Finally, after squinting at me for some time, first through her glasses, and then not, Ai-Ma leaped, long-legged, over the mess of her desk and grabbed me so hard in her long arms that I almost couldn't breathe.

CHAPTER 20

Demonic Dentistry

Oh, my sweet candied dung beetle of a girl child! Oh, my sweet moon entrail of a chitty-boo! Oh, forgive me for not recognizing you right away! Come give your old Ai-Ma a kiss!" Neel's rakkhoshi grandmother crooned and cajoled, cradling me in her huge warty arms like I was nothing more than a baby.

"Ai-Ma!" I hissed. "Let me down! What if the dentist comes in?"

"Don't worry, he's on his cockroach break!" Ai-Ma continued to sing and croon to me, dribbling long strands of saliva on my head. "Oh, my stinky baby-ta, oh, my fleshy human maybe-ta . . ." she sang tunelessly as she rocked me, kissing me again and again with her slobbery lips.

I gave the old woman a peck on her hairy, leathery cheek, and she finally put me down. I slipped back on my disguise in case the dentist returned from his break earlier than planned. And thank goodness I did, because not a few seconds had gone by before the front door swung open, and a little snarling dentist with bristly hairs all over his body and a mirrored headband stepped into the office door. Was he a khokkosh? A porcupine? A giant dung beetle? I couldn't really tell.

Not even paying any attention to either me or the mess of her desk, Dr. I. M. Pagol tossed Ai-Ma his small briefcase, which she caught with her teeth.

"Miss Mooneypenny, I presume," he cackled, "is the next victim in the room?"

I tried not to laugh. Ai-Ma looked nothing like someone named Miss Mooneypenny, but who was I to judge the fake name she'd chosen? After all, I was the one in a red wig, bird mask, and eye patch.

"Hi, boss! His Royal Snaky Highness is in the dental chair!" Ai-Ma warbled in a terrible fake falsetto.

The strange dentist snarled, taking out a metal dental pick from his pocket and chewing on it. "Good, great, grain." He rubbed his hands together. "Can't wait to cause some pain!"

"Super, boss! No one causes pain better than you! You're the best!" Ai-Ma twitted like she was performing in some old-time play. "Your new hygienist will be assisting you!"

She gave me a jaw-shaking pat on the head. I noticed her wig was hanging off one ear a little crookedly, revealing part of her balding head, but decided not to say anything.

"A new hygienist, I'll be gum! What happened to my old one?" The dentist gave me an appraising look. The fact that a little trickle of drool escaped his sharp fangs as he did so only made me more nervous.

"You were behind on my salary, so you said I could eat her," Ai-Ma said, giving me a broad wink as if to say it wasn't true. I wasn't exactly sure. "I'll send her in after you turn on the sleeping gas." Ai-Ma handed the little creature a pair of pliers so big they were practically as tall as he was. He snorted and clapped at the sight of the instrument.

"Oh, toss it! Oh, toss it!" he begged like a very ugly dog with a bone.

Ai-Ma did, and the strange little dentist leaped up but missed the pliers, getting hit squarely on the head. Ouch, that must've hurt! But the animallike creature just blinked away the blood now dripping down from his forehead. "At the count of ten!" he begged, "Oh, try it again!"

"Six and a half, twenty-five, thirty-seven, one hundred two . . . TEN!" Ai-Ma counted, then tossed it.

This time, he did a somersault and caught the pliers in midair between his back feet. Ai-Ma clapped, indicating that I should too. I noticed that along with the giant pliers, the dentist also dug through a filing cabinet to pull out a rusty-toothed saw. He dragged both instruments behind him into the adjoining examination room, where I was assuming Sesha already was.

I didn't have time to be nervous at the thought of my evil bio dad being so close, though, because as soon as Dr. Pagol closed the examination room door behind him, a square tile from the ceiling moved aside to reveal Naya's enthusiastic face. "Hi, Your Royal Highnosity!" she whispered a little too loudly. "It's super awesome up here! Like a slumber party minus the part where we braid each other's hair!"

"I'm sure it is!" I hissed. "Now keep your voice down and tell me when you've hooked up the sleeping gas!"

Naya moved aside with a slight *oof* noise, and Mati gave me a thumbs-up from the ductwork. "We're ready whenever you are. As soon as the dentist pulls the fang and you get ahold of it, give us the signal, and we'll flood the place with sleeping gas so that you and Ai-Ma can get away!"

Before I had a chance to ask anything else, the dirty ceiling tile slipped back into place. And it wasn't a moment too soon, because the dentist soon popped his hyena-like face around the door. "Hurry up, you bleepedy-bleep! Send that pirate now, or I'll make you weep!"

"Don't speak to her like that, you nasty little . . ." I began to say, but Ai-Ma pinched me hard with her bony fingers. Ouch, that hurt.

"She's on her way, boss!" the old rakkhoshi crone sing-songed. She smiled, her three crooked teeth poking this way and that, and the dentist shuddered at the sight.

"All right, fine! But no eye-patch contests on my time."

He disappeared around the corner, and Ai-Ma gave me a bracing look. "Your turn now, my fart-flavored lollipop! Just help the dentist, get the fang, and then give the signal."

I headed toward the examination room, but remembered a very important detail as my hand was just turning the knob. "What's the signal?"

"Why, this of course!" Ai-Ma put her right hand under her left armpit and made a trumpet call of rude noises.

I shook my head. Figured.

Inside the room, I was a bundle of nerves. I couldn't see Sesha right away, what with the sea of torture devices between me and the examination chair. Finally, when I saw him, though, it was a strange anticlimax. The Serpent King had a small breathing mask on his nose. His mouth was a little slack and his eyes were closed. He looked pretty much the same otherwise—the thick black hair and moustache, the rings on his fingers and silk clothes. But without his wit and his cruel words, without his flashing green eyes, he looked a lot less scary. That and the fact that he was drooling a little bit and making strange burbling noises with his mouth.

At the sight of him lying there, knocked out and helpless, I had a horrible thought. What if I just fired an arrow at him now, and was done with it? I could still take his tooth, and he'd never hurt Neel, or me, or my moon mother again. He was violent, and scary, and more than deserved it. I mean, this whole game show thing was obviously some kind of twisted plan to take over the Kingdom Beyond from the Raja, or who knows what. In which case, I'd be saving hundreds, maybe thousands of lives. A voice inside me seemed to urge me on, whispering, "Do it, do it." But could I? Could I injure, or even kill, my evil bio father while he slept? I itched my snake scar, then reached down for my bow, and yet, something stopped me. For some reason, I thought of Ma's and Baba's faces, and how disappointed they would be in me. I couldn't attack someone who was unconscious. Not even someone as purely evil as the Serpent King. He was a monster, it was true. But if I attacked him like this, then I would be too.

But I'd be lying if I said that I wasn't seriously tempted.

"What should I do?" I whispered. The little dentist, who seemed to be dancing some kind of spiky-booted jig on Sesha's silk-kurta'd chest, turned around, and gave me a condescending sneer.

"Weren't top of your class in hygiene school, eh?" Dr. Pagol cackled, tossing back a few sharp-looking dental picks like they were candy. "Just pull as hard as you can when I say!"

"Sure, okay."

"Yo ho ho and a bottle of rum!" shouted the dentist as he attached the pliers to Sesha's fang. "Grab me and pull hard, dum dum!" I grabbed on to his armpits and pulled with all my might. The little creature was squirmy and kind of disgusting to touch, but after a few minutes of tugging, we both stumbled backward, Sesha's fang now between the teeth of the dentist's pliers. It was long, and white, and glistening with some sort of poison. And it was the key to freeing Neel from his dungeon.

As soon as I saw the serpent tooth, I gave the armpit-farting noise signal. Immediately, I heard the whoosh of the sleeping gas being pumped into the room. Only, Naya must have made some kind of mistake, because the little dentist didn't fall down asleep, like I was expecting. Instead, he started giggling like he was an honorary member of Baba's early morning laughing club. (Yes, as totally weird as it sounds, a bunch of adults get together at the Parsippany community park to laugh every morning in unison, because it's, like, good for your blood pressure or arteries or whatever.)

"You're really good at that armpit song!" the dentist giggled, snorting and rolling around a bit. "Do it again! Again! For even more long!"

The other problem was, whatever pipes my friends had connected, they'd obviously shut off the actual sleeping gas to Sesha's mask. Because in less than a minute, the Serpent King's eyes popped open.

He was confused, both because he had just been knocked out, and by my costume. "They must not be paying dentists enough," he lisped through his missing front fang. "If you have to moonlight as pirates?" And then he too began to hoot and laugh. Clearly, no one had the policeman's anti-laughing sickness.

The dentist was now rolling around on the ground, clutching at his stomach. "Yo ho hoo! A pirate's life for you!"

"Ai-Ma!" I yelled even as I whipped off my hygienist's robe. I carefully dropped the bloody fang from the pliers into my backpack. The wig and patch I also threw off, but I was careful to leave the bird mask on, to protect myself from the effects of the laughing gas now heavy in the air.

"Wait a minute, who are you? What are you doing with my tooth?" Sesha was still laughing, but he was growing less confused by the second. "I know you! You're that daughter of mine! Give that back! Give it here! How much sharper than a serpent's tooth is a thieving child!"

He reached for me, a bit unsteady on his feet, just as Ai-Ma came whipping through the door. "Come on, my adopted sweet grand-boo-boo!" she yelled, throwing me over her shoulder and leaping out of the window with one long-legged stride.

"Miss Mooneypenny, my hairy dumpling dear!" the dentist half chuckled, half wailed. "What will I do without your ugly face and figure here?"

"You can shove this terrible job in your dung-beetle wing nut!" yelled Ai-Ma, yanking off her cardigan, glasses, and wig with one swift gesture. "I quit!"

"Wait! Wait!" Sesha giggled and snorted, but he was sounding more like himself with every second. "Henchmen!

Get them! They have my tooth! Don't let them get away! Bring my daughter to me!"

And just like that, Sesha was flinging uneven green bolts of energy at us in between giggles. Poor Ai-Ma cried out when they caught and singed her skin. Over Ai-Ma's shoulder, I nocked arrow after arrow in my bow, but they didn't seem to bother Sesha. And as if the flying bolts of pain weren't bad enough, at the Serpent King's cry, the scraggly lawn outside the dentist's office was filled with snakes of all kinds: boas, rattlers, pythons, and mambas. They slithered viciously in our direction, surrounding Ai-Ma in a trice. They hissed and snapped at us.

"Oh, dear, my licorice-toad dung drop!" Poor Ai-Ma exclaimed as another of Sesha's bolts singed her skin. "I'm afraid this getaway isn't going according to plan!"

Ai-Ma was right. With the green bolts of pain whirling all around us now, and the deadly snakes writhing at our feet, there was no way we were going to get away. And with one arm occupied with holding me up, Ai-Ma couldn't even fight off our attackers.

"Put me down, Ai-Ma. Let me help you fight!"

"No way, my sweet dumpling pants, what we need is a set of wings!" Ai-Ma pointed at the sky, but at what, I wasn't sure.

"I've got you, Grandma!" said a familiar voice. I couldn't see who it was but breathed a sigh of relief as Ai-Ma and I were both swept up into the sky. The snakes hissed and writhed in anger at our escape.

"Get back here, you piratical daughter!" lisped a one-toothed Sesha from the dentist's office window. The dental bib was still hanging crookedly around his neck from a chain. "I'll get you for thisss!"

I was so relieved to have been plucked out of danger that I didn't even register who had saved us for a few minutes. It was only when I finally looked up that I saw who was flying above us. As soon as I saw who it was, my relief turned to horror, and I screamed.

CHAPTER 21

The Flying Fangirls Revisited

At first, I tried to tell myself I was asleep. This had to be a nightmare, like the Rakkhoshi Rani visiting my room. Only, that hadn't been a nightmare at all, had it? And neither was this. But I couldn't believe my eyes, even as my brain slowly processed the information it was receiving.

Our flying rescuer was Naya. Naya, that selfie-taking, cutesie pie, multi-ponytailed optimist. Naya, the new kid in my school who'd stowed away on my intergalactic rikshaw ride. Naya, who had emigrated from the Kingdom Beyond to Parsippany, just like me and Ma and Baba. It was Naya all right, but in her full rakkhoshi form, with huge wings sprouting out of her shoulders.

"I'm sorry, Your Royal Highness, ma'am! I can explain everything, really I can!"

Apparently now that she had taken on her rakkhoshi form, she was speaking in the rhyming way of her people.

"Explain?" I shrieked from Ai-Ma's arms. Naya had Ai-Ma under the armpits and was flying like that, holding up the old woman even as the old woman held on to me. "There's nothing to explain! You're rakkhosh and a liar! Just wait until I tell Mati!"

"Not to contradict your prose," rhymed Naya, flapping her huge wings. "But Miss Mati already knows."

That's when I realized Naya wasn't the only air rakkhoshi flying in the skies above Demon Land. All around us were flying skateboarders, and when I saw them all together like that, I realized where I'd seen the girls before. Oh no. This couldn't be happening. It couldn't. But it was.

"You're the flying fangirls!" I screamed. "The ones who chased me and Neel last fall!"

"Prince Neel is a cutie, Prince Neel is sweet!" cackled some flying rakkhoshis to the left and right of us. "Prince Neel's toes are a great treat!" They did a little pep rally–type cheer as they flew, rolling their arms in circles and pumping their fists in the air.

And then some other girls joined in. "We all have his posters up in our rooms. Neel's so dreamy, he makes our hearts bloom!"

I should have known! Naya's clueless giggliness, her fangirl behavior with Buddhu and Bhootoom, her familiarity with all the back issues of *Teen Taal* magazine. She was one of the flying fangirls we'd run from last fall! And she'd had the guts to pretend to be my friend! I bet she had just been waiting on the chance to snack on my limbs this whole time!

"Let me down! Just let me drop!" I yelled, aiming my arrow upward at Naya's face. "I don't want to be rescued by the likes of you!"

"Num num gumdrop!" Ai-Ma grabbed on to me tighter, breaking my arrow in the process. "Don't say that! I couldn't bear it if something happened to you!"

It's not like I didn't appreciate the irony. Here was Ai-Ma, a three-toothed, near bald, drooling, and hairy crone of a rakkhoshi. Yet, her I trusted. She was one of the few good ones. Then there was adorable, perky Naya, refugee to Parsippany. And she was a rakkhoshi too. But as opposed to Ai-Ma, Naya's identity terrified me. Maybe it was that Ai-Ma had never disguised what she was, nor had she chased Neel and me across the skies, threatening to eat our toes. Or maybe it was the horrible realization, deep in the pit of my stomach, that if Naya was already living in New Jersey, passing herself off as human, then other rakkhosh could do the same. There really would be nothing to stop those lines of rakkhosh refugees in Demon Land from fleeing to my dimension. I closed my eyes, willing away the image of my parents being attacked again, being hurt again by rakkhosh. A wave of nausea rolled over me. I was obviously no hero if I couldn't even tell ally from enemy, friend from foe. I felt my snake scar throb on my arm.

"Kiran, I know it's a lot to process!" It was Mati, riding up on the back of Bangoma. Right next to her was the skateboarder Priya on Bangomee. She smiled, revealing wickedly sharp teeth, and then blew out fire from her mouth like she was a dragon. I shuddered, holding back a scream.

Mati shouted at me again, "Since the game show began, with the roundups and sending of demons to the detention center, we've been working in the interspecies resistance. There are some rakkhosh willing to work with humans besides Ai-Ma, you know."

She said it like it was no big deal. But it was a huge deal. My cousin was making a huge mistake, and she didn't even know it.

"You weren't even around last fall!" I yelled at her. "When Neel and I were fighting for our lives, fighting to save you and Lal. You don't know what went on—you were trapped in that magical sphere the whole time."

We'd landed in a field somewhere back within the borders of the Kingdom Beyond. Naya had let Ai-Ma down, who had in turn let me down gently on the grass. I tried not to freak out at the sight of all the rakkhoshis around me. At least half the Pink-Sari Skateboarders weren't human, and most of those who were rakkhoshis were either fire or air clan—and so were breathing out flames or had huge wings. Their fangs, horns, and claws were out now, and they looked like the monsters they were.

I felt a hand on my shoulder as Mati pulled me around to face her. "Don't you dare throw last fall in my face. It wasn't my fault I was a sphere! And besides, you think that being a hero back then is all that counts? Where have you been in the meantime?"

"I didn't know what was going on here! How could I? You guys didn't call or write or anything!" I could tell I'd made a good point, because Mati looked guilty at this. I pressed on, my bow and arrow still at the ready. "Look around you, Cousin. Is this who you want to be working with? What are you thinking?"

"What am I thinking? I'm thinking I didn't have a choice. Not when Lal and the Raja have declared this partnership with Sesha and the entire kingdom's got *Who Wants to Be a Demon Slayer?* fever. When rakkhosh families are fleeing Demon Land in fear. When our own leaders are risking so many lives—for what? The jewels of any society are its people, not some . . . some . . . stones!" Mati's face was flushed. She was usually so calm. This was the angriest I'd ever seen her.

Around her, the other skateboarders gathered, making a tight circle of bodies and faces swathed in blinding pink fabric.

"Whose side are you on?" I shot back. "They're killers, or have you forgotten?"

I felt, more than heard, the low grumble of anger around me. It was early evening, and the sun was setting, making multicolor streaks across the darkening sky.

"Your Royalness, there's really no need . . ." began Naya, but I whirled on her.

"No need?" My voice sounded screechy and thin to my own ears. "No need to protect myself? No need to defend myself against someone like you—pretending to be my friend when you were all the while waiting to snack on my bones?"

"No! Princess! How could you think that?" Naya looked like she was going to cry, and half stumbled over a clump of dry grass in her effort to move away from me.

"I don't like it either, Princess," snapped Tuntuni. "But

it's not always so easy to figure out who are the heroes and who are the monsters."

"Oh, what, now you're on their side too?" I snapped.

"There are no sides!" Mati protested, her voice rising in pitch.

Someone growled and snapped her teeth. It was Priya, breathing fire and looking like she couldn't wait to take a bite out of me.

"Please, sister!" begged Naya, standing between Priya and me. "No violence."

"She can be violent if she wants to, you! Who are you to tell her what she can't do?" shouted another rakkhoshi skateboarder.

At this, one of the human skateboarders jumped in. "Hey! Leave her alone, demoness!"

All around us, as Mati and I argued, things were getting more heated among the rakkhoshis and the human skateboarders. In the darkening twilight, it was sometimes hard to tell which was which.

"Kiran, stop being so emotional!" Mati yelled. "Use your head for once!"

She sounded so much like Ma, I saw red. "For once? What are you talking about? Oh, I suppose I should be like you, all calm and rational all the time? Like *this* was rational, leaving the palace to form your own half-demon girl group? What was this, like, a rebellion against your dad or something?"

"Don't talk about my father!" Mati snapped.

"He's my uncle! I'll talk about him if I want to!" I yelled back. "You know, why am I even here? This is bananas! I'm not going to hang out here with a bunch of rakkhoshis, wondering who's going to break down and try to eat me first! You want to take that risk, that's on you. I'm going to go get help from the only rational friend I have left! Lal!"

Priya the fire rakkhoshi was getting more and more antsy, even though Naya was trying to calm her down. "Don't act all innocent, Princess! Why should we trust you anyway?" Her arm muscles flexed and bulged, as if she was imagining hurting me. "Your hair and skin are getting greener every time I see you! Here we are risking our lives for you, and you're probably just a spy for your dear old daddy!"

And then Priya and a few other rakkhoshi girls took up the call, "Hao! Mao! Khao! Is that traitor flesh I smell? With curry leaves and turmeric, let's cook the rascal well!"

As fast as I could, I nocked an arrow in my bow, but before I could shoot it at the fire-breathing girl, Mati tried to jump in my way. Unfortunately, because of her one shorter foot, she stepped kind of awkwardly and almost fell in the process.

"Stop, Kiran! You don't want to do this!" Still stumbling, Mati tried to grab my weapon.

I reached out a hand to steady her. "Get out of my way, Cousin! I don't want to shoot you by accident!"

"Your Splendid Highness, I think—" began Naya, but I cut her off.

"I don't want to hear what you think! If you're so proud of who you are, why did you lie? Obviously because you had something to hide—like your true nature!"

"That's rich!" shouted Priya. "You lecturing us about hiding our true nature! Why don't you look at yourself in a mirror?"

I felt my insides turn to fire. Yeah, okay, I'd noticed the green color spreading in my hair and on my arm. But whatever was going on with me, I didn't need help from any rakkhoshis. I turned around to look at Neel's grandmother. "Can you get me back to the palace, Ai-Ma?"

"Neel is my precious jewel-boy grandbaby. I will do anything for him. And for you, num-num." Ai-Ma held out her arms to me. "Come, I will take you anywhere you want to go."

"Stay out of this, you half-dead old woman," snapped Priya, teeth bared and flames coming out of her nose.

Before I could punch the rakkhoshi in her fiery nostrils, though, Ai-Ma raised herself to her full height. Her eyes became like darkened caverns, her teeth flashed like razors, and her nails glinted and lengthened. She looked younger too, her hair thick and flowing, her skin unwrinkled. It was almost as if the years dropped away and she became the beautiful, powerful rakkhoshi she had once been, before her memory and everything else had started to go.

"Do not mistake me, little bean pole demoness, for anything less than what I am!" The air shook and the sky thundered. Priya gulped and backed up a little, as did most of the other Pink-Sari Skateboarders, rakkhoshi and human.

"Your Highness—" Naya tried again, but I interrupted with a wave of my hand.

"I can't. I just can't! You lied." I felt so weary as I looked at Mati and Tuntuni too. "You all lied. I can't trust any of you."

As I reached out to her, Ai-Ma returned to her regular (if still giant) size and shape. She picked me up in her warty arms.

"Cousin, let's talk about this. We need you," Mati said. "Neel needs you."

But I didn't owe her, or Naya, or any of them an answer. "To the palace, Ai-Ma," I said, and the old crone started galumphing off in the direction of the royal residence.

Only once did she turn around, to scowl terrifyingly at Naya, who apparently thought it would be a good idea to fly after us.

"Wait—" Naya tried, but old Ai-Ma wasn't having it.

"Scram! Shoo! Begone! Hato, little demon chitty-boo!" she yelled, flapping her floppy arms in Naya's direction.

Without another word, Naya turned around and flapped her wings back to where the rest of the PSS were waiting. I turned my face away from her and her betrayal.

As we went, I formulated a plan. I didn't need a skateboarding girl gang behind me to find Neel, especially since half of them were demons. I could do it on my own. I'd get help, that's all. That was it. I'd get help from the wisest person I knew in the Kingdom Beyond, with the exception of Albert Einstein. I didn't care if he was some eccentric hermit in the woods like Lal said. He was our best chance: the world-famous demonologist K. P. Das.

CHAPTER 22

A Demonologist of the Highest Caliber

Ai-Ma left me in the woods surrounding the royal palace well before dawn the next day. It was unsafe for her to stick around too long, what with the production company having hired soldiers to round up any and all stray rakkhosh. When I got to the palace, though, I was surprised to see tons of people out and about in the early morning. No one paid attention to me. They were all glued to the outdoor TV screens that had been set up all around the palace complex.

"What's going on?" I asked a courtly lady who seemed to have only gotten half of her fancy outfit on before getting mesmerized by whatever was on the screen.

"It's the crown prince!" she gushed. "His second test just began!"

I looked up at the closest screen to see Lal, whirling and clashing his sword as he fought off no less than twenty rakkhosh and khokkosh. I was impressed at how fierce my gentle friend looked with his weapon. I would have stayed and watched more, but then I saw that Suman Rahaman was already out with his camera crew, taking interviews of bystanders, discussing Lal's fighting technique and how long people guessed it might take him to defeat so many demons.

I knew I wouldn't get another chance to slip away. Once Sooms and his cameras caught me, I'd be stuck. And so I took off, as quickly and quietly as I could, toward the royal stable.

"Do you know the way to K. P. Das's hut?" I asked the horses, and even though Snowy looked confused, Raat nodded his great head.

The teacher. I know. I know.

I'd honestly been hoping to take Snowy, who I was more used to riding. But Raat seemed so grateful to fly with me, to have something to do except worry, that I couldn't disappoint him.

It wasn't a long flight to begin with, and the black pakkhiraj horse was bigger than Snowy, which also meant he had more power. He beat his strong wings, and I felt the wind rushing by me at a dizzying pace. I felt so free and happy that almost all of last night's doubts were gone. So what Mati and

Tuni had lost all sense of reality and were working with demons? So what Naya had turned out to have been fooling me this whole time? Lal and I could do this by ourselves. I would find out where Neel was being kept, and then tonight, after Lal had passed his second test (he had to! I couldn't think of the alternative), we'd go together to the right ocean. I'd make that one-breath dive and break open the bee box and get Neel the heck out of that detention center already.

Teacher will help find my boy? the black pakkhiraj asked into my head as we landed.

"I hope so, Raat." I petted the animal's sleek nose, scratching and stroking the velvety hair with my fingers. "I hope so."

I grabbed my backpack and weapons from the saddle bags, then looped the black stallion's reins around a tree trunk. The horse whooshed out a bunch of hot air into my hand.

"I know you miss him, boy." I put my forehead to the pakkhiraj's and felt my own emotions mixing with his. I tried to lend him strength and comfort but wondered whether he was the one who was actually comforting me. "I do too. That's why we're here."

I gave the loyal horse one last chunk of dried bee nectar (the best food for a pakkhiraj) and made my way toward the distant hut. The path up the slight hill was lush and overgrown. Mosquitos swarmed around my ears and the sun beat uncomfortably down on my neck as I trudged forward. Finally, I saw a little clearing with the clay hut a bit ahead of me. "Hello? Dr. Das? K. P. Babu? Anyone there?"

"Get out of here, you petni, you shakchunni, you daini!" Someone I couldn't see yelled out in a wheezy, shaky voice. "I'm giving you until three!"

"Wait, let me introduce myself . . ."

"Forty-one!"

"I'm a friend of the Princes Lal and Neel . . ."

"Three thousand two and a quarter!"

"Come for your help . . ."

"Three!"

Jeez, could no one count in the Kingdom Beyond? But I had no time to think about that anymore, because I suddenly found myself being pelted by something wet and slimy. A storm of wet slimy things actually. Fish! And more fish!

"Blargh! Blach! Stop! Stop!" I put up my hands to protect my face, but the onslaught of rapid-fire fish kept flying at me, flapping on my skin with their scaly cold.

"Eat that, you mechho bhoot! Don't come begging here for fish again!" I realized there was an old man under the thatched eaves of the hut, turning the handle on some kind of a seafood-shooting cannon.

"I'm not a bhoot! I swear! Look at my feet—they're right side around!" I held up my left leg with its silver combat boot.

"It's a trick!" said the old man, but the speed at which he was pelting me with dead fish seemed to slow down a little. He didn't approach me, though. Instead, he uncorked and held out an empty beaker—the kind we did experiments with in Dr. Dixon's science classes. "If you're not a ghost, then you should be able to easily get into this glass container."

Maybe Lal was right and K. P. Das had gone off the deep end a little. "I'm a human being, I can't get in that beaker."

"Are you sure?" The little man waved the science container at me. "A real human being would be able to get in!"

"Please, sir!" I put my hands together in a respectful namaskar. "I'm Kiranmala, a friend of the Princes Lal and Neel. I've come for your help."

"Kiranmala?" K. P. Das finally put down the beaker and peered at me. His eyes were huge behind Coke-bottle glasses and the hand that adjusted the yellowing white shawl on his kurta-clad shoulder was thin and trembling. "The one they call Princess Demon Slayer?"

"I don't know why they call me that, but yes, the same." I approached the old man, trying to walk with my feet as forward pointing as I could make them. I pulled out his book from my pack. "I'm a big fan, sir. I've read your textbook now cover to cover!"

That seemed to put K. P. Das at his ease. "Oh, an autograph seeker! How wonderful! Here, I will happily oblige!" The demonologist grabbed my wrist and, before I could pull away, scrawled his name on my hand. "So, how did you like my chapter on skondokata bhoot? Brilliant stuff, am I right?"

"Headless ghosts?" I recalled the gory illustrations in that chapter and tried not to grimace. "It was . . . ah . . . one of my favorites."

"Very good taste! It was mine too!" K. P. Das beamed. He pushed up his glasses with one hand and yanked up his dhoti with the other. "You won't find that level of research in any other volume on the creatures. And my index! I am kingdom-renowned for my ability to write indices and bibliographies! I've been recognized multiple times by the Royal Demonological Institute for my efforts, you know. I was even the runner-up for the purple medal of knowledge." The old man's face became shadowed with bitterness. "But I cannot believe that ridiculous poser Madan Mohan got the award. For his motivational motion device! A stupid trick to run from rakkhosh! Imagine! There was clearly some hanky-panky with the selection committee there."

"That's terrible!" I tried to pretend I had no idea who he was talking about. "Neel told me that you were the best in the business, sir."

"Kind of him to say so!" Now the old professor looked downright delighted. "Very kind indeed! Come into my office, my dear! I'm so sorry for mistaking you for a bhoot! How about a nice cup of tea and a digestive biscuit to settle your nerves?"

I shook off the remains of the fish scales that were still stuck to my face and hair and followed him into his hut. He'd set it up like an office, with a desk, a few cane chairs on one side and a rolling high-backed office chair on the other.

The professor puttered around, heating up some tea on what looked like a Bunsen burner—the kind Dr. Dixon sometimes used to show us cool blow-up chemistry experiments. After pouring out the tea into two dirty glasses, he dug out an incredibly dusty carton of biscuits from one of his desk drawers and offered me one. I took a gingerly bite. It was the stalest thing I'd ever tasted. I secretly spit out the mouthful into my hand the first chance I got.

K. P. Das settled behind his desk, leaning back on the towel he'd placed upon his office chair. He sipped at his tea, made a face, then asked me, "Now, you wanted to interview me and write my memoir, correct?"

I sighed, trying to hold the hot tea in the glass cup without burning myself. "No, sir. I wanted to ask about your student Neelkamal. He's being held prisoner in the dungeon detention center of the Snake King's new undersea hotel. Only, I don't know where the place is."

"Undersea hotel?" muttered K. P. Das, taking another slurp of his tea and making another face. He then dumped the contents into a desk drawer and tossed the glass in there too. "It's very hard to get into the TSK undersea hotel casino without an invitation. Well, if that instructional video is to be believed. Although they did do that very nice segment on *Lifestyles of the Rich and Monstrous*."

"You've seen that instructional video too?" I asked, surprised. Maybe Mati was wrong in how secret that interception was. "I've seen that video. And I'm prepared to do everything it asks. I already have a fang from the Serpent King himself."

"You do?" K. P. Das scooched toward me in his rolling chair. I put my tea down, then took the tooth out of my pack to show him. I was sure to hold it only through an old gym T-shirt. No need to poison myself, after all.

The professor's eyes got a bit glassy behind his giant glasses, and he rubbed his hands at the sight of the fang. "You wouldn't want to give that to me, would you? For research purposes? That could be my ticket to a Demonological Institute medal this year!"

"No, I need it to free Neel!" I tucked the tooth back into my bag before K. P. Das could grab at it. "I've been to Sesha's underwater fortress, but I need your help figuring out which ocean he's under." The professor kept his eyes on the tooth, so I added, "But maybe I can give it to you after I'm done with it?"

He perked up at that. "I bet that Madan Mohan won't have the chemical composition of the Serpent King's tooth to submit to the Royal Demonological Institute awards committee! And just to show you I'm sorry for thinking you were a ghost before, I'll throw in an ointment for your little snake skin problem!"

Snake skin problem? The professor's words opened the door I'd kept closed inside, the one in which I'd stuffed the worry about my green skin and hair. Was I turning into a snake? Was Sesha's wish coming true? I hadn't wanted to admit it to myself, but I had noticed that the skin near my snake scar had become an even deeper green and kind of scaly. I'd been trying to ignore it up until now, but the truth was, I was looking more and more like Sesha's logo every day. And it was completely freaking me out.

"Why am I turning green, Professor?" I asked urgently. "Is it something to do with my connection to the Serpent King?"

The little man didn't answer, but rustled through stacks of dusty papers on his desk until he found the yellowed sheet he was apparently searching for. He spent several minutes studying the paper. First reading it with his glasses on, and then with his glasses pushed up to his forehead. Finally, he put his glasses on upside down and read the paper that way. Even this didn't seem to satisfy him, because he then shoved the paper into his mouth, chewing thoughtfully.

"Professor Das," I said a bit louder, to make myself heard over the sound of the little man chewing on his own scientific notes. "Am I growing evil?"

"Evil?" Khogen Prasad Das peered at me so owlishly he reminded me of Bhootoom. He swallowed his notes with a dramatic gulp before coughing a bit and saying, "No one turns good or evil by magic. That's not how it works. You become evil when you choose to act against your conscience again and again. Being good or evil is about the decisions you make each and every day. It's not something that just happens to you."

His words relieved some of my anxiety at least. "Well, then, what's going on with my green skin and hair?"

The little man ripped off another page from a leather-bound notebook, sniffed it, then chewed on it like it was a piece of gum. "You obviously left something of yourself in the fortress last you were there. What I can't understand is if you made it there before, why you can't remember where it is to get there again?"

"I've never been to Sesha's hotel fortress . . ." I began, and then I stopped myself. "Well, except in Essence-Tyme, I guess."

The little professor blinked at me, his eyes all buggy through his glasses. "And you left something there of yourself?"

K. P. Das took out a huge mortar and handed me the heavy pestle. He gestured at me to start pounding as he threw into the stone bowl a weird assortment of ingredients: ginger, garlic, cumin, chilies, and then an entire melty bar of Cadbury's milk chocolate, which he licked off his fingers.

"My hair. I had to chop off a bit of my hair to get free from there," I said as he gestured for me to start pounding.

"Yes, well, that's obviously it, isn't it?" he gave me a skeptical look. "Didn't anyone ever tell you not to leave a part of yourself behind when in an undersea serpent hotel?"

"Um, no?" I said as the professor kept tossing various spices and other ingredients into the mortar.

"Honestly! What do they teach young people in schools these days anyway?"

"A lot of test-taking skills?" I sneezed as the professor poured some black seeds into the bowl for me to pound.

"Well, you've got to be a bit more careful, child," scolded the professor. "You are the jewel who can cement his power; you are the tail to his head. The all is one, you know!"

Why did I keep hearing that phrase? "What does that mean, 'the all is one'?"

"Oh, just the metaphysical unity of the multiverse, the meaninglessness of space and time, of any traditional sense of linear existence, you know! All that good stuff!"

The problem was, I didn't know. I'd barely understood anything he'd just said. "Um . . ." I said, but the professor smiled vaguely, made a clucking noise, and patted my head in a "there, there" sort of gesture. Then he took a big scoop of the noxious, chocolaty paste from the mortar, tasted it, and nodded.

I pointed at the smelly mixture the professor had just eaten a bit of. "Should I eat some of it too? Is this what will get rid of my snake skin problem?"

"Mmm?" K. P. Das looked startled. "Oh, no, this mixture has nothing to do with that!"

"Then it's to help us find which ocean Neel is being held under?"

"No, no! Nothing to do with that either!"

What? I felt like bashing the little man in the head with the heavy pestle. "Then what is this you've been making?"

"Oh, I've been improving the formula for KiddiePow, trying to reduce the side effect of chest hair growth." K. P. Babu peered under his kurta and groaned. "Darn. Furry as ever. You won't believe how many mothers are touchy about a little extra chest hair on their babies and toddlers."

I slammed the pestle down into the mortar and stood up. "Professor, are you going to help me or not?"

"Well, don't get so testy, my dear! Of course I'll help you with your seven oceans problem! The snake skin problem, well, that's something else entirely now that I know about you leaving your hair!"

The little man tut-tutted around, pulling notes and papers out of his file cabinets and desk drawers, even from as unlikely places as under his seat cushion and from inside his biscuit tin. Some of these he nibbled on, some he chewed and swallowed, and some he simply smelled and licked.

"All right!" he finally shouted. "I've got it! Come with me! We've got to gather up those fish I threw at you before!" He ran back out of the hut, picked up two baskets made of twigs, and gestured that I should help him gather up all the slimy fish he'd shot at me earlier out of that tennis-ball-thrower thing.

After we'd picked them all up (yuck), the professor grabbed my wrist and pulled me toward a small pond. I waited, totally confused, as K. P. Das attached a rope between his two bare feet and then—zipitty-zip!—climbed up a tamarind tree at the pond's edge. When he was a little way above my head, the old man asked me to hand him seven of the fish we'd collected, one at a time (double yuck). "That one! No, that one!" He pointed. "The slimy one! The other slimy one!" Carefully, consulting some notes he'd made on the back of his arm, the professor hung the seven fish from one of the tree's longest branches.

To come back down, the professor climbed awkwardly from my head onto my shoulders, and then started climbing down me, placing a foot in my hand, another uncomfortably at my waist. I helped K. P. Das as gently as I could down to the ground.

The little professor straightened his dhoti and proudly indicated the tree. "These seven fish I've hung are from each of the seven oceans in our dimension, and their blood runs with the color of that ocean," he explained. "If you are a true friend to Neelkamal, when you look down into the pond, you will see only one fish—the fish from the ocean where he's being held."

I looked down at the pond, where I could see all seven of the fish reflected. How was this supposed to work?

"You must concentrate. Draw on your inner resources," K. P. Das told me. *What if I didn't have any inner resources?* I wanted to ask, but didn't. Then he pointed to my bow and arrow. "When you see only one, you must shoot that fish—right in the eye. But you can only do so by looking down, at its reflection."

This exercise, shooting a fish hanging from above you while only looking down at its reflection, sounded familiar. I think it was a part of one of the epic stories that Baba liked to tell me sometimes. *Inner resources,* the little man had said. Okay, I guess it was time for me to try and find some.

I tried to put everything else I'd just been thinking about out of my mind and focus on finding out where Neel was being kept. At first it was really hard, as my mind kept jumping around, as antsy as the monkey Buddhu. I kept worrying about my green skin, my parents, the game, Mati, Naya, Sesha, everything.

"Remember, everything is riding on you, Princess," K. P. Das said in solemn tones.

"No pressure or anything," I mumbled under my breath.

I gave myself a little mental shake. The professor was right. I had to get it together. This was no game, and no joke. Neel's freedom, if not his life, depended on it. I nocked an arrow in my bow, then did Buddhu's breathing technique: in for four, hold for four, out for four, to try and still my mind. I pictured Neel's face, pictured him riding on Midnight next to me, fighting beside me, mad at me, laughing with me. I pictured him captured in that awful fortress, egging on that disloyal demon Bogli, forbidding me from rescuing him. I pictured Raat's love and his brother's loyalty. I thought of my arrow like an extension of my own will, reaching up to find its mark, straight and true. I imagined I could feel the little puncture of the arrow as it went into the correct fish's eye, showing me the way to save my friend.

Then, finally, when I felt still and steady, humming with concentration and power, I opened my eyes. Holding my bow pointing skyward, I peered down in the pond water, hoping I'd see one, and not seven, fish. And I did this time. I saw only a fish of glittering gold swaying above me from the tree branch. With another deep breath, I thought of Ma and Baba, imagining I could feel their hands on my shoulders, guiding me forward. And then the words came into my mind. *The all is one*, I thought. The all is one. I let my arrow fly.

My arrow hit the golden fish's eye and I didn't need to see the shower of honey-gold blood pouring down into the pond to know the answer. Neel's mother had even told me with that rhyme she had recited back in my bedroom. But I'd been too stubborn to listen. Some hero I was.

Elladin, belladin, Honey-Gold Sea, she had said. And I knew that Neel was being held in a fortress under the Honey-Gold Ocean of Souls. Now I just needed to get myself there.

CHAPTER 23

A Prisoner Parade

You'll be off to the Honey-Gold Ocean of Souls right away, I presume?" asked K. P. Das. "Don't worry, you'll find your skin problem answer when you get there."

"I have to wait anyway until moonrise tonight," I explained as I mounted Raat. I was relieved to hear the professor didn't think the green hair and skin situation was permanent. I'd hate to think how that'd go down in middle school. "Plus I want to go back to the palace and get Prince Lalkamal. He'll be waiting for me."

"Lalkamal? Why didn't he come see me? He was always such a good boy. Got such high marks in my class, unlike that distractible brother of his."

I turned the pakkhiraj around to face the teacher. Raat tossed his head impatiently. "Lal did well in your class?"

"Oh yes!" K. P. Das polished his thick lenses on his dhoti. "One of the best I've ever taught! His final demonology exam was wonderful—I always thought he should publish it, give up this royal-shoyal stuff and become a scholar! Very honorable profession, you know!"

"Yes, yes, I'm sure it is," I said in a faint voice. I hadn't remembered wrong, then, after all. It was such a small thing, but why would Lal lie about failing demonology class? About not turning in his final?

As Raat and I flew back to the palace, I was still wondering what reasons Lal could have for not telling the truth about something so silly like doing well in demonology. Was he afraid his father would find out how smart he was, and think it was somehow a bad thing? Was he ashamed about being book smart? Why? That was ridiculous, I thought, even as I remembered my own embarrassment in science class. But Dr. Dixon's class felt like a zillion years ago. By the time I was bringing Raat down in a field outside the royal palace, I was still not sure what all this was about.

We'd just landed, and I was just trotting Raat through the early evening dusk in the direction of the stables, when I heard, then saw, a loud band party coming in my direction. They were dressed in bright red costumes with gold braids and played white instruments. It was an obnoxiously loud racket: five drums, five brass horns, and a conductor in a fancy red turban with a plume of starched turban folds sticking straight up. For who knows what reason, Neel's pakkhiraj horse turned toward the music, like he wanted to join the parade. It was all I could do just to hang on as the stallion trotted along beside the band.

"What are you doing, boy?" I tried uselessly to tug him the other way.

Someone there. Like my boy, but not my boy, said the horse mysteriously. Needless to say, Raat was not quite as verbally gifted as Snowy, and I had a lot more trouble understanding what he meant.

"What's going on?" I shouted at the band's conductor, who pumped his baton up and down in time to the song. "Are you a wedding party or something?"

"No! A victory party!" yelled the conductor over the racket. There were torchbearers walking all around the band so that they were lit up by flames of flickering light. "Not only did Prince Lal pass his second test with flying colors, but we have just caught two demons trying to sneak into the palace grounds!"

That's when I saw what was behind the band: a squadron of soldiers dragging a wheeled cage. The cage was coming up a rise in the road, and it was surrounded by so many villagers that even from Raat's back, it was impossible for me to see what kind of monsters must be inside—probably some little doito or danav from the nearby woods.

Soon, the crowd grew as I was joined by palace servants and the lords and ladies who were called out by the band's noise. I was regretting not stabling Neel's pakkhiraj. The poor horse, initially curious, was now starting to get skittish in the crowd. He seemed terrified of all the fiery torches. His eyes grew big, and he started breathing heavy out of his nose. Finally, I dismounted. His sides shuddered as I tried to lead him through the crowd by the reins.

"It's okay. It's okay. Calm down, boy," I whispered. But when I reached out to him with my mind, I couldn't even understand any language. Just panic.

What made it worse was the crowd all around us. It was totally impossible for me to see now that I was on the ground, and I was feeling way claustrophobic. The people around me jeered at the demons, while some even threw rotten food and garbage at the cage. Most of the nasty stuff bounced off, but some clearly hit the prisoners inside as I heard wet thumps and squishes. Raat neighed and tried to break free of my hold. I dug out some more hardened bee nectar from my pocket, cooing at the frightened animal, looking for a way to get him out of the crowd.

So much hate. Scared. Want my boy. I want my boy.

I couldn't blame the pakkhiraj. The force of hatred was thick in the air.

"Our heroes are gonna destroy you cannibals!" someone shouted, waving a fire-lit torch.

"Eat garbage, monster!" yelled a delicate-looking court lady, her features ugly with anger. "Time to get slayed!"

I was getting a little freaked out, and starting to worry about getting trampled, when I felt someone grab my arm and pull both me and Raat safely away from the crowd.

"Princess Kiranmala is here!" boomed the captain of the guard, lifting my hand in the air as if I'd just won a boxing match.

Then someone standing right next to him lifted up my other hand. "Let's hear it for the Princess Demon Slayer!"

It was Lal, grinning at me and looking as handsome as ever in full princely armor, a shining sword at his side. Just seeing his honest and earnest face made me feel twenty times better. Things couldn't be so bad if Lal was here.

The mood of the crowd shifted. Someone took up Lal's lead and began happily chanting my new name: "Princess Demon Slayer, Princess Demon Slayer!"

Before I could say anything, the soldiers lifted me back up onto Raat's back. Lal himself took his reins, and

I was paraded around like some kind of victor returning from war.

No. False. No. False. No.

I couldn't make heads or tails of the pakkhiraj's panicky thoughts, but I did understand his fear. I tried as best as I could to emanate calm, slowing my own racing heartbeat, relaxing my own muscles, hoping the animal would sense my emotions. Lal was here, I kept repeating in my mind. Lal was here, and that meant everything was going to be okay.

From my perch on Raat's back, I saw that the gathering wasn't as scary as I'd initially thought. There were actually plenty of families with kids, and at the edge of the crowd were food vendors and toy sellers with everything from popcorn to balloons to pinwheels. There were novelty booths with baseball-style hats that said *Who Wants to Be a Demon Slayer?* and T-shirts with Lal's and my faces on them. A group of adorable little kids threw flowers at us, and all around us were grinning faces who seemed to take great delight in seeing Lal and me together. These were people who obviously believed we were the heroes they needed. I felt myself relax even more.

Lal waved like I should bend toward him. The crowd went wild, as if he was calling me down for a kiss. But it was just his mouth near my ear. "Not bad for a sixth grader from Parsippany, eh, Princess?"

Trying not to be embarrassed by the fact that the crowd had the totally wrong idea about Lal and me, I let myself enjoy their cheering anyway. I smiled back at the prince's friendly face. "It's not bad at all."

I wanted to tell him about my visit to K. P. Das, about discovering where his brother was being kept, even about my green skin worries, but all that would have to wait until we were somewhere less noisy. For now, I would just sit back on Raat and let myself enjoy the people's attention. I felt like a filled-up balloon, all floaty on their admiration. I tried to ignore the skittish horse under me—he obviously had some kind of panic disorder, I'd have to talk to Neel about it when he came back—and started waving back to the crowd, just like Lal was doing. They cheered and called out our names even louder.

It felt great. I mean, so what if the stories that were being told about us weren't entirely true? I had actually just done something really amazing—I'd hit that fish in the eye without even looking up at it and found out where Neel was imprisoned. So what if the recognition I was getting wasn't exactly for the right thing? It still felt pretty darn good. I caught a glimpse of myself on the giant palace posters, my bow and arrow in my hand, leaping over a building as I fought a snarly-toothed rakkhosh. Did it matter that the details were wrong if the sentiment was right? I *was* a hero. I was a star. And wasn't that the story that really counted?

Then, as the soldiers paraded me past the cage itself, my soaring emotions were basically flushed down the porta potti. A wave of nausea came over me, like a hand had reached inside my gut and squeezed my intestines tight. I saw for myself the prisoners the soldiers had caught. And I understood why Raat was so upset.

Inside the glowing magic bars of the cage was Ai-Ma, her shoulders hunched and face grim. There were some disposable teacups hanging from her few strands of hair and little burn marks like someone had thrown hot tea at her. Off her skin hung strange patches of vegetable peels and plastic bags too, like people had been using her as a target for throwing garbage. And then I saw who was with Neel's rakkhoshi grandmother. The old crone's gangly arms were wrapped around someone with garbage hanging off her wings and horns, but also her goofy little collection of ponytails. Naya.

They stood, the old woman and the girl, each not making a sound, quietly holding hands. The people around the cage screamed at them, words so horrible and angry they made my ears ache. My heart sank to my toes. They'd caught them because of me! Because Ai-Ma had brought me here and Naya had obviously followed us, even after we'd told her not to.

I let out a gasp, and Lal looked up. "Good hunting!" he said, grinning in a way that made me dizzy with confusion.

"The only good rakkhoosh is a dead rakkhoosh!" shouted someone in a shrill voice, and I recognized Ms. Twinkle Chakraborty, leaning down over the edge of the palace balcony. At a gesture from her, an assistant emptied an entire garbage can on top of the passing cage. The contents of the can landed on Ai-Ma's and Naya's heads with a wet thump. Naya stumbled a little at the force of the hit, but Ai-Ma helped her straighten up. "Oh, my num-num," I heard the old woman say in a sad voice. "Don't let them see you're afraid."

That seemed to excite the crowd more, and the scene around me drifted again toward the scary. I felt like I was in one of those old movies where the mobs chase a monster with pitchforks and torches. All around me were open, red mouths, jeering and shouting insults. Raat shuddered and tossed his head, a thin froth of saliva forming at his mouth.

False boy. No. False boy.

That's when I saw them, the cameras all turned on me, the lights blinding my eyes. There was Suman Rahaman, just to my right, eagerly waiting with his microphone. And then it appeared in midair before me, the harmonium. The keyboards played and the accordion pumped and the mellow baritone warbled out my name. This was my second test, it sang. Fighting, and killing, Ai-Ma and Naya. A great cheer went up from all the assembled spectators.

Fighting and killing Ai-Ma and Naya? No. No. No. No.

A sweet-faced village girl of six or seven was sitting on her father's shoulders not a few steps away from me. On her pigtailed head was a *Die, Rakkhosh, Die* baseball hat. Her father was wearing a T-shirt with an image of a rakkhosh and a bright red X through it.

"Are you excited to slay the rakkhosh on TV?" she asked in her pure little voice.

The crowd caught her last words, and started chanting, "Slay the demons! Kill the rakkhosh! Kill the beasts!"

"Of course she's excited! This is the Princess Demon Slayer's second test!" boomed the captain of the guard. "The entire multiverse is watching! She's not going to let us down!"

Naya said something from her cage, but I couldn't hear her words. I saw Ai-Ma squeeze the girl's shoulders tight.

"Shut up, you!" One of the soldiers banged his sword against the cage, making both Ai-Ma and Naya jump. And then the soldiers started clearing the crowd. "The Princess Demon Slayer's second test is about to begin! Give her room! Make space!"

The crowd did as they were told, shouting my name.

I felt disgusted. Disgusted at them, disgusted at myself. There was only one choice here. I looked straight into the face of the little girl, the one who had asked if I was excited to slay Ai-Ma and Naya. "No, I'm not excited to slay them," I said as loudly as I could. "I'm not going to slay them."

Lal shot me a surprised look.

"But why don't you want to kill the rakkhoshis?" the little girl persisted.

Why didn't I want to kill Ai-Ma and Naya? The answer was clear. I thought about Ai-Ma carrying Neel and me to safety, protecting us from other rakkhosh who wanted us for a meal. I remembered her saving my mother despite being tempted by her human smell. I thought about Naya saving my butt not once, but multiple different times. I remembered what it was like when she and I were traveling through the wormhole, our atoms and cells mingling together, crunching down, and re-expanding. I wondered if some of her atoms got mixed up with mine, or maybe if they had never been that different to begin with. I remembered K. P. Das's words. Being a monster or a hero wasn't about who you were, or what you looked like, or where you were from. Being a monster or a hero was about what you chose to do with every minute of your life.

I looked at that little girl's sweet face and made my

decision. I didn't understand everything about why Mati was working with the rakkhosh, but I trusted my cousin. I didn't understand how Ai-Ma could be both the kind soul she was and a monster, but I trusted her grandmotherly love. And I didn't understand why Naya had lied to me about being a rakkhoshi, but she'd proved herself loyal, and I was at least starting to trust her friendship. Most importantly, I trusted my own instincts. And right now, my instincts were telling me that this horrible scene was so, so wrong.

In the end, I didn't answer the little girl's question in words, but in action. The captain of the guard was right next to me. In a swift gesture, I aimed an arrow right at his waist. "Princess Demon Slayer?" the man asked in alarm. But he was too late. "Ai-Ma, catch!"

My arrow traveled, straight and true, hooking his key ring and then heading on toward the rakkhosh cage. It flew between the bars, where Ai-Ma caught it between her teeth.

"Fly, Naya!" I yelled. "Fly to the Honey-Gold Ocean! That's where Neel is!"

Naya opened the cage with the keys, but she hesitated. The crowd was already turning on me. "I'm not going to leave you!" she yelled.

But Raat had understood my words. *Fly*, he repeated, *fly to my boy. Fly.* He was already unfurling his powerful black wings, taking a few steps backward from Lal so that he could explode into flight.

"Hey, stop!" Lal yelled, but I couldn't tell if he was talking to Naya and Ai-Ma or me. "Stop them!" he said again, pointing at the now-flying rakkhoshi and the old crone on her back. That little loss of concentration was all I needed. I jerked Raat's reins out of Lal's hands, danced the pakkhiraj this way and that to avoid a bunch of soldiers, and finally let the horse soar into the evening sky above the palace complex.

"Wait, no! Come back! Kiran!" Lal yelled as his brother's pakkhiraj horse took off into the sky, narrowly missing his head. The crowd screamed and some of them applauded, probably thinking this was all a part of the spectacle of *Who Wants to Be a Demon Slayer?*

I felt a surge of power like I'd never felt before. Neel was right. I didn't need to play by anyone else's rules. No one else but me could shape my legend.

As I flew higher into the sky, the crowd started to get a sense that all wasn't right. Maybe it was the angry exclamations of the soldiers, or Suman Rahaman shouting into the cameras, "She's gone AWOL! The Princess Demon Slayer is no hero—she's siding with the rakkhosh!"

Some people now were starting to boo and shout at me, but I didn't care.

And then we were flying hard, Naya with Ai-Ma piggy-back and me on Raat's strong back. The midnight horse's mane flew in the wind. For the first time since all of this mess began, I knew for sure I was doing the right thing, on the right side.

"Oh, my delicious snotty candy cane!" Ai-Ma crooned. "You saved us!" I noticed that she was holding Naya's phone and was clicking shots of us escaping. Except that her finger seemed to be over part of the camera lens, but I wasn't going to tell her that now. The old crone looked way too happy as she snapped away. "Look, boo-boo! I'm taking pictures for the demon-net!"

"Thank you, Your Princessness! Oh, thank you!" Naya burbled. "Promise me you'll let me post about this as an Instagreat story! It'll go viral for sure!"

The soldiers sent a storm of arrows after us, but Naya and Raat did some impressive evasive maneuvers. They'd be behind us at some point, but for now, we had the advantage and that felt pretty good.

"Are you both all right?" I asked. "I'm so sorry that happened to you!"

"Monsters!" sniffed Ai-Ma, and I was afraid I had to agree.

"Let us go and save my grandson!" cried Ai-Ma, and Raat bucked and neighed happily.

We're coming, boy. We're coming. We're coming!

CHAPTER 24

The Honey-Gold Ocean of Souls

I flew with Naya and Ai-Ma to the Honey-Gold Ocean of Souls. On the way, I tried to talk to the two rakkhoshis about Lal. "I don't understand it. He was so okay with me killing you both on live TV."

Even midair as we were, Ai-Ma piggybacking on Naya, they exchanged a funny look. "He is the crown prince, my bean-pole dung beetle," said Ai-Ma. "He and the Raja did agree to partner with Sesha on the show."

"I think that was that new minister of the Raja's! That Minister Gupshup—he's up to something!" I insisted. "I just can't believe Lal would be so mean! His own brother's half-rakkhosh!"

Again, Ai-Ma and Naya exchanged that look. "Your Splendiferousness, I know you're surprised, but we're not.

This has always been the way humans treat rakkhosh—no matter if we're violent or not. And the false news you speak of, that's always been around—think of all the tales telling of rakkhosh being evil!"

"But . . ." I stopped, embarrassed. Naya was right. I had heard stories my whole life about how rakkhosh were villains. Was that not entirely true? Oh, this was all so confusing. I buried my face in Raat's mane for a minute to gather my thoughts.

Luckily, our conversation was cut short by the fact that we were there, at least according to Mati's moving map. We landed on a cliff above the Honey-Gold Ocean, the moonlight bathing us in light, and dancing across the black waves like diamonds. I felt my mother's strength and power washing over me. I didn't know if Neel could hear me, but I turned my face up to the disc of my moon mother's silvery face, and whispered, "I'm coming, Neel. Hang in there."

Ai-Ma spun some sort of land rakkhosh dryness spell over me so that my clothes, pack, and weapons would stay dry as I dived into the water and down to the TSK hotel and casino. It would also give anyone looking at me the illusion I was full serpent. "Not too hard, since you're half-green already," said Ai-Ma, and I gulped. My arm was greener than it had been even this morning, the color almost down to my wrist. "It should last long enough for you to get past the lobby and into the dungeons."

Unfortunately, her spell didn't include any scuba gear or extra oxygen tanks.

"That kind of magic is out of my pay grade, dear betel bum," said the old crone, picking at something that looked like a bug that was stuck between her few remaining teeth.

I looked away, trying not to grimace, and at Naya. "Sorry, I just fly," she said.

Raat, for his part, snuffled at my shoulder, as if he wanted to go with me. Then he thoughtfully chewed on my hair, which I took for a sign of affection.

"Why do I have to dive down from way up here again?" I peeked down the edge of the cliff at the golden waters below.

"It'll give you the momentum you need to get to the bottom, Your Majosity," explained Naya for the umpteenth time. But to her credit, she didn't sound impatient. Despite her fangs and horns and talons, not to mention her wings, being out, she still seemed like the same old upbeat sixth grader I'd met in New Jersey. Which was weird. How could one person be so many contradictory things at once? Course, I was one to talk.

I looked at my two companions' faces—one old and familiar, one young and relatively new, both kind souls, both demonesses. I should, by rights, be their enemy. But I knew for a fact that I would have been no hero if I'd let the game go on. As Neel had said, I didn't have to play by their rules. I didn't have to be bound by anyone else's game. I sighed, rubbing my neck, trying to build up my courage to dive.

"Um, Your Highnosity?" Naya's voice was weirdly tense.

"What?" I looked up, and caught her looking out toward the lightening horizon. Raat neighed in recognition. Even though it was small still, I realized they were looking at the form of a snow-white pakkhiraj horse with a red-clothed rider on its back.

"Lal and Snowy," I breathed. I didn't realize he'd be behind us so soon.

"Not just that, look behind him!" said Naya, pointing. And sure enough, behind the white pakkhiraj was a whole army of flying horses, carrying what looked like a battalion of pantalooned and mustachioed guardsmen. And with them, a flying camera crew and Suman Rahaman!

"Well, that's not good." I wished I'd paid more attention to those word problems in math class, so I could try to calculate how long it would take them to get to us.

"Caramel toadstool, dear, I'm sorry, but that may not be our only problem," said Ai-Ma. I realized the old crone was looking in a different direction. And from that direction, there was the far-closer shape of a giant flying chariot pulled by six enormous, bridled snakes. The chariot itself glowed a magical green, and I didn't need binoculars to know who was inside.

"Sesha and Naga," I breathed, catching sight of my birth father and brother in the flying chariot. And then I was distracted for a minute from the doom that was gaining on us from multiple directions by Naya's flying thumbs.

"We're about to be attacked from multiple directions and you're *texting*?" I shouted. "Stop that already!"

"I'm texting Mati, Tuni, and the PSS!" Naya said, her thumbs never stopping motion. "We're going to need some backup!"

"It's time for you to go, dung cakes," said Ai-Ma firmly. "Me and the moody horsie and Miss Moyna Sunshine here will handle whatever comes our way."

"No, I'm not going to leave you . . ." I said, but it was too late, because with a fierce shove of her giant hand, Ai-Ma pushed me over the edge of the cliff and into the water.

"Good luck, toadstool beetle dung! Go rescue our boy!"

Raat reared and neighed, as if wishing me good luck.

I fell like an ungraceful stone, cannonballing into the waves. The impact was terrible, like I'd run into a wall of bricks. But then I was under the water, fighting my instincts to swim upward. I let the serpent side of me take over and imagined myself able to breathe comfortably underwater, pictured myself slithering, instead of desperately swimming, down to the bottom.

Somehow, the ocean was so bright with golden light that I could see even deep under the waves. Conscious of the soldiers, the snakes, and the camera crew potentially all chasing me down here, I swam as fast as I could. How long could Naya and Ai-Ma hold everyone off? How long would it take for Mati, Tuni, and the PSS to get Naya's text and come?

But I couldn't help them now. I had to get to Neel. In fact, if I could get him out quickly enough, we could both be more use to Ai-Ma and Naya than just me alone. I kept swimming down, my chest practically exploding from the pressure, my eyes and throat burning, my brain telling me I needed a breath. But just when I didn't think I could make it, just when I thought I'd let go and drown, there, among the stingray and schools of silver fish, was the huge, gaudy TSK hotel fortress that I'd seen on *Lifestyles of the Rich and Monstrous*. The outside was super tacky, the entire building made to look like it was made of snakes. Through the undulating motion of the water all around me, the building seemed almost like it was breathing. But that was just my vision playing tricks on me and my oxygen-deprived brain.

There was a curving driveway with tacky golden stat-ues, and underwater limos driving up to it. I swam furiously toward the revolving doors, pushing my way past a number of flashily-dressed fish monsters with cigars and jewel-encrusted wristwatches.

"Hey, watch it!" they protested.

I burst into the bright lobby of the hotel. I was dry because of Ai-Ma's spell, but dragging in breaths like a drowning person. I noticed that the doors, walls, pillars, everything, were stamped with that TSK symbol—the Ouroboros—the rounded snake eating its own tail. There were serpents and demons and ghosts and talking fish all over the place, streaming in and out of the casino, throw-ing their luggage carelessly toward the overworked bellboys, talking in loud voices. Luckily, no one gave me a second glance, and from a quick look in one of the lobby's gilded mirrors, I could see why. I looked like myself, but myself as a serpent. I gave a shiver. Is this what I really was inside? Would I ever turn back? I didn't have any answers, but I realized, I also didn't have any time to think about it. Because I knew I had to find Neel before Sesha, Naga, and the Raja's guards got here.

I tried to move faster, but it was hard. I shook my head, trying to get over my dizziness, and the weird feeling that everything in the hotel—the walls, the gold-encrusted chairs and sofas, the ornate pillars—were kind of waving around. I shook my head, hard, and took in some more deep breaths. My brain needed more oxygen, that was all. But when I put my hand on one of the giant pillars in the lobby, I pulled it back right away, grossed out by the fact that the golden marble had felt warm and fleshy under my hand.

I tried not to scream as a skondokata—one of K. P. Das's headless ghosts—approached me from the right. The creature was in a front-desk uniform, complete with a lapel pin like an Ouroboros, and seemed to be asking me if I needed help. Only, I couldn't understand anything the ghost was saying as his head wasn't in the right spot, but in his arms. I backed away as quickly as I could and tried to think. How was I supposed to find the dungeon inside the hotel fortress?

That's when the strangest thing happened. I had the bizarre feeling the parquet floor under my feet kind of *tilted*, so that I shuffled and slid toward where I needed to go—a huge bank of gold plated elevators. But that wasn't possible. A floor couldn't move like that. Nor could a pillar. I must be feeling seriously seasick or something. I had a bad history with barfing on roller coasters, so maybe this weird, topsy-turvy feeling was something to do with that.

"D'ya hear? The boss is coming!" I heard a serpent in a housekeeping uniform tell the skondokata as I passed by.

Oh no. That must mean that Sesha and Naga had made it past the pakkhiraj and two demonesses. Plus, I realized as I looked into a big gilded mirror, the snake disguise of Ai-Ma's spell was wearing off. I was still looking green-tinged, but not really scaly or that snaky anymore. I had to hurry.

I shuffled quickly along on the maybe-moving floor toward the elevators, trying not to be too noticeable. Each door had that symbol, the snake eating itself, and that darned saying *The all is one*. I pushed the down button. As soon as I did, I shuddered and pulled back my hand, trying to shake off the feeling that the button had kind of *throbbed* under my finger. I was so creeped out, I practically dived toward the first elevator that opened and jammed my finger into the *D* for *dungeon* button. This button didn't seem to have a heartbeat, thank goodness. I was so relieved by this that it wasn't until I'd stepped all the way in and the doors were closing that I had the strange sensation that I wasn't in an elevator at all, but had entered the mouth of some kind of living creature, complete with rubbery lips and teeth! The elevator doors stayed open for a nerve-shattering moment, and then slammed shut, plunging me into total, moist, mouthy darkness before the entire car plummeted swiftly downward.

"Waaaaaa!" I screamed, not able to control myself, slamming into the soft floor as the elevator crashed downward, landing with a teeth-jarring thunk. When the doors opened again on the dungeon floor, I jumped out as quickly as I could. I could swear the elevator gave a little burp as it closed up again and sped away.

I shivered, rubbing my hands, trying to get rid of the oogly feeling of having been in the hotel's mouth. I looked around cautiously at my surroundings, an arrow nocked in my bow. I was in a place opposite to the fancy, crowded lobby. It was a plain, totally empty, steel-lined hallway. Luckily, I didn't see Bogli or any other guards around. I knew I didn't have much time, so I ran farther and farther into the belly of the dungeons. I came to a few turns along the way, and let my instinct guide me—right, left, and right again. I prayed I was going in the right direction.

At the far end of the final hallway I turned down were two heavy steel doors. And in front of the doors? Oh, just great.

Witches.

CHAPTER 25

The Second Test

They were two horrible-looking daini: long toothed and knobbly kneed, spindly necked and fiery eyed. The women's bony forms were draped in dirty white saris. And behind them—up and down the length and breadth of the stainless-steel wall—were cameras. Cameras without operators, but trained right on me. I blinked in surprise as a dozen bright lights came on at the same time, dazzling my eyes. And then I heard it, the sound of the magic harmonium again, singing again that this was my second test.

"This is my second test? But . . . but . . . it can't be . . . I failed my second test. I was supposed to fight two rakkhoshis and I refused . . ." I sputtered. I couldn't think of any reason to lie anymore. I hadn't played by the game's rules. Which meant it was supposed to be over. How had the producers even known I was coming here?

The two daini grinned creepily at me. I expected them to speak in soul-rattling tones, but when they flapped open their rubbery lips, one started humming some cheesy game show music and the other started speaking in a silly, overly loud announcer-type voice.

"Welcome! Welcome! Welcome! To the multiverse's most popular game show, *Who Wants to Be a Demon Slayer?*" It was almost like they hadn't even heard me.

"Oh, look, studio audience, here comes our contestant," said the second witch.

I looked around in alarm, but except for the cameras, there was no studio audience—that I could see, anyway. I bit my lip. I had no choice but to play along and hopefully pass the test fast. I had to get to Neel before Sesha, his minions, and the Raja's soldiers got here.

"Let's learn a little bit more about our contestant, shall we? What's your name, dearie?"

"Uh, Kiranmala," I said into the microphone the crone pulled out from somewhere in the folds of her sari.

"That's an interesting name, Uhkiranmala. Tell us what you like to do for a hobby! Chew on the entrails of souls?

Entrap innocents inside tree trunks? Crochet macramé leg warmers?"

"I like to, uh—" I began.

"No one wants to listen to your boring hobbies, human!" the second daini cut me off. "Let's hear a word now from our sponsors!"

"1-800-Samosa Drones!" she sang out, like it was a little company jingle. "Just call us on the phone, and we'll drop one into your mouth by drone!"

"Hot, delicious!" said the first witch, her tongue kind of lolling and dribbling drool. "And so convenient!"

The first witch picked up the questioning. "So, Uhkiranmala, how does it feel to be on a game show created by your own biological father, the Serpent King? Terrifying? Unnerving? Like someone is eating at the last, dirty bits of hope you had caked to the bottom of your emotional frying pan?"

"If you knew who I was all along, why did you ask?" I said in frustration, peering over my shoulder down the still-empty hallway. "Look, I don't mean to be rude, but I'd like to get to the bee box as soon as possible!"

"Well, dear contestant, the prize you seek is behind one of these two locked doors!" As the second daini said this,

the first daini hummed some other game show music under
her breath—lots of trombone noises and gong sounds. "The
rules of this second test are simple—let's review them for
first-time viewers of our show, shall we?"

The sisters took turns explaining the rules. "After the
buzzer goes off, one of us sisters can only answer your
question with the truth, and the other can only answer
with a lie."

"It's a part of our supernatural contract with the station
higher-ups."

"And behind one of these two doors behind us is . . ."
The daini made a dramatic drumming noise with her
floppy lips.

"The crystal box containing the soul bee you seek!" said
the other sister, and they both did a fake *rahhhhhhhh* cheer
noise, like the studio audience was going nuts.

"But what's behind the other door?" I asked.

"Behind door number two is the prisoner Prince
Neelkamal!" More *rahhhhhhh*ing.

I felt my spirits lift. Wow, both things I sought—Neel
and the soul bee whose wing was the key to freeing him
were each within my reach. I tried not to get too distracted
by the fact that Neel was so nearby. Could he hear us? Could
I somehow send him a signal?

"But here's the catch, dear contestant!" As she said this, the witch's eyes kind of goggled in her bony skull.

Dang. I knew there was a catch. There was always a catch.

"What is it?"

"We will tell you shortly, but first, another very important word from our sponsors!"

"Not another one," I moaned.

"No show can go on without corporate sponsorship," scolded the witch.

The other daini pulled out a makeup box from her sari. On the cover was a really gross "before" and "after" shot of a beautiful woman smiling at the camera, and then her rotting corpse being picked over by vultures.

"Dead and Lovely!" she said in a mellow, fake-doctor sort of voice. "The fairness cream so good that it will fool even vultures into thinking you're so pale because you're actually dead!"

"Ewwww . . ." I protested. "Why would anyone want to make their dark skin lighter, or look like they were dead?"

But the witch shushed me with a terrifying glare. "Dead and Lovely—the preferred skin-whitening cream of ex–cricket captain and heartthrob anchorman Suman Rahaman. Dead and Lovely—when fair skin simply isn't enough!"

"We now return to our regularly scheduled program," said the other witch, as if the disgusting commercial hadn't happened at all.

"What's the catch with the doors?" I asked, trying to hurry the supernatural sisters along.

"Okay, so, if you don't choose the door containing the soul bee first, you can't unlock the prisoner's door."

"And also . . ." added her companion, "if you choose the prisoner's door first, then my sister and I get to eat your and the prisoner's livers for a snack!"

"While they're still in your bodies!" Both daini chomped their dangly teeth in anticipation.

"But don't be sad, even if you lose, there's still plenty of nice departing gifts we have for you," said the first witch, while the second pulled out a bunch of nonsensical items from her supernatural sari.

"Two resealable bags full of cockroaches!"

"A cup of curdled chocolate milk! Plus, a curly straw!" added the first.

"A gift certificate to the Dead and Lovely beauty salon! Get one of their famous exfoliating facials—peels your skin clean away down to the bone!"

Needless to say, none of those items made it worth having my and Neel's livers eaten up while we were still alive.

"So, how do I know which door is the right one?" I asked.

"We're not unfair, oh, dear contestant."

"We will allow you one question that you may ask either of us!"

"Either of us!"

"And it doesn't even have to be a yes-or-no question!"

The sisters bounced this way and that up the wall of the hallway and onto the burbling and moving ceiling. They hung upside down up there, their feet planted into the ceiling like it was nothing more than sand, before each scampered back down the opposite wall to take her sister's place in front of the other door. Then I heard a buzzer go off. The contest was on.

I rubbed my neck, my fingers tracing the crescent-shaped scar there. I wished I could call on my moon mother for help, but she was unreachable, high and bright in the sky. I had to do this alone. I heard the cameras zooming in and knew there were hundreds, if not thousands, of intergalactic viewers, watching for my every reaction.

Think, Kiranmala, think. I tried Buddhu's breathing technique again. Okay, no matter what I asked, I had no way of knowing which witch I was speaking to, the truth-teller or the liar. And so, no matter what they answered, I had no way of knowing if they were speaking the truth or a lie.

"Bing-bing-bing-bing, bing-bing-bing, bing-bing-bing-bong, bing-bong-bong-bing-bong-bong," ticktocked the sisters cheerfully.

"Stop! You're making me nervous!" I desperately ran through scenarios in my head. If I asked the truth-teller daini which was the door to Neel, she would tell me the truth. But if it ended up being the lie-teller, she would tell me the other door. If I asked the lie-teller daini which was the door to the bee, she would tell me the door to

Neel, and if I asked the truth teller, she would tell me the actual door.

"We're going to need an answer, dear contestant!" said witch number one, licking her slobbery lips a little too conspicuously for my taste. "Or would you like to forfeit?"

"That's not very sporting of you, is it, sister?" argued witch number two. "I like a bit of a challenge before I enjoy my liver tartar." Then, with a wink at me, she added, "Or maybe I'm lying."

"Or maybe my sister's not lying. Or maybe I'm lying about my sister not lying," said the first witch. Both sisters burst out in a fit of grotesque giggles at this.

But their wordplay gave me an idea. "Wait a minute, I think I have my question."

"Aw, shoot, do you really?" whined the first sister.

"Yes, I do."

My heart was beating faster. Did I actually have the answer? I had to think it through. If I asked either daini what her *sister* would say if I asked her which was the door with the bee box, I might actually get the answer I needed. The truth teller would truthfully tell me that her sister would point to Neel's door. And the liar would obviously tell me that her sister would point to Neel's door too. So, no matter which witch I asked this question to, I would have to take the door they didn't point to.

I turned to one of them. "This is my question: What would your *sister* say if I asked her where the bee was?"

Both witches stared at me, their gums flapping, their radish-teeth waggling, their wiggly necks woggling in disappointment. "We'll give you a second chance, girlie—that doesn't have to be your question."

"No, thanks, I'm happy for that to be my question," I said, asking it again.

Rolling their eyes and gnashing their teeth, cracking their knuckles and flapping their feet, the sisters showed me the wrong door.

And I chose the opposite one.

CHAPTER 26

Rescuing My Prince

I knew I'd chosen the right door when I stepped into a room made of glass. As we were deep under the sea, this meant the room was like an inside-out aquarium. There was seaweed and coral below me, schools of fish of all colors floating by above. The space was brightly lit, and my breath caught in my throat as I saw what was in the center of the room. On a crystal stand, on a broad crystal platform, sat a beautiful little crystal box. It looked as clear and shimmery as a piece of ice, or a diamond. And in the crystal box was the soul bee, letting off a golden glow that lit up the whole space. As I walked toward it, it started buzzing, like it knew what I was there to do.

I'd never really thought before about the fact that I'd have to hurt the bee—rip off its wing—to free Neel. I remembered how the policeman at the registration center had torn off the bee's wing, and how the poor insect had wailed in pain. I hesitated, but only for a second. Because suddenly, the fish-filled ocean on the other side of the glass wall was filled with action. Entire schools darted around in agitation like there were predators coming. I had to hurry.

I grabbed the crystal box from the stand and ran back out of the room to where the witchy sisters still lounged in the wide hallway, crying over the loss of my liver.

"Our test center's just been canceled thanks to you!" the first witch moaned.

"We lost all of our corporate sponsors!" said the second.

But I didn't have time to deal with two witches whining about losing their corporate sponsorship from a samosa Drone company. I had to get my rescue on, and quick. I knelt at Neel's cell.

There was a slot in the locked door, like the kind that might be used to slip a meal tray into the room. I hadn't seen it before and wondered if the daini guards had somehow made it invisible to me during the game show contest. Now I put my eye to it, and saw him. I couldn't believe it—there he was! Not separated from me by Essence-Tyme, but a solid, heavy door. Unlike last time I'd seen him, though,

Neel was just lying there. It wasn't right. Neel of all people was always active—riding Raat, fighting our enemies, giving me a hard time. I didn't think I'd ever seen Neel so still: not cracking jokes, or being sarcastic, or raising his eyebrow all handsome-like. This wasn't right at all. I felt goose bumps rise on my arms as the fear rose in my heart.

"Neel!" I shouted. "Neel!"

And pop, just like that, he rubbed his eyes and sat up. "Kiran? Is that you?" He awkwardly shuffled over to the door with his arm and leg chains clanking. "What are you doing here?" He reached his fingers through the door slot.

"I'm here to rescue you!" I said breathlessly. "There's not a lot of time!" I let myself grab his fingers and hold on. It felt wonderful. His fingers were dry, and dirty, but it was him. It was Neel. And I was holding his hand.

"I told you not to rescue me!" Neel said then, pushing my hand away. "Go away! Go home!" He waved in a shooing gesture, like I was some annoying fly, a bee buzzing at him through the door slot rather than his rescuer, his chance at freedom.

I had made it through so much to save him—demons, ghosts, witches, riddles, passwords, intergalactic wormhole driving. I'd disobeyed my parents, stolen the Serpent King's tooth, fought with my cousin, and escaped angry soldiers. And Mr. Princie-Pants had the gall to actually be annoyed by my coming here! Oh, this was rich.

"Listen up, dude," I began hotly, but then my attention was captured by a terrible noise. Somewhere down the long corridor, someone was coming. Oh, man, my time was up.

"Neel, I don't have time to argue about this." I grabbed the serpent's tooth from my backpack, being careful to protect my hand with my old gym T-shirt. With one bold stroke, I cracked the crystal box. I grabbed the glowing bee inside by the wing, trying not to freak out as it wiggled under my grip. It took all my self-control not to shriek, drop the buzzing bee, and run away. "I'm getting you out of there!"

But as I put my fingers on the bee's wing, preparing to rip it off, Neel practically screamed himself. "Stop! That's my mother's soul!"

I paused, my fingers hovering in midair above the buzzing insect. "What did you say? Your mother's what?"

And then, in a smelly, sulfuric cloud of smoke, who should arrive before me but the Rakkhoshi Queen herself— not hazy like through Essence-Tyme, but real and in the flesh. Her golden sari hugged her curvy form, and her hair and ears dripped with jewels. Hanging from a golden belt around her waist was also something else—Neel's sword.

"Well, speak of the . . ." I mumbled to myself, wondering how the Queen had gotten ahold of her son's weapon.

"Ack! What a reflux headache! My head is cutting circles!" The Rakkhoshi Queen belched and rubbed at her temples. "What took you so long, Moon Is Made of Green Cheese?"

"Mother!" Neel yelled from inside the locked doorway. "She's about to kill your soul bee! Don't let her!"

"Don't let her? What are you talking about, my imbecilic offspring? Why do you think I've been visiting your little lunar lady friend here for these past weeks? It wasn't to partake of Parsippany's great foodie scene. Although, those baklava at that Greek diner were excellent, I must say." The rakkhoshi seemed to remember then why she was there, snarling and pointing the sword in my direction. "Do it, Green Lanterna! Get my son out of that detention cell!"

But still, I hesitated. Why, I don't know. Probably a part of my new realization that heroes and monsters weren't always that easy to tell apart. I wanted to save Neel, but now that I knew the cost of it—killing, or at the very least, injuring his mother—I couldn't bring myself to hurt the bee.

"Do it!" the Rakkhoshi Queen screamed, a sound full of frustration and anger. I realized that for whatever reason— a sense of self-preservation?—she couldn't destroy her own soul. "Do it!" she screamed again even as Neel shouted from behind his prison door, "Don't! Kiran, please!"

I looked at the struggling bee in my hands. Its light was fading, and the fight leaving its small body, like it knew what was coming. "I can't," I whispered.

"Ohhh, YOU!" she shouted, like she was so frustrated, she couldn't even come up with an appropriate insult. And then, with an incredible effort that seemed to use every ounce of her power, the demoness lunged at me. I screamed. I really thought she'd just had it and was going to kill me, but it wasn't me she was after. Her sharp talons grabbed the bee out of my hand, and in one swift motion, she tore off its wing.

Her scream—or was it the bee's?—was something awful to hear. Deep and horrible, like someone was being cut in two. The demoness dropped the sword and then fell down heavily next to it. Neel started pounding on the inside of his prison door. "Kiran! Kiran! What did you do?"

But of course, I hadn't done anything. The Queen had sacrificed herself to free her son. She writhed now on the floor, her arm at a horrible, unnatural angle. She was in obvious pain but still had enough power to glare at me. "Open. The. Door!" the Rakkhoshi Rani commanded with a huge effort.

I had to ignore Neel's pounds from the other side of the door, his demands to know what exactly was going on, how upset he sounded, and how furious he was with me. My hands trembling, I grabbed the torn bee wing from the rani's hand and slipped it in the tiny lock on the door. Not only did I feel the prison door give way under my hands as I did, but I heard Neel's shackles fall off with loud jangles and thuds.

The moment the prison door opened, Neel shot out into the hall. But before he even bent down to see how his mother was doing, the hallway grew colder and a familiar voice made both of us look up.

CHAPTER 27

The Arena

Welcome, intergalactic viewers! Welcome, live satellite audience!" said Sesha, the Serpent King. "Welcome to Princess Kiranmala's final test on *Who Wants to Be a Demon Slayer?*"

I whipped around to find not only Sesha sitting on a high throne in the center of the hall, but that suddenly, in addition to the cameras on the walls, there were ginormous TV screens everywhere. They were stacked floor to ceiling, lining the walls five or six high. And on the screens were the eager faces of hundreds of viewers. They were sitting in stands in fairgrounds, they were in the Kingdom Beyond's palace courtyard, they were in huge movie theaters in the Kingdom of Serpents. I saw with a startled cry that one screen was even broadcasting my own living room—from where my parents were watching me with horrified expressions!

"Ma! Baba!" I cried, reaching toward them.

"Daughter!" I heard Ma's voice call. "Darling Garland of Moonbeams! Do not . . ."

"I'm okay, Ma! Don't worry, Baba!" I yelled at the exact same time. "I'm sorry!"

But with a flick of his hand, Sesha shut the sound off that screen. I could see my mother's mouth still moving, but I couldn't hear what she was saying. She and Baba were clutching at each other, and the expressions on their faces almost broke my heart. With an effort, I tore my gaze away from them.

"What is this?" I looked around at all the television screens now encircling me, the low wall all around me, the hungry eyes of all the viewers up and down the magically widened hallway. But I didn't need to wait for the answer, because I realized that the dungeon hallway had been transformed into something that looked, for all the world, like a gladiator arena.

From who knows where, Sesha had made a harmonium materialize in front of him, and now he played it. "A princess split in two—is she boringly good or evil true?" he warbled in a deep baritone. Oh man. Why hadn't I realized it? It had been him singing those harmonigrams all along. "Will she embrace the skin she's in, or fight against her birth and kin?"

From behind the Serpent King emerged another figure on the dais, that obnoxious seven-headed serpent, Naga, my brother. Naga butted into Sesha's song, "Just in case you didn't get it, this is your last test, oh, Sissster!"

This was super bad. Super-duper-with-extra-cherries-on-top bad. I took a quick look at Neel, who was cradling his mother's glassy-eyed head in his lap. She was alive at least, but taking in deep, raspy breaths and not looking particularly healthy.

I looked around the arena, realization dawning even brighter. This wasn't all put together at the last minute. Sesha had known I'd be here. He'd wanted me to come. He'd set me up to do this. And it all made sense now—the instructional video for how to get here, how easy it had been to get away on Raat's back with Ai-Ma and Naya. "You wanted me to get Neel out of detention like this all along? This was part of the game show the whole time?"

Sesha clapped, slow and mocking. As he did, the satellite audience clapped too. "Of course that was the plan!" He waved his hands at the screens, and instead of the satellite audience, I saw Naya, Mati, Tuni, and me plotting together on my palace balcony. Then Sesha played a video of me in my ridiculous dental hygienist's costume, assisting Dr. I. M. Pagol. Me escaping with Ai-Ma after fighting with the rakkhoshi skaters. Finally, I saw myself flying on Raat's back to the hut of demonologist K. P. Das. Then I was shooting down the fish by just looking in the pool. I saw the prisoner parade with Ai-Ma and Naya, I saw us flying here to the Honey-Gold Ocean of Souls, I saw me diving under the water, I saw me making my way to the dungeons, I saw myself solving the witches' riddle. I saw all of it.

"Everything I've done since I got here has all been a part of the game show? You had hidden cameras everywhere? This has all been a part of your sick plan?" I felt like I needed a shower. I couldn't believe it—all those decisions I'd made, all that planning we'd done, Sesha had been watching the whole time?

"Yes, dear audience!" Sesha boomed, and the screens switched back to the viewers. "That's my evil, snaky offspring all right! She may not have given in to temptation in the dentist office, when I was so vulnerable. She may not have decided to kill me then, but you know what they say about the poison not falling far from the fang! Use the touch pad on your remote control to vote for your favorite sneaky, snaky move committed by the Princess Demon Slayer! Was it when she plotted with her little friends to steal my tooth? When she refused to kill the rakkhoshis like a true hero should? When she let Prince Neel's mother sacrifice herself even though he expressly asked her not to save him? Use your remote to vote or text Kiranmala001 for tooth steal-ing, Kiranmala002 for sparing rakkhoshis, or Kiranmala003 for letting the Queen sacrifice herself!"

"This is totally bonkers," I murmured. "Bonkers!" Nothing I'd done had been out of the eyeshot of Sesha. He'd been watch-ing and recording and laughing at me this whole time. He'd obviously planned, all along, for me to injure the Rakkhoshi Queen. As I thought this, I turned back to Neel. "How is she?"

My friend's face was a mask of pain. His mother's muti-lated soul bee flopped helplessly in her loose fist, but even half-unconscious as she was, the Rakkhoshi Rani mustered enough power to yell, "Get off me! You are no son of mine! You half-human weakling! Get away from me!"

"Mother?" Neel's face was confused, and I could see he didn't want to believe his mother's words even as he was hurt by them.

"Idiot," gasped the weakening queen. I could tell, even if Neel couldn't, that the Queen was faking it, pretending not to love Neel so that he wouldn't be distracted from whatever fight was coming.

"Wah! Wah!" Sesha started clapping, slowly and dra-matically. "What a shad, shad scene!" he drawled. "Mummy doesn't love you, is it? You'd have plenty to talk about at your next therapy appointment—if you were going to get out of here alive, that is!"

Neel jumped back, his eyes full of hate and tears. From the ground, he picked up his sword, pointing it in Sesha's direction. I was already in fighting stance, my bow raised. Sesha thought he could convince me that I was evil. He'd set me up, again and again, to fail. But I hadn't. My heart was thudding so loud in my chest, I was sure everyone could hear it. And then, I realized with a start, that the sound wasn't my heart at all, but the hotel itself, throbbing like a live heart under the ocean. The fortress beat with Sesha's life force even as the soul bee had buzzed with the demoness's.

"Don't come any closer," Neel warned, taking a protective position right in front of his gasping mother. All around us, as if sensing the danger we posed to its master, the fortress thudded and hummed. The floor under our feet got slick, and it was hard to keep my footing. The arena itself was our opponent.

Sesha snarled, his lip curling above razor sharp teeth and two perfectly formed fangs. I couldn't believe it. The whole scene at the dentist had been an act. I must have "pulled out" a tooth that had already been pulled earlier. And he'd lain there, pretending to be knocked out, so that I would be tempted to kill him and embrace my evil side? Why? Because it would get him better ratings for his show? It was all so twisted.

The Serpent King pointed at Neel with a menacing finger. "Look where you are, little half demonling. This isn't just any fortress—you are inside the deepest heart of my power. And you stand here, in my underwater dungeons, in the arena of *my* hit game show and threaten to k-k-k-k-kill me? Are you k-k-k-kidding?"

Naga, the brainless follower that he was, copied our father, "Yeah, are you k-k-k-kidding?"

"So, you deep disappointment of a daughter, how do you like the TSK hotel—Honey-Gold Ocean of Souls location?" The Serpent King asked this of me like he really cared about my opinion. "It could have been your inheritance. If you had joined me willingly, that is."

"I don't think so, you slimeball!" I started firing my moon-magicked arrows at my snake father, but he just raised a mocking hand, and they all fell short of reaching him.

"How dare you fire on our father?" hissed Naga, charging toward me from the dais. "Die, sssissster! Die!"

"Oh, really, Naga? Didn't take you too long to fall back in line with dear old Daddy, did it?" I fired two arrows at a time, and then three at my seven-headed brother serpent.

"Last time I saw you, you'd quit working for him because he wouldn't stop insulting you."

That made Naga pause, but only for about a milli-second. "He promised he'd stop doing that."

"And you believed him because he's so trustworthy? Good move, Bro!" I felt my power grow and expand, as I made it rain magical moon arrows on the serpent's hooded heads. Since swords weren't particularly useful except at close range, Neel kept unnecessarily directing me—"Aim for that head!" "No, the other!" "Now that ugly one!" "The other ugly one!" "Watch out!" As I fired, I threw down my backpack from one shoulder, watching its contents scatter partially over the floor. It didn't matter. The heavy thing was throwing off my aim.

"Father!" Naga whined. He looked like a slithery porcu-pine now, there were so many magic arrows hanging off his skin. "Shhhe's hurting me!"

"Oh, shut up, you dolt!" Sesha snapped his fingers, and Naga was hurled back from us, landing mewling in the corner.

"You promised you'd stop saying mean things like that!" the seven-headed serpent cried, but our father ignored him.

"And so, we begin the third test." Sesha was playing now for the hungry crowds. "Are you ready, satellite audience, to see a hero being born? Will the Princess Demon Slayer claim her destiny or will she die trying, and pass into song and legend?"

My parents were banging desperately on the other side of their TV screen now, and I willed myself to look away. What was coming next? What would my poor, loving Ma and Baba be forced to watch? I couldn't even guess.

I turned my gaze toward where Neel's mother lay on the floor. Her bee's light was almost gone. She was getting weaker and weaker, too weak to even speak. Neel had run back to her side, ineffectively stroking at his mother's hair. The demoness wasn't exactly a hero. She had tried to kill Lal and Mati, hurt Neel and me. She was infuriating, and frightening, and totally untrustworthy. But she was his mother, and she was willing to sacrifice everything for her son. Just like Ma and Baba were willing to do for me. I realized what I had to do.

"Fine, we'll fight!" I stood squarely in the middle of the arena, facing Sesha. Out of the corner of my eye, I saw Neel give me a startled look. All around us, viewers on the TV screens gasped with shocked delight.

"That's what this has been all about, right? Why you captured Neel, why you set up this whole game show in the first place? Fine, I'll do it. You win. I'll fight Neel if you fix, or heal, or however it works, his mother's soul bee!"

"Kiran, you'd do that for her?" Neel said, his voice tight and full of emotion. His dark eyes danced over my face, warm and open for the first time in what felt like forever.

"I'd do it for you," I said. And I saw his expressions change quickly from gratitude to hope to guilt to defeat.

"I could never fight you," Neel said finally. "I never would." But his eyes told me what I needed to know. He didn't hate me after all. Even in the midst of our current horror, I felt something heavy and painful lift from my heart.

"Oh, that's rich! That's really, really wonderful!" Sesha all out guffawed, after watching our discussion with the interest of a TV viewer himself. "Is that what you thought, you little imp? That I wanted to have you fight your puny half-demon friend for my own pleasure?" Sesha looked out at the TV audience. "Isn't that wonderful, viewers? Aren't children just precious?"

The audience on the TV screens cheered, but a little less than before, as if they too were confused by what was going on.

"You don't want me to fight Neel?" I asked. "That's not my third test?"

"If I wanted that kind of cheap entertainment, I wouldn't have gone to all this trouble!" Sesha was laughing so hard, he actually had to catch his breath and wipe his eyes. "No, what I want is altogether different. I want to kill you, my youngest child. I would have thought that was utterly obvious. Oh, yes, I want to kill you and the Rakkhoshi Queen both."

CHAPTER 28

The Truth about a Prince

At Sesha's admitting he wanted to kill me, the Kingdom Beyond audiences on the TV screens let out collective gasps and exclamations of "Princess Demon Slayer!" "No!" "The game was rigged after all!"

"Silence!" Sesha shouted at the on-screen spectators, and they obediently quieted. Ma and Baba were still on mute. I couldn't even look anymore at that screen with my parents, though. I didn't think I could keep it together if I saw their faces.

"So," I said slowly, playing for time. "The entire *Who Wants to Be a Demon Slayer?* game was a big joke? I'm sure your sponsors won't like that, will they? The whole killing-Princess-Demon-Slayer bit of your dastardly plan?" I looked directly at one of the cameras on the wall. "Hey, Princess Pretty Pants people! You really want to partner with TSK industries on your product? What about you, KiddiePow? Or you, Samosa Drone, Inc.? This evildoery isn't exactly on message for any of your companies, is it? Well, I guess with the exception of Dead and Lovely skin cream."

"Shut up!" I knew I'd gotten to Sesha when he blasted a bolt of green lightning at the camera into which I'd been speaking. Like the witchy sisters, the Serpent King obviously felt strongly about his corporate sponsorships. I felt a little spark of triumph. I'd figured him out, and I'd gotten to him.

My happiness was cut a little short, though, by the fact that Sesha then shot a bolt at me, encasing me in one of his green orbs of pain and torture. Immediately, I dropped to my knees inside the floating bubble. The sharp, hot pain on my skin and in my bones was so intense, I couldn't stop from crying out.

"Leave her alone!" yelled Neel, charging at Sesha with his sword raised. They clashed, sword to green bolt, making an enormous explosion of light every time their weapons made contact. Through the mossy haze of the orb, I saw that as Neel charged at the Serpent King, the hallway seemed to get longer, making it harder for him to reach his goal. When Sesha charged, the floor itself buckled and softened under Neel's feet, making his every step treacherous.

"Neel!" I yelled, even through the torment. "The hotel's alive! It's fighting dirty!"

But I was too late. The floor turned oil-slick slippery under Neel's feet, throwing him off balance and making him skid halfway across the arena, clunking his head painfully on the wall. Even with their volume down, I could hear the audience shrieking. Several viewers jumped up or covered their eyes. Of course, despite their disapproval or even disgust, none of them stopped watching.

"Neel, stop!" I moaned through the pain as my friend struggled to get back on his feet. "Don't. It's useless!"

Sesha raised his eyebrows. "Good advice. You're not as stupid as you look, Daughter. Too bad I have to kill you for my plan to work. You might have been better company than that reptilian rube in the corner." He pointed mockingly at where Naga still lay, half-dazed. Then the Serpent King waved his hands and broke the spell of the orb around me. I knelt, gasping on the ground, and Neel dashed over to me to help me to stand again.

"Why?" I panted through my pain. It was all I could manage. My skin was burned and bruised, my insides felt like molten lava. I struggled desperately to catch my breath.

This whole ridiculous game had been because Sesha wanted to kill me? Not incorporate me into his snaky minions, but outright kill me? I remembered Zuzu's warning. I remembered how adamant my parents had been about my not coming here. Neel had been the bait, yes. But not so that I would fight him. He had been the bait that caught both me and his mother—because Sesha knew that we would both try to free him.

"Why are you doing this?" I asked again, hanging on to Neel's arm for balance.

"Why, because of the Ouroboros, of course!" Sesha said this in a loud, booming, game show announcer way. On the screens, there was that image again, the snake eating its own tail. "I've been watching that TV show from your dimension—Shady Sadie the Snaky Lady! And I've learned quite a bit about the study of alchemy. That's where I found the story of the Ouroboros. If the head of the great serpent—that's me—eats its own tail—that's you, my youngest child—why, I get to do it! I get to cheat this annoying cycle of life and death and rebirth! I get to be as wide and all-powerful as the galaxies themselves! I get to live forever!" He cackled evilly and rubbed his hands.

Sesha really was such a cliché. A cliché that was going to kill me, yes. But still a cliché.

"And all this nonsense about the Chintamoni and Poroshmoni Stones? What about them? Were they just a distraction?" I sputtered, even as I exchanged a panicky look with Neel.

"Oh, no, that's the best part of all!" Sesha gave a shrill whistle, then laughed in an über-movie-villain way. "I can't just kill you outright to fulfill the Ouroboros spell. I must kill you in a special way—with the power of two neutron stars!"

"I was right," I breathed. "The stones are neutron stars!"

"Not just yet. Not in this form." Sesha wiggled his finger at me. "Right now they are simply jewels. But through the alchemical power of all four rakkhosh clans—a quadruple power held by only the Rakkhoshi Queen—they can become stars! Get on out here, my trusted henchman!"

"Yes, Your Majesty!" The person who walked out onto the dais handed the Serpent King two shimmering stones—one white and one yellow. It was the Thinking and Touch Stones, the two jewels that would be changed, through the power of the Rakkhoshi Queen, into two neutron stars. They were the two objects that would kill me and give Sesha immortality.

You would think my attention would be on those stones, the cause of all this drama and misery, the weapons with which my birth father would very soon try to kill me. But I barely paid them a glance. Instead, I was staring openmouthed at the person who brought them in. The TV audience gave a collective gasp too.

"It was remarkably easy to convince the Raja that the Poroshmoni Stone should be given to his son for safekeeping," drawled Sesha as he took the two jewels into his ringed hands.

But I still wasn't listening. I was too slack-jawed with shock at who had brought Sesha the jewels. I couldn't. Bloomin'. Believe it.

"Brother!" exclaimed Neel. "I knew it!

"Lal?" I practically screamed. "How could you?"

"How could I what?" drawled Lal, his handsome face unrecognizable in its malice. "Fool you? Very easily, my dear. Have my brother get put in detention? A bit trickier, but it was manageable. I just wish I wasn't caught up in that farce of a second test, and could have stopped you from talking to K. P. Das."

I narrowed my eyes. Wait a minute, Sesha had known—he'd been watching—when I went to speak to the old demonologist. And he had wanted me to dive under the Honey-Gold Ocean of Souls to rescue Neel all along—he'd even set up this gladiator arena for it. Then what was it that Lal didn't want me to find out from his old teacher? That's when it hit me. Raat's strange reaction to Lal, Lal's own weird lies about not liking demonology, how the crown prince never called me Just Kiran like he used to.

"You're not actually Lal at all, are you?" I said slowly, the pieces all falling together in my head.

"What are you talking about? Has your *lurve* for me melted your little brain?" Lalkamal sneered. "Or are you angling for more canoodling? More stolen kisses and hugs? Don't be shy just because my big brother is here!"

"*Canoodling?*" repeated Neel. "Kisses and hugs?"

From the TV screens, the audience started laughing.

"There was no canoodling!" I sputtered. "That was all that stupid propaganda machine. Anyway, I mean, gross! Besides which, that's not Lal!" I said this last part through gritted teeth.

"What are you talking about, Kiran? Of course that's my brother," Neel snapped. "Have you lost leave of your senses?"

The viewers on the TV screens all seemed to think so too. They frowned at me now, and one snake woman even seemed to be wagging her fingers at me. That was all I needed. To be shamed by a green-skinned snake woman watching me on an intergalactic TV game show.

"Enough with this!" Sesha pointed at Neel. "Get him, Prince Lalkamal! Kill your brother and be rid of his polluting, rakkhosh presence in the kingdom!"

Lal ran at Neel with his sword drawn, almost faster than the eye could see. At the last minute, Neel raised his sword to block his brother's, his face shocked. "Lal? Bro? Stop! What are you doing?"

The two brothers clashed weapons, swirling and slashing at each other. Lal was attacking and Neel was on the major defensive. He stumbled as he walked backward, blocking his brother's incredibly strong blows. "Lal! It's me!" said Neel, his voice strangled. "You don't want to do this!"

I had to do something, and now. Neel wasn't going to attack his brother, and that was going to get him killed. Sesha was paying attention to the princes' fight, laughing and cackling in delight. With everyone's eyes off me, I dived across the arena to where Naya's Lola Morgana thermos had come spilling out of my backpack before. Before anyone could understand what I was up to, I twisted the lid open.

"If you're the human being you claim to be, Prince Lalkamal, then you should be able to get into this thermos, right?" I shouted, remembering how K. P. Das had tried to get me to do the same thing. "You should be able to get into this easy as pie!"

"Stop!" sputtered Sesha. "Don't listen to her!"

The viewers on the screens leaned forward eagerly, their eyes shining with anticipation as they waited to see what happened next.

I held my breath too, not sure if he would fall for it. But

the challenge seemed to appeal to the crown prince's vanity. He stopped attacking Neel, and lowered his sword.

"Of course I can get in there! I'm a human being, aren't I?"

"Well, that's the question!" I taunted, waving the thermos. "Are you a human being? I have my doubts! You're going to have to prove it by doing something only a real human could do! Get in this thermos!"

"You doubt me?" The prince's eyes grew an unnatural red. "Just watch!"

Transforming into a burst of vapor, the creature pretending to be Lal shot himself into the Lola Morgana thermos. As soon as the ghost was in, I shut the thermos with a resolute bang. Neel looked absolutely—as Buddhu might say—gobsmacked.

The audience went wild. They obviously thought this was all a part of the show. "Princess Demon Slayer! Princess Demon Slayer!" I heard someone begin to chant, and hundreds of voices from all over the kingdom joined in. I held up the thermos like a trophy and took a little bow, shooting Sesha a sly grin as I did.

The Serpent King wasn't having any of it. "Oh, shut up, all of you!" he snapped, turning the volume off all the TVs.

"If that was a ghost who stole his form, then where's my real brother?" demanded Neel.

"That's for me to know and you never to find out!" snapped Sesha.

But from inside the thermos, a faint little voice called out something. I couldn't make it out until I held it up to my ear. "A peanut where my garden grows. A pike all the way from my toes to my nose!"

Of course! Thank goodness ghosts couldn't resist riddles! I could have kissed that Lola Morgana thermos. I could have even kissed ghost Lal (well, okay, maybe not).

"New Jersey!" I told Neel. "The real Lal's stuck in a tree trunk somewhere in New Jersey!"

Neel stared at the thermos, finally getting that the guy he thought was his brother had actually been a ghost. He looked up at me, mouthing the words *thank you*.

The TV screens, all muted now, were a flurry of visual activity. People were jumping and pointing and screaming and fainting. Some had left their stands and others had crowded up to the camera and seemed to be yelling into it.

I saw why. Sesha had lifted the white and gold stones above his head, one jewel in each hand. There was a tremendous light shooting off them, like a laser beam, right in my direction.

CHAPTER 29

The Final Test

I thought I was a goner for sure, when another familiar voice echoed throughout the arena. "Let my grandchildren go, you snake!"

Sesha lowered his arms and turned around to see, as did we all.

It was Ai-Ma, joining us in the hallway, tall and strong with protective love. Right behind her was an army of pink-sari'd girls on skateboards, all rakkhoshis, including Naya, looking fiercer than I'd ever seen her.

"Your Highnosity!" Naya waved. "We're here to help!"

"Um, hi, Naya!" I looked over her shoulder for Mati, before I realized the dive would have been too dangerous for any of the human PSS, or for Tuni.

The flying fangirls gave me a little cheer, their faces apologetic. "Princess Kiran, strong and true! Don't you worry, we'll save you!"

"Henchmen!" Sesha yelled into the air. He sounded just like a movie bad guy. "Intruders in the fortress dungeons! Get them!"

The TSK hench-snakes flooded down the hallway from behind Sesha, falling upon the rakkhoshi skate-boarders. At the same time, a recovered Naga took aim at Ai-Ma herself.

"Ai-Ma!" Neel called as he leaped forward with his sword raised. "Look out!" Turning to me, he yelled, "Please, Kiran, protect my mother!"

I stayed where I was, protecting the Demon Queen's body. Long distance, I fired arrow after arrow at Naga. But still, he headed toward Ai-Ma.

"You think you're a match for me, you sad old bag of bonesss?" Naga hissed and lunged but Ai-Ma brushed him aside with a magical sweep of her hand.

"Naughty boy! You must show more respect for elders!" Neel's grandmother cackled, her three teeth gleaming from her slobbery grin. "Shame, shame, puppy shame! All the donkeys know your name!"

Love had made Ai-Ma into a phenomenon to behold. She whirled and struck out at Naga, her arms such a blur, it

looked like she had as many arms as he had heads. The seven-headed snake moaned, all fourteen eyes goggling in surprise as Ai-Ma tied the seven cobra necks together like a giant birthday bow. "Grandma to the rescue!" she declared as she put the vicious snake out of commission.

But now it was Sesha's turn to lunge at Ai-Ma. "Stupid cow, you think you can save anyone? Stupid like your demon daughter! You came to save your daughter and grandson, is it? Well, you can keep them company in death!"

Like it had before, the hotel tried to fight dirty for its master, making the floor and walls shift in ways as to throw the rakkhoshi off balance. But Ai-Ma was sprightlier than she looked, and scampered up the walls and onto the ceiling, like the witches before her had done. She stayed one step ahead of the living fortress. She and Neel now had Sesha on the defensive for a moment, but then the hotel redoubled its efforts, warping and burbling its walls, floor, and ceiling to throw everyone but Sesha off their stride. The skateboarders, including Naya, who had been leaping and wheeling over snakes—and getting the advantage over the slimy reptiles—were now put on the defensive by the aggressive moves of the evil fortress hotel.

"Did you disgusting vermin actually think you could stride into my property, *again*, and destroy it? Did you actually think I wouldn't destroy you first?" Sesha snarled. "No, it's time for me to taste immortality! It's time for evil and good to stop being in balance! It's time for me to win!"

That was when I made a horrible mistake. The dungeon hallway buckled and thrashed, throwing Neel off his feet and to the floor with an audible "Ouch!" He looked weak after his weeks in the dungeon detention center, and so tired. I saw Sesha raise his hands, as if to finish the prince off right then and there.

"No you don't!" I left the rakkhoshi's side to run and help Neel to his feet. But right at that moment, Sesha grabbed his chance, aiming the two stones in his hands not at me, but at the fallen Rakkhoshi Queen! The light coming out of the stones—golden and white—united and flared, streaming in a laser-like beam toward Neel's mother's fallen body.

As the light hit her, the Demon Queen screamed. At her piercing cry, all of us—snakes and skateboarders, Ai-Ma and Sesha, Neel and I—froze in place. Naga had no choice, since he was still tied up like a giant bow.

Neel's mother had her eyes open now, and she was thrashing about on the ground, a thick silver smoke coming out of every pore. "Stop!" I cried, trying to run back to her. "Please, Serpent King, stop!"

"Why? Not long now before these mere stones are transformed into stars! And then, my last-born child, I will use them to kill you! The head of the serpent shall swallow the tail, and immortality will be mine forever!"

On the screens flashed rapid-fire images—a snake encircling the world, a snake churning up life from a cosmic ocean, a snake winding its way up from the bottom of a meditating monk's spine, up, up, up to the heavens until it became a constellation. Then came the Ouroboros—the snake biting its own tail. Its eyes glowed bright and fierce—one yellow and one white—expanding out and out until their energy merged together in fierce fireworks of intergalactic power.

Neel's mother was floating up off the ground now, her glowing body losing its form, becoming water and then fire, earth and then air, over and over again. She was the Demon Queen, and so had powers from all the clans. Why hadn't I paid more attention to that passage from K. P. Das's book about the demon clans and their connection to alchemy? If only I'd understood. It was all connected: my fate, the fate of demon-kind, the fate of serpent-kind, the fate of human-kind, all of it. The all was one.

The glowing bright Demon Queen hovering above us was everything in the universe and the universe itself all at the same time. She was power and vulnerability, she was mother and monster, she was life and she was death. I saw the direction of the beam change and realized the stones were sucking away her magical life powers. They grew—in size and brilliance—even as she diminished.

"Mother!" Neel cried, trying to get to her. "No!"

We stood there in stunned silence as the Rakkhoshi Rani dimmed, becoming dark as an ocean, still as a beginning place. It was sad, but it was also beautiful. She was creating a celestial power. She was giving birth to twin stars.

That is, until her mother Ai-Ma leaped at her. "No! I won't let you do this to my daughter!" As she jumped, Ai-Ma called to me, "The jewels, my num num! Break the connection and get those jewels!"

I knew it was useless to try to fight Sesha directly, and so I ran over to Naya, jumping on the skateboard behind her. "Let's fly, girl!" I pointed at the dais.

Naya gave a huge whoop and let her wings unfurl. I had the skateboard in my hand as she flew me toward Sesha and then let me drop. I landed right next to him on the dais with so much momentum I practically bowled right through him on Naya's skateboard.

"What?" he exclaimed as I picked him up on the board too. He was so topsy-turvy he dropped the jewels.

"Neel!" I shouted. Neel dived for the halfway-to-star stones, which he tossed at Ai-Ma with one ferocious throw.

I saw one of the screens come to life with the words, *Prince Neelkamal being recruited by both the intergalactic cricket and rickets leagues on account of his fantastic bowling arm. Princess Demon Slayer a possible skateboard athlete in this year's X Games.*

Ai-Ma caught the glowing stones in midair. She was right next to her daughter's floating body when she brought the yellow and white jewels together over her head in a resounding thunder crash. The light of the stones dimmed again, their power flowing back into the Rakkhoshi Rani's body. But that's when the strangest thing happened. We all—me, Neel, Naya, Priya, and the other PSS—got sucked toward Ai-Ma as if by a tornado. In the swirling, whirling force of the storm, I saw reflections of other faces as well: Mati, Tuni, the real Lal, my parents, even Zuzu and Jovi. What was going on? I looked down at my body to realize I too was losing my borders and boundaries, I too was becoming one with the others—until the distinctions between us all seemed to dissolve. It didn't matter who was rakkhosh and who was human, who was hero and who was monster, who was near and who was far. We were all connected. We were all creators and destroyers. We were all children and we were all elders. We were all mortal and we were all stars. I remembered the lines of the rakkhoshi's poem. *Elladin, belladin, Honey-Gold Sea. Who seeks immortality?*

We were humming with the promise of the universe's mysteries. We moved and danced around the Rakkhoshi Rani, like the stars in Shady Sadie the Science Lady's video had done, spinning faster and faster in their cosmic dance. But then I saw Ai-Ma again—distinct from the mist that we were all now lost inside. The powerful old grandmother brought the Chintamoni and Poroshmoni jewels together over her head again, with the words, "Thought and Touch, stones of space, free my children with your grace."

A light—blinding and hot—shot out from inside of me and from around me. We sparked and glowed, exploding out everything that had come before. Exploding out old ideas, old habits, old prejudices. My body was mine and it wasn't mine anymore. I wasn't entirely sure if I was a star that was dying or one being born anew.

"Neel?" I called out. I was afraid and reached out for his hand.

"Here, Kiran!" I heard but didn't see him. "I'm here." I felt his firm hand in mine.

"Naya?" I called next.

"I'm here, my friend!" said the girl's voice, and I felt someone grip my other hand.

"The all is one," I heard Ai-Ma's voice call. "The one is all."

I don't know if it was the magic of the jewels or the magic of all our interconnections or even if it was some other-worldly magic only possessed by grandmothers, but Ai-Ma flung us all out of the light, throwing our dizzy and crumpled bodies to the floor. As she did so, the room exploded in a shower of golden and silver sparks. We were ourselves again, parts of stars no more.

But when I looked for the gentle old rakkhoshi, all I saw was the glowing white orb of light, raining gold and platinum upon us all. On the floor beneath where she had been were the Chintamoni and Poroshmoni Stones in their original size and form. I picked them up and tucked them into my pack for safekeeping.

The magical gold and platinum rain now pouring over us was an alchemist's dream. It coated our skin, clothes, hair—making everyone glitter and glow. The precious metal soothed the burns where I'd been hurt by Sesha's magical orb. They changed the color of my hair and skin back to normal. The metallic rain acted as a powerful healing medicine on the Rakkhoshi Rani too, bringing her back from her near death, giving her form, healing her mangled arm. And as she straightened up from the floor, an expression of blood-violent hatred on her face, I saw, for the first time in my life, my bio father the Serpent King actually look afraid.

"Now, Pinki," he cooed, "you don't want to do anything rash."

Pinki? I thought. Neel's mom's name is Pinki? But there were more important things to worry about right now. Like the TV screens and cameras, which all seemed to have been blown to smithereens by the force of the neutron star explosion. Like the one person who was missing from our midst.

"Ai-Ma," Neel said frantically. "What happened to Ai-Ma?"

The world was blurry through the precious metals on my eyelashes, and the tears in my eyes. I watched everything happening as if from very far away. Watching but not watching, caring but not caring. All I could think of was the sweet old rakkhoshi who had sacrificed herself to save us all.

"Don't you 'now, Pinki' me!" In the meantime, the Demon Queen was rounding on Sesha with her arms raised above her head. "'Rash'? You want to see rash? Rash like imprisoning my boy to lure me and little Luna Loo Loo here? Rash like relying on some ancient 2-D myth to try and cheat death? Rash like killing my mother?" Her eyes were so dark with rage, they were like the velvety black of outer space. Her dark hair spun out from her head, shooting electric-like sparks from each strand. Her teeth elongated, and her talons seemed to grow as we watched, becoming a twisting jungle of sharp nails.

I was surprised when Neel stepped in between her and Sesha. "Mother, I just got you back. I'm not going to lose you now too."

"I don't understand!" yelled Sesha, his own teeth clenched and bared. Like the rest of us, he too was coated in gold and platinum, looking like someone had dumped glitter all over him. "It should have worked! You!" He pointed a long green nail at me. "You are the reason for my failure. You are the poison infiltrating my plans and my power!"

"You better believe it!" I shouted. "And I'll keep poisoning, I mean infiltrating . . . I mean . . ." I looked to Neel for help, but he just shrugged. "Oh, bite your own tail, you snaky loser!" I finally concluded.

"Forget the Ouroboros!" Sesha snapped his teeth. "Just come to Daddy and die!"

He shot green bolts at me, but the Rakkhoshi Queen deflected them. I rained a torrent of arrows down on the Serpent King even as I expected the hotel to fight me back. What I didn't expect to see was that there was no more hotel between Sesha and me. What I didn't realize was that the very building around us was dissolving.

The gold and platinum rain falling all over us was incredibly powerful. It had not only healed me, and brought Neel's mom back from the brink of death, but it seemed to be attacking the Serpent King's fortress. Where the glittering pieces of precious metal hit the wall, ceilings, and floors, the solid substance of the hotel around us was corroding away. And because this particular building was at the bottom of an ocean, that meant the fortress was springing a zillion leaks of ocean water. Oh, this wasn't good.

"No! My fortress! My beautiful hotel!" wailed Sesha. "I'll get you for this! This isn't over, Daughter, mark my words! I will see you in the coming war! The snake shall find its circle! I will conquer you, and immortality!" Arms in air, he created a flash of green light into which he, Naga, and a few of his closest hench-snakes disappeared.

The Rakkhoshi Queen raged acrid red smoke from her ears and nose. "Oh, no you don't!" she snarled, diving after Sesha as he vanished. She caught the last bit of Sesha's green magic and disappeared with them. As she did, we heard her voice call out, "Oof! My reflux! Take care of each other, dum-dums!"

Neel gave me a look that made my toes seriously melt. "I assume she meant us."

"Probably," I agreed. But then I had to return my attention to the total catastrophic chaos happening around us.

There were snakes being sucked out of the holes in the fortress and into the ocean. The PSS girls were the next to go. As soon as a hole opened up that was big enough, Priya got sucked out. Naya tried to hang on to her but the force of the ocean was too great, and the speed at which the hotel was disintegrating was too darn fast.

"Your Highnosity!" my silly, goofy rakkhoshi friend Naya yelled, racing over to me through the now waist-high water. "Be prepared to swim!"

The fortress was taking in more and more of the Honey-Gold Ocean, the very walls around us convulsing and weeping, like the hotel knew it was at the brink of destruction. "We're going to have to swim up, Kiran." Neel was now on my left side, and Naya was on my right.

"Don't worry, I have you, Your Highnosity," said Naya, grabbing ahold of my arm.

"Who are you again?" asked Neel, peering over at the rakkhoshi without any recognition. "Why do I feel like we've met?"

I saw Naya squirming with embarrassment and decided to help her out. "It's a long story, Neel, but we don't have time for it right now." I held on to his arm. "We gotta start swimming before we all drown down here! I've got to let my parents know I'm okay, and plus, I think I missed a huge math test. I'm going to be in some serious trouble if I don't get some studying in."

The water was already nearly chest deep, and rising fast. There was very little left of what used to be the TSK hotel-slash-fortress (Honey-Gold Ocean of Souls location).

The water was almost to our necks when I gave both my friends a squeeze on the arm, Neel on one side and Naya on the other. Naya whooped, and Neel gave me another toe-curling grin.

I didn't know what came next—where we'd go first or how we'd save Lal. I didn't know what dangers we'd face—or how in the world I was going to pass that math test. What I did know was there would be plenty of danger ahead, especially with my serpent father still on the loose and talking about some kind of coming war. But I also knew that I wouldn't have to fight alone.

"To New Jersey!" I said, raising my fist.

"To New Jersey!" Neel and Naya shouted as the water rose, taking us with it.

We swam hard and strong toward the surface, and the light.

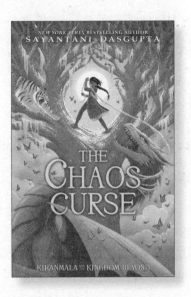

"**R**akkhosh!" I shouted again. I looked over my shoulder and realized that no one had pulled out a weapon or anything. Naya looked seriously hurt, and the Pink-Sari Skateboard girls—demonic and human—all seemed to be laughing at me.

"No kidding they're rakkhosh!" Priya shot little flames out of her mouth with the words. "So are half of us. Or have you forgotten, Princess? And if I'm not wrong, you yourself freed these sad saps from the detention center when you destroyed dear old Daddy's underwater hotel."

"Stop being such an anti-demon bigot!" Mati scolded. "I would think you would know by now that no one type of creature has the market on monstrosity. Rakkhosh can be good or bad, based on their choices—just like human beings!"

I felt a twinge of shame at my cousin's words, but getting over my fear of rakkhosh was easier said than done. But even as I relaxed my guard, the rakkhosh who had come up out of the waves made a tight circle around me. I gave a little yell and whirled, not sure where to aim my bow and arrow. "Some help, please!" I shouted.

But what the rakkhosh did next shocked me into lowering my weapon. Some kneeled, some gave me a respectful namaskar, some salaamed, and some even touched my feet with their warty hands.

"From demonic detention you did us free," rhymed one green-skinned and boil-covered fellow. "We are yours, if ever you need."

"My friends, all, please rise up. The resistance is happy to have your support," said Mati. "We have much work to do to get the kingdom back from Sesha's rule."

Author's Note

Game of Stars (Kiranmala and the Kingdom Beyond Book 2) is an original story that, like the first book in this series (*The Serpent's Secret*), draws from many traditional Bengali folktales and children's stories. These are stories shared by grandparents, parents, aunties, and uncles in West Bengal (India), Bangladesh, and throughout the Bengali diaspora to generations of children. I've used many of these stories as a basis for inspiration while writing both books in the series, and as a way to tell my own story as an immigrant daughter.

Thakurmar Jhuli and Rakkhosh Stories:

Folktales involving rakkhosh are very popular throughout all of South Asia. The word is sometimes spelled "rakshasa" in other parts of the region, but in this book, it is spelled like the word sounds in Bengali. Folktales are of course an oral tradition, passed on verbally from one generation to the next, with each teller adding spice and nuance to their own version. In 1907, Dakshinaranjan Mitra Majumdar collected, wrote down, and published some classic Bengali folktales in a book called *Thakurmar Jhuli* (grandmother's satchel). This collection, which involves separate stories about the Princess Kiranmala, the brothers Neelkamal and Lalkamal, and the monkey and owl princes Buddhu and Bhootoom, is also full of tales involving rakkhosh and khokkosh, as well as stories about the Kingdom of Serpents. The giant birds Bangoma and Bangomee make an appearance in the story of Neelkamal and Lalkamal, as do pakkhiraj horses. The Demon Queen appears in the original Neelkamal and Lalkamal story, as does the lovably goofy rakkhosh grandmother, Ai-Ma. Lalkamal and Neelkamal never meet Kiranmala in their original stories, but brave Kiranmala does have two brothers named Arun and Barun, whose lives she must save. A version of the Serpent King appears in this collection as well, although not exactly as he appears in this book. Also in *Thakurmar Jhuli* is the idea that rakkhosh have soul bees and cannot die unless their soul bees are killed. *Thakurmar Jhuli* stories are still immensely popular in West Bengal and Bangladesh, and have inspired translations, films, television cartoons, comic books, and more. Rakkhosh are very popular as well—the demons everyone loves to hate—and appear not just in folk stories but also Hindu mythology. Images of bloodthirsty, long-fanged rakkhosh can be seen everywhere—even on the back of colorful Indian auto rikshaws as a warning to other drivers not to tailgate or drive too fast!

Stories of Bhoot, Petni, Shakchunni, and Daini

Stories about bhoot, or ghosts, are very popular in Bengal. Bhoot are not exactly like the white-sheeted, chain-rattling notion of ghosts in the West, but are their own kind of horrible monster creature. Different types of bhoot also have different personalities and traits—petni are female ghosts (women who usually died unmarried) and shakchunni are the married version. They, like many other types of ghosts, want nothing more than to capture a human being and put them in a coconut or other tree trunk for safekeeping while taking over their physical form and then trying to inhabit the human being's life. If you're ever walking by a haunted coconut grove or lake, particularly at dusk, never turn around when you hear your name being called—or your soul is up for grabs! Petni and shakchunni can also be identified by their backward-facing feet (a dead giveaway!) or when they use their supernatural powers to do housework—like when they reach their extendable arms out a window to pluck lemons, or stick their own feet into the fire because they're too lazy to go get firewood. Other kinds of bhoot mentioned in this story include mechho bhoot (fish-eating ghosts) and skondokata (headless ghosts). Although traditional Bengali bhoot aren't fond of riddles (I made that up), they are sometimes fooled when they are convinced to enter sealed bottles. Daini are witches, and unlike bhoot, are actual living beings. In traditional Bengali stories, they often capture and kill children or conduct other evil spells. In this story, our sister witches are simply slightly (okay, very) wicked game show hosts.

Abol Tabol and Sukumar Ray

Sukumar Ray can be considered the Dr. Seuss or Lewis Carroll of the Bengali literary tradition. His illustrated book of nonsense rhymes, *Abol Tabol*, was first published in 1923, but like *Thakurmar Jhuli*, it is an evergreen Bengali children's favorite. The character Mr. Madan Mohan in this book and *The Serpent's Secret* was inspired by two nonsense poems from *Abol Tabol*—the first about a man with a bizarre contraption on his back that dangles food in front of his face ("Khuror Kal"), and the second about an office worker who is convinced that someone has stolen his very hairy and very much present moustache ("Gopf Churi"). Two other characters in *Game of Stars* were also inspired by Sukumar Ray's poems—the police constable who is prohibited from laughing, whose "illness" was inspired by a poem called "Ram Gorurer Chhana," and Chhaya Devi, purveyor of shadows, who was inspired by a poem called "Chhaya Baji."

Tuntuni

The wisecracking bird Tuntuni is another favorite, and recurrent, character of Bengali children's folktales. The father of Sukumar Ray, Upendrakishore Ray Chowdhury (also known as Upendrakishore Ray), collected a number of these stories starring the clever tailor bird Tuntuni in a 1910 book called *Tuntunir Boi (The Tailor Bird's Book)*.

Alchemy

There are a number of references to alchemy in this book, which was the philosophic and prescientific practice concerned with the transformation of elements. Most notably, alchemists in Asia, the Middle East, and Europe often searched for the elixir of life, as well as a substance or stone that could transform one metal into another. There is evidence that there were alchemists as long ago as the Bronze Age Indus Valley civilizations of Mohenjo-daro and Harappa (located in current day Pakistan), who searched for the elixir of life to give them immortality and ways to transform other metals to gold.

In *Game of Stars*, I refer to the Ouroboros, or the snake biting its own tail, which is a symbol Egyptian in origin and also seen in ancient Greek magical texts. The Ouroboros made its way into the European medieval tradition of alchemy, coming to symbolize cyclicality, introspection, and the cycle of life and death. The phrase "the all is one" appeared on a third century Egyptian image of the Ouroboros, from the papers of a woman philosopher, author, and alchemist named Cleopatra (sometimes mistaken for the queen of the same name). Although neither the Ouroboros nor the phrase "the all is one" are South Asian in origin, I included them in this story because both ideas seemed consistent with Hindu philosophy, and, honestly, they intrigued me.

I also include reference to the Chintamoni (also

spelled Chintamani) and Poroshmoni (also spelled Para-smani) Stones. Here, it's important to note that *moni/mani* means "jewel," and these stones appear in both ancient Hindu and Buddhist texts and are often considered equivalents to the European Philosopher's Stone. It is unclear if they granted wishes, changed other metals into gold, granted immortality, or all three. Sometimes the stone is pictured in Hindu texts as in the possession of Naga, the Snake King (not the same character as in this book!).

Astronomy

Like in *The Serpent's Secret*, there are many references to astronomy in this book, most notably the 2017 discovery of a kilonova—the distant collision of two neutron stars—which was detected by the Hubble Telescope and other instruments as light and gravitational waves, ripples in the universal fabric of space-time. It is from this spectacular collision that scientists now postulate much of the gold and platinum in the universe was created. Although I conflate these neutron stars with the Chintamoni and Poroshmoni Stones, this is entirely made up on my part. Like in *The Serpent's Secret*, rakkhosh in *Game of Stars* are the manifestation of black holes. Even though this pairing of folktales and cosmology may seem strange, I did so to tear down the stereotype that cultural stories are somehow unconnected to science. In fact, like in every culture, traditional Bengali stories are often infused with stories about the stars and planets. That said, please don't take anything in this book as scientific fact, but rather use the story to inspire some more research about astronomy, as well as different cosmological beliefs about how the universe began (there are several from different cultures I refer to in this book)!

Game Shows, Products, Social Media, and Communication Culture

The game *Who Wants to Be a Demon Slayer?* is somewhat modeled after the popular show *Who Wants to Be a Millionaire* in India (*Kaun Banega Crorepati?*). It is also inspired by many popular Bengali game shows including *Didi Number One* and *Dada-giri*, shows that I sometimes watch on "intergalactic satellite" with my children in the United States. They are so popular that there was, in fact, a stampede at one of these game show registration offices, and people do actually hire tutors to train them before going on these shows. Some of the ridiculous products in this book are inspired by real products, like KiddiePow™, which is inspired by the many vitamin supplements advertised to South Asian mothers worried about their children's nutrition, and Dead and Lovely, which is inspired by the many types of "fairness creams" sold all over South Asia and connected to the region's long history of imperialism and colorism. In other words, these products perpetuate the internalized racist idea that lighter/fairer skin is somehow better. Princess Pretty Pants™ isn't inspired by a real doll, although perhaps it's inspired by all such dolls that talk, walk, and otherwise uphold a certain type of feminine beauty standard. Mr. Madan Mohan's Artisanal Moustache Oil™ is not a real thing either, but I do have a much-hipper-than-me cousin-brother, Saptarshi, who makes some pretty amazing homemade products for his plentiful beard and moustache. Similarly, Samosa Drones isn't real, although I thought it up based on a certain online bookseller suggesting they might use drones for book deliveries.

Essence-Tyme is inspired by video conferencing technologies, while Instagreat and Instachat are inspired by social media applications. In this book, I was thinking a lot about how immigrant families are in fact at the forefront of such technologies. Contrary to the stereotypes about us, immigrants often are the first to get satellite or digital TV, use video conferencing technologies, and buy imported products—all to feel more connected to their distant families, communities, and cultures.

Pink-Sari Skateboarders

The Pink-Sari Skateboarders of this book were inspired by at least two groups of Indian women that to me exemplify female power. The first is the Gulabi Gang—a group of modern-day pink sari–clad women activists in Northern India who, armed with bamboo sticks, go after domestic abusers and other men committing violence against women in their rural communities. The second group are the young women involved in India's slowly emerging skateboard and surfing scene, some of whom are featured in the movie and organization *Girl Skate India*. I'm particularly inspired by Kamali Moorthy, an eight-year-old skateboarding prodigy from a small fishing village in the South Indian state of Tamil Nadu (go look her up—she's super cool!).

Food

Green coconuts (daab) are a very popular roadside treat in South Asia (like in a lot of tropical places), and very good for getting hydrated after being out in the sun! Fish is a big part of Bengali culture in general since it is a watery area—West Bengal and Bangladesh are on the Bay of Bengal and intersected by innumerable rivers. Therefore, the fact that Bengali bhoot want fish isn't strange, and fish chops, like fish cutlets, fish fries, and such, are a very popular food. Similarly, begun bhaja, or battered and fried eggplant, is a very common dish found in Bengali meals, which usually consist of rice and daal (lentils) as well as many types of vegetables, fish, and sometimes meat. Digestive biscuits are a kind of flat, not very sweet cookie eaten with tea. Drinking tea (black tea, usually with milk and sugar), of course, is a big part of Bengali culture as well.

Other Random References

Two of the riddles in this book can be attributed to American logician Raymond Smullyan—the riddle told by the police constable ("...this man's father is my father's son") and the truth teller and lie teller puzzle put to Kiranmala by the sister witches near the end of the book. I have a great deal of affection for logical puzzles and riddles in general and Raymond Smullyan in particular because my own father, Sujan, adapted and translated many Smullyan puzzles into Bengali, and his Bengali children's book, *Dhadhapurir Golokdhadha* (The Labyrinth Riddle of Riddle Land) is based on logical puzzles, including Smullyan's.

The scene where Kiranmala has to shoot the eye of a hanging fish simply by looking down at its reflection in water is inspired by a similar test that the hero Arjun underwent in the Indian epic *The Mahabharata*. *Green Eggs and Ham* and "ooblecking" are both references to Dr. Seuss books. "Elladin Belladin Shoilo" is a common singing children's game in Bengal. "Aguner Poroshmoni," is a popular song written by Bengali Nobel Laureate Rabindranath Tagore. A harmonium is a keyboard instrument common in Bengali music. It is played with the right hand only, while the left pumps at the bellows behind it. An auto rikshaw, often called a tuk-tuk in other parts of Asia, is a small wheeled vehicle without walls hired like a taxi to go usually short distances. As far as I am aware, it is not safe to fly auto-rikshaws of any sort into outer space. So please, I beg you, do not try it at home.

Acknowledgments

There were many heroes who saved me in the writing of this book, without whom, the second installment of Kiranmala and the Kingdom Beyond would never have come into being! First and foremost, let me thank the teachers, librarians, booksellers, families, and young readers who have read, enjoyed, reviewed and shared the previous book in this series, *The Serpent's Secret.* Your supportive notes, tweets, questions, and demands to know "what's happening to Kiranmala next" have made the process of writing *Game of Stars* such fun!

I heartily thank my brilliant agent Brent Taylor and his colleague Uwe Stender, for believing in this series from the beginning. Thank you for paving the way for Kiranmala into the multiverse.

I have no words with which I can adequately thank my editor Abby McAden, who makes this process so joyous, besides putting up with my terrible jokes, and anticipating my every question great and small, profound and ridiculous. Thank you also to her assistant, Talia Seidenfeld, knower of all things. In my gratitude, I shower you both with intergalactic gold and platinum—barring that, a good deal of glitter.

Vivienne To, you have outdone yourself again! I thank Vivienne and the wonderful Elizabeth Parisi for their artistic vision on the cover and all the interior art. To Rachel Gluckstern and Melissa Schirmer, my production editors, Jackie Hornberger, my copyeditor, and to the rest of #Team Kiranmala, including the ever-wonderful Ellie Berger, David Levithan, the intergalactic marketing and publicity legends Rachel Feld, Vaishali Nayak, Lizette Serrano, Emily Heddleson, Tracy van Straaten, Lauren Carr, and Crystal McCoy—thank you again and again! Thank you to Anne Marie Wong and Preeti Chibber and the team from Scholastic Book Clubs as well as Robin Hoffman and the team from Scholastic Book Fairs for getting this series into the hands of so many readers. Thank you to my publicist Jennifer Romanello for being everywhere at all times. You are the best.

Gratitude to the best critique group around—Sheela Chari, Veera Hiranandani, and Heather Tomlinson—who keep me learning and growing as a writer. Eternal love and hugs to my writing sister, Olugbemisola Rhuday-Perkovich, and to my oldest sister-friend, Kari Scott, who now needs to buy new boots to match Kiranmala's new ones. (Everyone needs a childhood best friend this supportive!) I'm also indebted to the dynamic brother-sister duo of Mallika and Gautam Chopra for their invaluable support and advice on this series.

Thank you to the We Need Diverse Books, Kidlit Writers of Color, and Desi Writers families for being your awesome selves! Thank you to Kerri Cesene for your artistic support and camaraderie, and to Jovi Geraci—who is nothing like the mean girl named after her—for being your incredibly awesome and supportive selves. I couldn't make it through without you both.

Thank you to my narrative medicine/health humanities colleagues at Columbia and around the country who continue to teach me that stories are the best medicine. Lots of gratitude as well to my former pediatric patients and my current undergraduate and graduate students, who teach me, inspire me, and fill me with hope for the future of this planet. Thank you to my extended family in India and this country, as well as my wonderful Bengali immigrant community of aunties, uncles, and dear friends.

To my loving and ever-supportive parents Sujan and Shamita who inspire me with their own creativity and brilliance, and cheer me on every step of the way. To my husband Boris and my darlings Kirin, Sunaya, and Khushi—for reminding me who I am, keeping me anchored, and loved, with my feet on the ground, even as we turn our faces toward the stars.